Through The
Snow Globe

Through the Snow Globe

ANNIE RAINS

KENSINGTON
PUBLISHING CORP.

www.kensingtonbooks.com

KENSINGTON BOOKS are published by

Kensington Publishing Corp.
119 West 40th Street
New York, NY 10018

Special book excerpts or customized printings can also be created to fit specific needs. For details, write or phone the office of the Kensington Sales Manager: Kensington Publishing Corp., 119 West 40th Street, New York, NY 10018. Attn. Sales Department. Phone: 1-800-221-2647.

The K with book logo Reg US Pat. & TM Off.

ISBN: 978-1-4967-4086-1 (ebook)

ISBN: 978-1-4967-4084-7

First Kensington Trade Paperback Printing: September 2023

10 9 8 7 6 5 4 3 2 1

Printed in the United States of America

For Sonny, Ralph, Doc, and Lydia:
If I had a snow globe to shake and a second chance,
I wouldn't change a thing with you

Chapter 1

'Twas the Night Before December 4th

"You think I'm an Elsa too?" Diana Merriman drew back as she faced her fiancé.

Linus placed his hands on his hips. Today he was wearing his lavender-colored tie with a print of tiny dogs playing fetch. She'd given it to him for their six-month dating anniversary. It was meant to be more of a prank than a staple in his weekly wardrobe, but it fit Linus's personality perfectly—equal parts fun, dorky, and unassumingly handsome. "I didn't say that."

"No, but you didn't say I wasn't one either." Earlier in the day, Diana's teenage patient had tossed this insult at her and Diana's thoughts had been simmering on it ever since. She'd only seen bits and pieces of the children's movie, and the character in question was beautiful and strong. Diana didn't think Addy meant for it to be a compliment, though. "Elsa is an ice queen, right?"

Linus chuckled under his breath, which only made her feel more hurt by the accusation.

"It's not funny, Linus." Diana narrowed her eyes as she folded her arms over her chest, applying pressure over her achy heart.

Linus reached out to touch her shoulder. "Hey, don't be upset. I didn't mean to laugh. It's not like you to be so sensitive with stuff like this."

Diana's lips parted. "What is that supposed to mean?" She could feel herself taking offense to even that statement. She was just stressed. She'd had a busy day, seeing one home health patient after another, and tomorrow was her interview with her boss for the big promotion she'd been pining over for months. That's all it was. She was tired and stressed, and she wanted Linus to side with her in this debate. He was her fiancé after all.

"You're not an Elsa, okay? I think what your patient probably meant was that you're hard to reach—emotionally. You can be a little"—Linus wobbled his head back and forth, a small grimace stretching the corners of his lips—"distant sometimes."

"I'm not distant," she objected. "I'm standing right here."

Linus slipped his dog-print tie from around his neck. "Well, I didn't mean it literally."

"What did you mean, then? Give me one example of a time when I was emotionally distant." Diana looked at him expectantly. She watched as the humor drained from his expression, a note of trepidation playing in her chest.

"Okay," he said, his tone suddenly becoming serious. "How about ever since I proposed this summer?"

Diana's throat tightened, remembering that night. She'd had no idea he was going to ask her to marry him. The question had taken her so much by surprise that she'd actually started crying for the first time in front of him. It was the happiest moment of her life. "What does that mean?"

"You said yes to forever, but you've been dragging your feet on setting a date ever since."

She shook her head. "No, I haven't. I've just been—"

"Busy? Or"—Linus folded the tie in his hands in half—

"distant. One can have a career and a personal life too. It's been done before."

Diana looked around their bedroom, searching for the right response. How had the conversation jumped from her teenage patient's insult to her and Linus's wedding plans—or lack thereof? She rolled her lips together, searching for yet another excuse to delay this discussion. She wasn't ready to discuss dresses or flowers and especially not a guest list.

"Let's get married this Christmas," he said, his expression shifting into a lopsided smile. It was the same smile that had stolen her heart nine months ago when she'd first walked into his father's toy store—the Toy Peddler. The same store that Linus now owned, following Mr. Grant's retirement.

"This Christmas?" she repeated, an invisible cord tightening around her chest. Her breathing felt like shallow gulps. "As in three weeks from now?"

Linus grinned. "It'll be perfect. My relatives from my mother's side are flying in. My dad's family all live within an hour's drive. Everyone will be here."

"Everyone" implied even more than the droves of Grants who'd come to Linus's parents' home for Thanksgiving. That's when she'd learned Linus had more aunts, uncles, and cousins than she had acquaintances.

"Imagine it. The lights. The trees. The poinsettias." He took a step closer, bracing her shoulders with his hands.

She tipped her head back to look up at him, and her heart did a little somersault in her chest. She loved this man. There was no doubt about that. He was *the one*, the only one, for her. Some part of her wanted to say yes so badly. There was another part, though, that envisioned herself as the runaway bride. A lack of love wasn't what made those brides-to-be bolt. No. Diana knew exactly what made women turn their backs on a perfectly good happy ever after—fear.

"What do you think? Having our wedding at Christmas

will take out most of the planning and a lot of the expenses. It'll just leave *us*."

"Us" and about fifty or so members of the Grant family to Diana's zero. She had friends, of course, but Linus had more. The church would tip to one side from the guest list's disproportion.

She tried to swallow, but her mouth felt parched. "My interview for the promotion at work is tomorrow," she finally said. "Let me concentrate on that before we make any rash decisions. Then we can focus on planning the wedding. I promise."

"Rash?" Linus asked quietly. The disappointment in his tone was evident. "We've been engaged for months and you've barely wanted to discuss wedding planning." He searched her gaze. "Why do I get the feeling you don't want to marry me at all? Was your yes to my proposal out of pity?"

"What? Why would you ask such a thing?"

He lifted a shoulder. "I don't know. I'm sure there's a lot of pressure when someone pops the big question. Maybe you didn't want to hurt my feelings."

Guilt consumed Diana. She hated that he would even question her sincerity. "I would never say yes if I didn't mean it, Linus. It's just . . ." She trailed off because she didn't have a good reason for delaying things. Not one he would understand, at least. He didn't know what it was like to grow up, abandoned by both parents and raised by a grandmother who didn't seem to want her either. Diana had issues, and she was the first to admit it. "What's the hurry?" she finally asked.

Linus's lips set in a straight line. "My grandfather used to say that forever is a myth. All we have is this moment." His eyes searched hers. "*That's* the hurry."

"Well, surely we have at least one more tomorrow," she teased, trying to lighten the mood. It didn't work for either of them, though. She was anxious and defensive, and Linus seemed deflated. The hurt feelings over her teenage patient calling her an Elsa were irrelevant now because she'd hurt Linus, which was the last thing she'd ever want to do. Maybe she truly was an ice queen.

Linus stepped back, pulling his arms down to his side. "Some part of me regrets asking you to marry me," he said, so quiet she almost didn't hear him.

"What?" Diana pressed a hand to her chest, reminding herself to breathe. Surely he didn't mean that. Did he?

"Not because I don't love you." He offered a humorless laugh. "The truth is, I love you so much I can hardly take a breath when I think about it. You're everything I ever wanted. And more. I don't know what I ever did to deserve you."

Tears burned in her eyes. She could feel the *but* trailing silently behind his sweet words. She waited, bracing herself. When he remained quiet, she prodded. "But?"

Linus shook his head. "I don't know. Maybe I moved too fast. Maybe you weren't ready. Maybe you still aren't," he said.

Diana didn't make a habit out of crying in front of people. Not even Linus. Her grandmother, Denny, had taught her to hold her emotions at bay until she was alone. Denny hadn't been as poetic with her words as Linus's grandfather, but she'd given out hard truths to help Diana survive the real world, which Denny had painted to be cruel and unforgiving. Diana had experienced a little bit of that, of course, but her world had been so much nicer since Linus had come into it. He made life seem magical in a way she'd never experienced. "All this because I asked you if I was an Elsa?"

"All this because I've been trying to talk to you about the wedding for weeks and there's never been a good time." He sighed wearily. "It's still not a good time. We should talk about this tomorrow, after your interview, when we're both clear-minded."

"Talk about what, exactly?" she asked, still working hard to hold in her tears.

"The wedding. And if there's going to be one this Christmas."

The *if* made her stiffen and she wondered if he meant more than he was saying. Maybe he wanted to discuss if there'd be a wedding at all. Maybe he truly did regret proposing.

Linus offered a half smile that didn't reach his eyes. Then he placed the folded tie he was holding on the edge of their bed, turned, and left the room.

Diana finally gave herself permission to let the tears stream down her cheeks. She climbed into bed and laid her head on her pillow, wiping her eyes futilely. Then she gave up and let the tears fall.

An hour later, she listened to the sound of Linus's breathing in the bed beside her. She'd pretended to be asleep when he'd returned to their room. She hadn't known what to say. An apology was probably in order, but from her or him? They'd both said regrettable things. This whole night had been a mess. The only bright side she could see was that tomorrow could only go up from here.

She twisted the diamond engagement ring on her finger while her thoughts ran laps in her brain. *This is silly. We love each other.* "Linus?" she finally whispered. "Linus, are you awake?"

His breathing continued, slow and steady.

She rolled to her opposite side, her eyes trying to focus in the dark. The shadow of his chest lifted and dropped steadily. "Linus?"

No answer. He was asleep, and once Linus was out, he was gone to the world. She'd just have to wait and smooth things over with him tomorrow. She didn't want him to think she regretted saying yes to his proposal. The only regret she had right now was going to bed angry. And asking Linus if she was an Elsa, like Addy had said. She regretted that too.

A No Good, Exceptionally Bad Day
December 4th

"Wake up, sleepy girl."

Diana blinked Linus's face into focus. "Already?"

"Afraid so." He was in his usual cheerful mood for early morning. The man had a spring in his step as soon as he got up, excited about each new day. It was one of the things that she loved about him, but at times she also found the quality annoying.

Diana slid an arm over her eyes to block the light as memories of last night filtered into her mind.

"How about we trim the tree tonight?" Linus said with no trace of frustration with her, despite going to bed upset.

"The tree?" she repeated, trying to will her eyelids open. Unlike him, she was not a morning person.

"You know, the tall green thing in the corner of our living room. We dragged it home from the lot last weekend?"

"Right." Diana's face stretched into a yawn.

"We can drink champagne to celebrate your new promotion and add the lights and tinsel. Who knows, maybe I'll even add a little tinsel to you."

Diana peeked out from behind her arm just in time to see him waggle his eyebrows. "Promotion?" She sat up now and looked at him with wide eyes. "Today's the interview," she remembered out loud. She'd tossed and turned so much in the night—her mind rehashing her argument with Linus and rehearsing today's meeting with Mr. Powell—that she was completely out of sorts.

"Don't tell me you've forgotten. That promotion is all you've talked about for weeks." What he didn't say was it was also her excuse to avoid setting a date and planning their wedding. She was grateful he didn't bring that up this morning. It would only make things tense between them again and today promised to be life-changing. A promotion at work would improve their financial situation. They might even be able to afford to leave this apartment and move into a house of their own.

She stood and hurried into her closet. The interview wasn't until this afternoon. First, she had a busy morning of home health patients to see. Grabbing a pair of scrubs with a sparkly snowflake print, she quickly started stripping down to change.

"I'm sorry for calling you an Elsa last night." Linus stood in the closet's doorway, watching her.

"Addy was the one who called me an Elsa. You just confirmed it."

"I only meant that you're beautiful like her."

"That's not what you meant, and you know it." Diana rolled her eyes playfully as she looked at him. Even though he'd likely already brushed his hair, it was disheveled on one side.

He cast a sheepish grin. "Well, you *are* beautiful. More so than any ice queen. Forgive me?"

She also needed to apologize. He was right. She had been avoiding the subject of marriage. Pulling her scrub pants up to her waist, she stepped toward him. "We'll set the date tonight," she promised. "While we celebrate with champagne and create the most festive tree that Snow Haven has ever seen."

Linus leaned in and kissed her. "I like the sound of that."

"Me too." And she did, even if she was terrified of being part of a family. She didn't know the first thing about having relatives who actually cared and wanted to spend time with her. What if she was horrible at it? What if Linus realized his mistake in choosing her and left? Or worse, if he stayed and it ruined his life?

"Tonight, then?" He pulled back. "I've got to get to the toy store. I have a meeting with a distributor this morning. Love you forever," he called behind him on his way out.

Diana's brain stuttered on that last word. *Forever is a*

myth. All we've got is this moment. Had Linus's grandfather been right about that? Well, if so, she intended to knock this day out of the park. "Love you too!" she called after him. "See you tonight!"

After he was gone, she hurried into the bathroom and washed her face. The front door squeaked as it opened down the hall. Diana turned off the faucet and peeked out, seeing Linus standing back in the doorway.

"My truck is out of gas," he said with a long face.

"You let it get so low that you can't make it to the station?"

"So low that it won't even start." He released a heavy sigh, his good mood visibly deflating.

Diana shrugged. "It's going to take me a few minutes to get ready, but I can drive you if you want to wait."

Linus shook his head. "No, I'll take the bicycle. It'll be fine. I've got to go. I don't want to be late."

All the reason she should drive him. He would only argue, though. Linus always rode his bike to work when the weather was nice, which wasn't exactly the case for today. The toy store was only a mile down the road and he enjoyed the exercise.

"Love you!" he called as he rolled his bicycle out of their apartment into the December morning. He didn't wait to hear her reply before the door was closed and he was gone.

Her stomach suddenly felt unsettled as she stood there. She guessed it was the argument they'd had last night. Even though everything seemed fine this morning, last night's feud felt bigger than their usual quarrels about him leaving dirty laundry on the floor or her not screwing the cap on the toothpaste. Had Linus really said he regretted proposing? Had she allowed the whole marriage thing to freak her out so much that it was driving a wedge between them?

She stared after the door for another second, some part of her wanting to run out the front door and wrap her arms around Linus. There was no time for that, though. They both had a busy day ahead. Today she was going to get the promotion she deserved and tonight she and Linus would begin planning the rest of their lives together. Whatever issues she had with family and commitment, she'd just have to get over them between now and then.

Linus's grandfather was mistaken. Forever wasn't a myth. It was hers for the taking.

Chapter 2

"Come on, Maria. It's cold out here," Diana mumbled under her breath as she stood outside her patient's door. She pressed the bell a third time.

It wasn't like Maria not to answer immediately. The old woman lived alone, though. Maybe she was in the bathroom. Or perhaps she'd gone off to stay with relatives and had forgotten to cancel her physical therapy appointment.

Diana wasn't even sure if Maria had family in Snow Haven, North Carolina. When Diana was working with Maria, she kept things professional. They focused on Maria's exercises so that the older woman could recover some of the strength and endurance she'd lost during last month's stroke.

Diana shivered beneath her lightweight coat. The temperatures had dropped sharply in the night, leaving a dusting of frost on the lawn. She rang the doorbell one more time and waited. Then, sighing, she turned to leave, stopping cold when she heard Maria's voice calling out from inside the house. Diana turned back and bent her ear toward the door. "Maria?"

"*Help!*"

All the air in Diana's lungs whooshed out in a puff of white frosty air. She attempted to turn the doorknob, but it was locked. "Maria, I'm here!" she called again, hoping her patient could hear her. "Hold on!"

Diana scanned the porch for some sort of obvious place to hide a key. She checked beneath a flowerpot and then a garden gnome. She checked the wind chimes and behind the loose shutter near the front window. There was nothing. Diana briefly considered kicking the door down, but decided the professional thing to do was to call 911.

Diana hurried back to her car where she'd left her phone and tapped her screen to make the call.

"Nine-one-one, what's your emergency?" the dispatcher answered.

Diana's hands shook as she clutched the device to her ear. "Yes, um, well, I'm sitting outside my patient's house right now. Her name is Maria Harris. I'm her home health physical therapist. Maria isn't answering the door, and I can hear her calling for help inside. I'm not sure what to do."

The operator asked several more probing questions and then assured Diana that help was on the way. The fact that Maria could call out was a good sign. Obviously, she couldn't get up to reach the phone for herself. Was she on the floor? Had she suffered a second stroke? The possibilities whirled through Diana's mind until the first police cruiser slid up to the curb, sirens wailing. An ambulance pulled into the driveway moments after the police. The lights of the emergency vehicles competed with the early Christmas decorations the neighboring house had already put up.

Diana helplessly watched, wondering how her morning had already become so eventful. Most of her days were just the opposite. She lived a routine life, seeing her patients one by one and coming home to Linus during the evenings. She liked her life as it was, even if lately she wanted something more. The promotion at work might help with that. And marrying Linus. Her life would change for sure once she joined the Grant family. That excited as much as it terrified her.

Diana leaned against her car and watched as a man worked to open Maria's front door. Finally, it swung inward and a team of police and paramedics disappeared inside. When two paramedics finally rolled Maria out on a stretcher, Diana rushed over.

"Maria! Maria, are you okay?"

Maria turned her head, searching the small crowd of uniformed men and women who had gathered on her lawn. She smiled warmly when her eyes connected with Diana's. "Oh, Diana. Don't worry about me. I'm fine, dear. I just took a little fall. I think my ankle might be broken." She flinched softly as she tried to move it.

"Broken?" Maria's right leg was already weak after last month's stroke. "What happened?"

"I'm embarrassed to say." Maria glanced sheepishly at the two male paramedics who'd stopped long enough to let her talk to Diana. "I was trying to climb into my attic to retrieve my Christmas decorations."

Diana's mouth fell open. "Maria, I told you to wait on that."

"Wait for what? For who? It had to get done, and I was feeling well enough this morning, so I decided to go for it."

Diana shook her head. "That wasn't safe. You injured yourself for a little holiday decorating?"

Maria looked offended for a moment. "Christmas cheer is important."

The paramedic standing on the right of the stretcher cleared his throat. "We're taking her to East Medical," he told Diana.

East Medical was the local hospital. Diana knew the place well. She had visited often when Grandma Denny had gotten sick. Diana had stood by her grandmother's side, hoping to return the favor of when Denny had taken Diana in. Denny hadn't provided the best emotional support when Diana was growing up, but Diana had never wanted for food or shelter. She'd had her own room, three warm meals a day, and when she was sixteen, Denny had provided her with a dented clunker for transportation to and from an after-school job. That same clunker had gotten Diana through physical therapy school.

The paramedic signaled to the other that it was time to continue toward the ambulance.

Diana took a step backward. "Take care of yourself, Maria. I'll be here when you're ready to begin PT again." She watched as Maria was carted into the back of the vehicle. Then, with her heart still racing from the chaos of the morning, Diana headed back to her car. Why had Maria attempted to climb into her attic? She could barely walk, which was one of the reasons Diana was treating her.

Diana plopped into the driver's seat and shut the door behind her, barring the frigid air. She took a moment to check her phone, hoping there'd be a text from Linus. He usually messaged her throughout the day, sending funny GIFs and random musings that she liked to refer to as Linus-isms. There was nothing waiting for her on her phone though. He must still be in a meeting with the toy distributor.

She tapped out a message to him.

Diana: *I hope your morning is going smoother than mine.*

When he didn't immediately reply, she shifted her car into gear and drove to her next patient's home.

Addy was a sixteen-year-old in remission from acute myelogenous leukemia. Addy had been an active basketball player on her high school team before that, and she was already looking at colleges. Cancer didn't care about the future, though. Or how old a person was.

Diana fiddled with the radio as she drove. All the stations were playing holiday songs, which she didn't mind. She sang along to Mariah Carey's "All I Want for Christmas Is You" as she headed to her next stop, entertaining Linus's idea of a

Christmas wedding. This might be a good song selection for the ceremony. Knowing Linus, he'd probably want to serenade her with it at the reception. He thought he could sing and Diana would never tell him otherwise, even though the man couldn't hold a tune to save his life.

Perhaps she should suggest eloping. Linus probably wouldn't go for that idea. Knowing him, he would want to share their special moment with his loved ones. He was a family man, and well, Diana wasn't a family woman, even though she'd always fantasized about being part of a huge family.

When she arrived at the Pierces' home, she slowed her car and parked along the curb. She walked up the driveway and porch steps and pushed the doorbell. Shuffled steps could be heard inside. They grew closer until Mrs. Pierce opened the door and smiled brightly.

"Ms. Diana!" The middle-aged woman with light brown hair and tortoiseshell glasses opened the door wider for Diana to enter the home.

"Good morning. How is Addy doing today?" Diana asked, getting straight to business.

Cecilia Pierce shrugged, clasping her hands together at her midsection. "She's barely come out to say hello. As far as I know she's just listening to music in there."

"Pain?" Diana asked.

"Well, you know Addy. She doesn't complain about stuff like that. I think she's comfortable, though."

"Good." Diana glanced down the hall where Addy's room was located. "I'll just go check on her, if that's okay."

"Of course. Thank you."

Diana turned and walked down the dimly lit hallway. Addy's room was the last door on the left. She knocked and waited for the girl to respond, mentally preparing herself to go inside.

Addy was thinner every time she saw her. Her leukemia had been aggressive, but she'd fought it like she would an opposing team on the court, and she'd won. Now she was weak, which was why her doctor had ordered physical therapy.

"Come in," Addy called from inside the room.

Diana opened the door and stepped inside. The light purple walls were adorned with boy-band posters and basketball memorabilia. She also had dozens of pictures of family and friends on her nightstand and along a shelf on her far wall.

Addy removed the earbuds she was wearing. "Hi."

"Hey, you. How are you doing?" Diana asked.

Addy was pale, but her blue eyes were still bright. That was a good sign. "Good."

"Your mom says you've been in here all day."

Addy rolled her eyes, looking like a normal teen girl. That was another good sign. "Because when I go outside this room, my mom hovers around me like I'm a porcelain doll about to shatter into a million pieces."

Diana set her bag down on the floor next to the bedside table. "She loves you."

"Well, she also smothers me, so . . ." Addy trailed off. Her gaze landed on Diana's diamond ring. "So when are you getting married anyway?"

Diana sighed and pulled up a chair. "I'm here to ask you questions, not vice versa."

Addy poked out her bottom lip, which was part of their routine. Addy pried into Diana's personal life, Diana shut it down, and Addy pouted. Or, as had happened yesterday, she called Diana an Elsa. "You're no fun at all."

"So I'm told. By you on a weekly basis." Diana reached inside her bag for her company laptop. There was a series of health-related questions she asked every week. Before she even got started, Addy began reading off her answers.

"I'm a five on the pain scale. I already went to the bathroom this morning. Number one, not two. I had some orange juice and a piece of toast for breakfast. No nausea or vomiting."

Diana smirked. "All right, smarty-pants. You're going to have to tell me all of that again once I get my laptop open and running."

Addy grinned proudly, but the humor didn't quite reach her eyes.

Diana began filling out her weekly status report for Addy. "You said a five on the pain scale?"

Addy shrugged. "Maybe not even that, unless you're considering my heart."

Diana looked up with concern. "You're having chest pain?"

Addy rolled her eyes. "No. My heart-heart. You know, the one with all the feelings."

"Right." Diana hesitated. Did she really want to open this can of worms and ask a teenager about her emotions? That was more Diana's best friend Rochelle's realm than Diana's. Rochelle was a pediatric counselor in town. She loved to discuss feelings. Diana, on the other hand, would prefer to discuss all the physical aches and pains of the body. "Let's get up and walk to the bathroom, shall we?"

Addy released an audible sigh. "It's so weird that walking to the bathroom sink is considered exercise for me. I used to run up and down the courts for an hour at a time."

"You'll do that again," Diana promised. "But right now, we're taking baby steps. Your body is building back what it lost during your cancer treatment. Come on, let's go." Diana clapped her hands, doing her best basketball coach impression.

It worked. Addy began to slowly shift and move. She looked like she was feeling more than a five on the pain scale as she dropped her legs off the edge of the bed and grimaced. Then she stood, took a breath, and walked toward the bathroom with Diana sticking close behind her just in case her legs gave out.

When Addy got to the mirror, she stood there and stared

at her reflection as if she hadn't seen herself in days. Diana wondered what the girl was thinking. "Am I still pretty?" Addy finally asked.

Diana's lips parted. "Of course you are, Addy. It's just hair. It'll grow back."

Addy's gaze cut to hers in their reflection. Her eyes glinted angrily. "That's something only a person with all the hair they could ever want would say. Would you look at an amputee and say it's just a leg?"

Diana drew back. "A leg can't grow back. Your hair can."

Tears swam in the girl's eyes. *No, no, no. Please don't cry.* "And I suppose you'll tell me that losing my boyfriend and my best friend is also no big deal? I can find new ones, right?"

Diana searched for words, feeling like the wrong ones might make this session combust. "I didn't know you had a boyfriend," she finally said.

"Well, I don't. Not anymore." Addy swiped at a tear that slipped down her cheek.

"Listen, whatever I said to upset you, Addy, I'm sorry. I didn't mean to hurt your feelings."

"It's not *just* hair," Addy said through clenched teeth. She leaned against the sink, bracing herself with her thin arms. "It's not even just cancer. This is my life—don't you get it?— and it feels like it's over right now. My biggest achievement today will be walking to the sink and standing here for five minutes. This sucks!" Her voice shook as more tears rolled down her flushed cheeks. "No one understands how I'm feeling, which makes me feel even more alone. Not to mention the fact that I *am* all alone in this room."

"Not true," Diana said. "I'm here."

Addy's gaze caught hers in the reflection. "I don't even really know you. You're just a stranger with a familiar face."

Diana flinched. Yesterday Addy had called her an Elsa and

today Diana was labeled a familiar-looking stranger. Teenagers could be harsh. "Addy, I . . ."

"Whatever." Addy turned from the sink and attempted to step past Diana. "Excuse me. I just want to go back to bed. I need to conserve energy. Isn't that what you're always harping on? Energy conservation?"

"Yes." Diana released a weary breath and stepped to the side. Going back to bed sounded like a good idea for Diana right about now too.

Chapter 3

At 2:00 p.m., Diana absently twisted her pearl earring, trying to stay focused on her meeting with Mr. Powell and not on the events of the morning that included Maria being carted off in an ambulance and Addy pretty much kicking Diana out of her bedroom. Then there was the fact that Linus still hadn't texted her back. He'd seemed fine when he'd left the apartment, but maybe he wasn't. Maybe he was more upset about last night's argument than he'd let on.

Well, she'd make things up to him tonight. After this interview was behind her. Last month, she'd put in for a promotion at Powell Rehabilitation Center, and she could only assume that's why her boss had asked her here today. She'd been working with the company for seven years, rarely missing a day and never garnishing a single complaint. It was time for something new, and this felt like exactly what she needed.

"This morning must have been scary," Mr. Powell commented.

Diana forced a confident smile. Despite the rough start to her day, she felt good about this meeting. This day was about to turn around for the better. She could feel it to her core. "I've never had to call nine-one-one before. It was definitely an experience," she said on a small laugh. "Not one I'd like to repeat any time soon." She sat up tall with her shoulders pulled back, mirroring the man sitting across from her. She wasn't exactly confident by nature, but she purposely presented herself that way.

Mr. Powell nodded. "Well, I'm glad you were scheduled with Ms. Harris. Otherwise, who knows how long she would have laid there calling out for help."

Diana didn't even want to imagine her patient being so vulnerable and helpless. "Maria is one determined woman. When she mentioned needing to get her holiday decorations down from the attic, I told her not to do so on her own. She's in physical therapy for a reason. I guess I underestimated how stubborn she was."

"Stubbornness is a good quality for patients to have. I used to find those patients worked the hardest." Mr. Powell chuckled. "And decorations are important to the holiday diehards. My mother was always one to drag out the Christmas items on the day right after Thanksgiving."

Diana wasn't sure what Maria and her holiday decorations had to do with Diana's promotion, but she smiled through the conversation even as her palms began to feel slightly damp. She crossed her legs and leaned back into her chair. "Anyway, the ambulance took Ms. Harris to East Medical. I'm sure she's doing fine by now. At least I hope she is."

"You haven't checked on her?" The skin between Mr. Powell's brows pinched behind his glasses.

The note of judgment caught Diana by surprise. "No, not yet. I had another patient to see after I left Ms. Harris's home." Surely Mr. Powell wouldn't have wanted Diana to cancel her physical therapy schedule. "I'll call her cell phone after I leave here, though. I might even stop by the hospital to visit."

This garnered a smile. "Good idea. And when you do, please tell Ms. Harris we would be happy to come to her home and put up her decorations for her. We don't want her getting reinjured, after all."

Diana's lips parted. "We?"

"The staff here at Powell Rehabilitation. As you know, we're a family-owned company, and our patients become like family to us. If Ms. Harris wants a festive home, it's easy enough to make that happen for her. In fact, William has already offered his help."

"William," she repeated. William Davis was one of Diana's coworkers. He was young, single, and high-energy. And he treated everyone as if they were his best friend, which bothered Diana for some reason. Best friends were hard won; they didn't happen in the span of thirty minutes. Diana had known her best friend, Rochelle, for two decades now. They'd met in middle school and, after a period of loathing each other, they'd found common ground and had worked their way to friendship. "That's . . . nice of him."

"It is. William goes above and beyond with his patients, doesn't he?" Mr. Powell asked good-naturedly.

He said it as if it were a good thing, but Diana didn't necessarily think so. "But Maria isn't *his* patient." She offered a wobbly smile to offset the sudden defensiveness rising inside her. She could feel her confidence melting away along with the antiperspirant that wasn't working.

Mr. Powell shrugged. "Like I said, we're a family here at Powell Rehabilitation. We're all one big happy family."

"Of course." Diana didn't know much about family, but she didn't think her workplace qualified. Work was one's professional life and family and friends was personal. The two shouldn't mix.

"That's why I called you here, Diana," Mr. Powell finally said.

That statement was Diana's first red flag. She'd assumed her boss had called the meeting to discuss the promotion she'd applied for. The one she was a shoo-in to get. But her promotion had nothing to do with William or Maria.

Mr. Powell pressed the tips of his fingers together in front of him as he looked at her over his glasses. "I like to shoot straight with my employees. You are one of the best therapists I have here at the company, Diana. I hope you know that."

"Thank you, sir." Confidence surged inside her once more. Maybe this was about the promotion after all. Perhaps, in a few hours, she and Linus would be toasting her new role with the company.

"But . . ." Mr. Powell said, hesitating for a moment.

Here came red flag number two.

". . . I don't see you in a leadership position at this time." There was a note of apology in his voice.

Diana swallowed as her mind struggled to process his words. A half dozen emotions hit her all at once. Disappointment. Confusion. Embarrassment. She didn't know what to say so she said nothing as she sat there numbly staring at her boss. She raised her hand to twist her pearl earring, a nervous habit that occupied her hands while helping her remember to breathe. Rotate—breathe in. Rotate—breath out. Rotate. Rotate. *Just don't hyperventilate in Mr. Powell's office.*

"Leadership requires a complex skill set of knowledge, experience, and heart. That's why I'm planning to promote William. I'm sure you understand, and that you'll offer him your best wishes," Mr. Powell said with an easy smile. As if this information were no big deal.

"*William?*" she repeated in a shrill voice, rotating her pearl earring faster now. "But William hasn't been here as long as me." *She* had seniority. This promotion was rightfully hers.

"Time is relative. With William's passion for patient care, and his rapport among the staff here, he'll make a great supervisor."

How was this happening? Was she dreaming? Having a nightmare? William would be her supervisor? *She* was the one who'd trained *him*. Was this because William was a man? Diana had never considered Mr. Powell a sexist, but what other reason would he have for promoting William over her?

"Practically every patient of William's turns in a Glow Card," Mr. Powell went on, oblivious to her scattered emotions.

Glow Cards were inserted in all the patients' informational folders given to them at their initial evaluations. Patients could fill out the print version or go online and complete a form there. In Diana's experience, most patients didn't complete the forms at all. It was optional, and it required that patients go above and beyond. William probably coaxed his patients into filling out those cards. Perhaps he even bribed them or filled them out himself.

"There's more to being a good supervisor than knowing how to complete the paperwork," Mr. Powell said offhandedly.

Diana drew back. "I'm sorry? Sir, I have a good relationship with my coworkers and my patients."

"Of course you do. I only meant to say that management isn't easy." He tipped his head in her direction. "Actually, I did receive one Glow Card on you in the last two weeks."

Diana felt her insides light up even though she was on the verge of either crying or throwing something. Maybe that crystal picture frame on Mr. Powell's desk. She'd never gotten a Glow Card before, even though her other coworkers got them a couple times a year. What were they doing differently? "One of my patients filled out a card?" she asked.

Mr. Powell wasn't smiling. Instead, he looked nervous for the first time in this meeting. He reached for a piece of paper on his desk and seemed to blink the text into focus before reading the comment that was left. " 'Diana Merriman is a qualified physical therapist. She seemed to know what she was talking about, even though I often found her bedside manner to be overly curt.' "

"Curt?" *How is that a compliment?* "Who wrote that?" Diana asked.

Mr. Powell shook his head, looking up from the piece of paper he was holding. "It doesn't matter. The fact that your patient took the time to comment on you is progress." He set the paper back on his desk. "And progress is always welcome. This will look good on your annual review in a couple of months," he said as if that was any comfort right now. "Diana, I want you to know that you're respected here. As I said before, Powell Rehabilitation is lucky to have you on its staff. I always depend on you to train the new hires."

"Which is part of the supervisor's role," Diana pointed out. Her forced smile felt more like an uncomfortable twitch now. "I'm not curt. I'm professional," she argued numbly.

"I don't disagree with that. Rest assured, William thinks very highly of you. You'll be in good hands with him as your supervisor. And I'm sure he can give you a few tips on improving your bedside manner."

"My bedside manner is just fine," Diana bit out. "I don't know who wrote that comment, but my patients all seem very satisfied with me, sir. Maybe I don't pry into their personal lives, but I am not curt."

"I'm sure." Mr. Powell stood and reached out his hand for her to shake. Apparently, this meeting was over. It hadn't really been an interview at all. Mr. Powell was just checking on Diana after Maria's injury and giving her the courtesy of finding out firsthand that she wasn't getting promoted. And that she'd gotten a Glow Card calling her "curt."

Diana stood on wobbly legs and reached out to shake Mr. Powell's hand. When she did, her arm bumped against the crystal picture frame on his desk—the one she'd briefly considered throwing. It wobbled in slow motion as she watched, paralyzed by her thick disbelief and disappointment. Then it fell to the floor at her feet, shattering into tiny pieces that looked like slivers of ice.

Maybe I am Elsa, the ice queen.

Diana gasped and looked up at Mr. Powell. "I am so sorry."

He lowered his arm and his smile vanished. After a moment, he cleared his throat. "Don't worry about it, Diana. I'll call someone to clean it up. Frames can be replaced, but good employees can't. Thanks for all your hard work here at the company. It hasn't gone unnoticed."

But it *had* gone unnoticed. She was a good employee while William was getting her promotion. His patient caseload would be cut to twenty-five percent so that he could focus on supervising the staff, interviewing and hiring new employees, and handling in-house issues. Those were all things Diana could do. Things she was already doing.

In a daze, she walked out of the facility. The cold air stung her lungs as she stepped onto the sidewalk and sucked in a shaky breath.

Don't cry.

She hurried through the parking lot, wishing she'd worn a coat. It was freezing out. Snow Haven was nestled in North Carolina's Blue Ridge Mountains. It was often cold enough to snow during the winters, but the white stuff rarely made an appearance in this valley town. The last time Diana remembered it snowing here, she'd been eighteen years old. Her grandmother had just passed away, and Diana had worn snow boots with her long black funeral dress. Grandma Denny would have approved. She was a very practical, no fuss kind of lady. Some might call Denny "curt." Most people, in fact, would probably describe her that way.

Diana's stomach clenched painfully as she approached her car and clicked her key fob. Had she turned into her grandmother without meaning to?

Holding back tears, Diana plopped into the seat behind the steering wheel and closed the door behind her. She cranked the engine with a turn of her key, listening to the soft hum of the motor while her thoughts ran rampant. She'd been looking forward to interviewing for the management position for over a month, mentally prepping and taking on extra work with patients and new hires to prove that she was management material. She was the most experienced, responsible, and, in her humble opinion, she possessed every quality a boss might look for in his choice for supervisor.

But apparently, she was wrong.

Diana sat in her car, clutching her steering wheel and wondering how she could have done that interview better, to prove to Mr. Powell that she was the right candidate for the job. What did it matter, though? It was too late. Mr. Powell had already made his decision before she'd stepped into his office, and there were no second chances in life.

After a few steadying breaths, Diana shifted the car into DRIVE and left the rehabilitation center's parking lot. She'd already taken the rest of the afternoon off because she'd had no idea if Mr. Powell would want to show her the new office that was now going to go to gum-smacking, loud-laughing William.

Diana didn't know where she was going. She could stop in and see Linus at the Toy Peddler, but he was working, and he kept telling her what a busy month December was for him. Maybe she should just give him space and go back to their apartment. She could have a glass of wine, take a hot bath, and maybe do some online shopping for the people on her Christmas list. She could pretend this day had never happened. *Yeah,* that sounded like a good plan.

Diana's phone chirped from the center console as she drove. She tapped a button on her steering wheel to answer.

"Are you going to meet me or not?" Rochelle asked.

Oh, crap. It was Rochelle's thirtieth birthday, and Diana was supposed to meet her at Sparky's for their traditional celebratory drinks.

"I, um, I'm actually not feeling well," Diana said. It wasn't a complete lie. She did feel pretty awful after the events of the day, which was proving to be even worse than yesterday.

"What? You're canceling? What's wrong?" Concern layered in Rochelle's voice. As a counselor, Rochelle always wanted to know what was wrong, and she got just as frustrated as Linus did when Diana insisted there was nothing.

"Everything's fine," Diana said.

"F-word alert." Rochelle had been calling Diana out on saying "fine" too often lately. "And, if everything's fine, there's no reason you can't have a birthday drink with me. Come on, Diana. I'm single and I need someone to toast me on my next several decades of being lonely on my birthday."

"You won't be alone for several decades." Diana rolled her eyes as she slowed behind a STOP sign and looked both ways. Seeing that it was clear, she pressed the gas and continued forward. "I'm sorry, Rochelle. Rain check."

Silence stretched out on the other line. Diana hated disappointing the people in her life. Linus last night and now Rochelle. William probably didn't have this problem. He probably never needed a moment alone with a glass of wine.

"*Fine*," Rochelle finally said, her voice quiet. "I hope you feel better."

"Thank you. Happy birthday, Ro."

"I don't know how happy it'll be since I'll be drinking alone at the bar. Talk to you tomorrow, Di." Rochelle disconnected the call without waiting for Diana's response.

Diana blew out a breath as she turned left onto Oakwood Drive. She slowed to a stop at a red light. All her thoughts—of Linus, Rochelle, Mr. Powell and her patients, one who'd called her an Elsa and another who'd labeled her curt—jumbled together as she sat there numbly. She needed to fix a lot of areas in her life, starting with her relationship with Linus. They were engaged, which meant they needed to set a date. Perhaps she could push the ceremony out until next Christmas to give herself time to prepare. This was their first Christmas together after all. Even though every other milestone in their relationship had been fast, it didn't mean this one had to be. They could take their time and Diana could adjust to Linus's world, which was far different from her own.

The car behind Diana honked. She blinked and saw that the light had changed to green. "Sorry," she said even though the driver behind her couldn't hear her, and she started driving again when something jutted out in front of her. Diana yanked her steering wheel left to avoid hitting a boy on a bicycle and then yanked it right to dodge a delivery truck whose lane she'd just merged into. It all happened in a quick flash, and then she was back in her lane and breathing heavily.

That was close! She glanced in her rearview mirror to check that the little boy was okay, spotting him pedaling hard and fast, heading in the direction of Linus's toy store. Expelling a breath, she pressed the gas pedal more heavily. She just needed to get home. There was something off about this whole day. She needed it to end, and end soon.

She was still shaking by the time she walked inside the little apartment that she and Linus shared. She slammed the door behind her, peeled off her winter coat, and carried it to the hook in the laundry room. After tugging off her boots, she headed straight for the wine in the kitchen. It was only four o'clock. Having a drink with Rochelle would have been acceptable, but maybe not enjoying one on her own.

Diana's mother had enjoyed drinks at any time of day. That was the problem when Diana was growing up. One of them, at least. It was why Diana had lived with her grandmother. Her mom drank too much and only remembered that Diana existed around the holidays. That's when Jackie Merriman came around with a single, wrapped gift and empty promises that she'd be more involved in the coming year. Diana didn't want to turn out like her. And even though Grandma Denny had come through, raising Diana as her own, Diana didn't want to take after her either. She wanted to be warmer to the people she loved. She didn't want to keep her guard up and her emotions hidden. That was easier said than done, though.

Deciding against the glass of wine, she headed over to the couch and laid down. Just for a moment. She needed to erase the stress of the day. In fact, she wouldn't mind sleeping the rest of this awful day away. She closed her eyes and waited for her mind to finally stop whirring with too many things. Finally, she drifted off to nothingness.

She awoke to the sound of someone knocking on her apartment door. She blinked the room into focus. The natural light from the windows was gone. What time was it? She must have been asleep longer than she'd intended.

The knock came again. It was probably Linus. He must have forgotten his house keys when he rode off on his bicycle this morning.

"I'm coming!" she called as she sat up on the couch. She took her time standing and walking to the door. She didn't want to fight with Linus tonight. Perhaps she'd cook them a hot meal and they could still have that glass of champagne even though she hadn't gotten the promotion. Then they could set a date. Not for this Christmas, but maybe for the next one. Or the one after that.

Linus knocked again, more urgently this time. In his defense, it was freezing outside. Diana walked more quickly, looking forward to having Linus's arms wrap around her. After a day like this one, she wouldn't mind disappearing into his embrace for hours.

She reached the door, turned the knob, and pulled, ready to do just that.

It wasn't Linus, though. Instead, there were two police officers on her stoop. Diana recognized the older one as Officer Crane. She had treated his mother last year after Mrs. Crane had broken her hip. Why hadn't she filled out a Glow Card for Diana? Diana had done a great job with the elderly patient. She hadn't been curt or distant. Her bedside manner had been impeccable.

Diana looked between the two men, who stood there with grim expressions. What were they doing at her apartment? Why did they look so upset?

Her knees buckled under the weight that suddenly hung heavy in her gut. Something was wrong. She could feel it. And no amount of saying that things were fine would fix whatever this was. "What happened?" she asked, bracing herself against the doorframe. The cold air felt harsh as it rushed through the doorway, burning her cheeks.

"Hello, Diana," Officer Crane said. Why did he sound so serious? "I'm here about Linus." He hesitated and Diana's heart did a free fall into the pit of her stomach. *No, not him.* She needed Linus. She needed him now.

"Just tell me," she whispered.

Officer Crane seemed to hesitate, his lips pressed into a thin line. "I'm sorry to inform you that Linus was in an accident tonight."

Chapter 4

Merry Eve of Christmas Eve

Three weeks later

The bitterly cold air nipped at Diana's cheeks as she slipped out of her last patient's home and descended the porch steps, heading toward her car parked along the curb. The forecast had been calling for snow for over a week, but at present, the air was too cold and dry for precipitation. It was prime conditions for black ice on the roads, however. Diana's visit with Linus at the New Hope Long-Term Care Facility needed to be a quick one so she could get back to her apartment before dark.

As she dipped into the driver's seat, her phone buzzed. Her body jolted upright at the sound. She had this running fantasy that someone from the facility would call and say, "Good news, Ms. Merriman! He's awake! It's a miracle!" Diana had seen Linus's chart, though. She understood the low probability of him waking up. He'd been lying lifeless for three long weeks, and every day that passed made his prognosis bleaker.

She pulled her phone from her purse and glanced at the caller ID. It was Linus's mother—again. Diana let the call go to voice mail, cranked her car, and waited a few minutes for the engine to warm before pulling onto the road.

Mrs. Grant had been calling a lot since the accident, saying she wanted to *"be there"* for Diana during this *"difficult time."* Diana was certain Mrs. Grant's intentions were good and Diana felt guilty for not answering or reciprocating. Mrs. Grant must have been struggling a lot as well. Linus was her only child and as far as Diana could tell, she doted on him.

Linus would want Diana to reach out to his mom—she knew that—and she would. Just not tonight. She was too overwhelmed and she wasn't used to having someone so concerned about her. Yeah, she had Rochelle, but Ro knew her well enough not to push too hard or too much. Mrs. Grant didn't understand that yet.

No, tonight Diana wanted to get to the facility before dark and see her fiancé. She wanted to hold his hand and talk to him despite the fact that he wouldn't be saying anything back.

As Diana impatiently drove the forty-five-mile-an-hour speed limit to the care facility, her thoughts swirled around like battered snowflakes. She missed Linus more than she ever realized she could. How had he captured her heart so completely in less than a year? Her life hadn't been the same since meeting him and it wouldn't be again if he didn't wake up.

Stop thinking like that, Diana. He's going to pull through. He has to.

If the tables were turned, Linus wouldn't give up on her and she wasn't going to give up on him either. It was rare, but there were cases of patients who'd woken after decades of being comatose. Linus had been asleep for only three weeks—but they had been the longest weeks of her life.

Finally, she pulled up next to an SUV that was wearing a red Rudolph nose over the hood ornament and had antlers coming out of each side of the front windows. She took in the image for a moment. She'd always enjoyed Christmas, but this year she was struggling to be jolly for obvious reasons. She would have skipped over the holiday altogether but knowing Rochelle, that would invoke an intervention.

Who would be in that intervention circle? Diana pondered as she locked up her car and hurried toward the expansive brick building with a blue metal roof. Mrs. Grant? William Davis maybe? Or perhaps Diana's eccentric neighbor, Mrs. Guzman, who always seemed to stop by at the most inconvenient times?

Diana pushed through the front entrance doors and let the heat envelop her. She stood there and let it soak in, thawing out her body. In the corner of the room was a comically large and heavily adorned tree that made it hard to forget the season. The ornaments were handmade by the patients. Linus even had one hanging on the tree, but Diana knew his hands hadn't touched the tiny star-shaped ornament made from popsicle sticks and lathered with glue and glitter. His eyes hadn't even opened to see it. It was more likely the work of one of the nursing aides here.

"Good evening!" an orderly said. He was wearing Grinch-themed scrubs.

"Hi, Ernest." At this point, Diana knew everyone at New Hope, even though she'd been coming for only the last two weeks. The first week after Linus's accident, he'd been in the hospital and she'd been by his side every moment that she wasn't working. She'd slept there, eaten there, and had managed basic hygiene with his in-room shower and a toiletry bag that Rochelle had brought over. Once Linus's condition had failed to improve and the powers that be had determined there was minimal hope, he'd been transported to New Hope. It was ironic that the facility's name was New Hope, seeing that this was where patients were sent when there was none.

"Merry eve of Christmas Eve! Santa Claus comes tomorrow night!" Meeka Jamison said. The charge nurse was wearing Frosty the Snowman–themed scrubs this evening.

"Ho-ho-ho!" Dr. Romani said in passing. There were no cartoon characters on his scrubs, but his scrub top was bright red and his pants were green.

"Happy holidays," Diana said, politely. She wasn't in the mood to be merry, though. She picked up her pace as she made her way to room fourteen and dipped inside, closing the door behind her and fleeing from all the good cheer. A steady *beep, beep, beep* greeted her from Linus's equipment. Her heart seemed to take on the same rhythm.

Beep, beep, beep. Thump, thump, thump.

She pulled in a breath, walked over to the bedside chair, and sat down, inspecting him for a long moment. His dusty brown hair was neatly combed, which was never the case in real life. The man was always running his fingers through the unruly waves. He was also clean-shaven tonight, thanks to one of the aides. They'd done a good job, no nicks, which wasn't like the awake version of Linus either.

"Hey. It's Di." She reached for his hand and held it in hers. It felt foreign, not like the hand she'd been holding for the past nine months. The muscles were soft from three weeks of not using them. There were no calluses along the palm from where he rode his bicycle every day to work.

Diana leaned forward just a touch and watched his face, looking for any sign that he knew she was here. She had this fantasy that one day Linus would just open his eyes and look back at her. How long had it been since she'd stared into those blue-gray eyes of his? Would she ever again?

His lips were a straight line. There was no crooked smile that came with his witty one-liners. He just looked like he was sleeping. No, not even that. Linus wasn't a peaceful sleeper. He typically tossed and turned, making creases and sporting laughable bedhead as he slept. She loved those things about him. She loved everything about him.

Wake up, Linus.

Resigned to the fact that his eyes weren't going to pop

open and greet her this evening, she reached into the large canvas bag she'd carried in and pulled out the tiny Christmas tree she'd bought for his room. Linus professed to love Christmas more than anyone else. Not having a tree would kill him a lot faster than the delivery truck that had knocked him off his bike three weeks earlier.

"I brought you this tree to cheer you up." She looked at Linus, speaking to him as if he could hear her. Maybe he could. Meeka had told Diana it was possible, at least. "I know, I know. You would prefer the real thing, but they wouldn't allow me to drag a Douglas fir in here. I asked."

She dipped to plug the little tree in and straightened, watching the colorful lights twinkle festively. "Multicolored lights," she said, glancing over at him. "I'm not sure, but I suspect this would be your preference." Next, she pulled out a box of silver-toned tinsel. "If you don't open your eyes, I might have to decorate you as well," she warned, remembering a similar threat he'd made just before his accident.

Linus didn't flinch. Didn't smile. The only reason she knew he was even breathing was because of the obnoxious beep of his bedside machines.

She ripped open the box of tinsel and added a few strands to the tree's plastic branches. "It's gotten colder outside," she said as she worked. "Too cold to ride your bike, although I'm sure you'd disagree." She waited a beat, carefully draping a single silver strand at a time. "Maria is doing well. Her ankle is healing up well since her fall. You should see her house. It's like *National Lampoon's Christmas Vacation* inside, thanks to William." Diana rolled her eyes. She was still bitter about William being made supervisor over her, and about him going to her patient's home to decorate it for the holidays. That wasn't his job. If anything, it would be Diana's.

"I know what you're thinking," she told Linus on a sigh. "And yes, it was nice of William to help Maria, but it crossed a boundary. I mean, we're professionals. We don't spend our spare time decorating a stranger's home. I have my own place to decorate." Not that she'd done any such thing this month. She had an excuse though. Her fiancé was in a coma.

"And my patient Addy is still trying to figure out what's going on with us," Diana told him. She set the box of tinsel down and worked to fan out the limbs of the tree that had gotten smooshed in her bag. "She's sixteen going on thirty. And *so* nosy. She reminds me of you in that way."

Linus would balk at that comment. He prided himself on keeping his nose out of other people's business. It wasn't his way. He was a proper gentleman, through and through. Before him, Diana had always gone for the bad boy type. The ones who rode a motorcycle instead of a Schwinn ten-speed. The bad boys Diana had gone for had never been any good for her, though. They'd just wanted a physical relationship, which was all Diana had thought she'd wanted too.

Falling for Linus had come as a pleasant surprise. She'd gone inside the Toy Peddler to buy a gift for one of her coworker's children. Linus had taken his time in helping her, suggesting only the worst toys first—dolls that peed or pooped. Or puke-themed slime. He'd later confessed that was his tactic in getting to know her. By the time he'd rung up the doll she'd eventually decided on—one that laughed and sang—he'd asked her to have dinner with him. She'd agreed, of course, and the rest, as they say, was history.

Linus was what she never knew she needed: a good guy with a big heart and more love than she knew what to do with—literally.

Diana sighed and turned away from the tiny tree. She could add the ornaments tomorrow. Taking a seat in the chair beside his bed, she took hold of his hand and squeezed. "Come back to me," she finally whispered, leaning over to give the back of his hand a gentle kiss. "Please." She didn't believe in Christmas miracles beyond the ones that happened in movies, but she needed one this year. She needed this one.

* * *

By the time Diana had gotten back into her car, it was dark and the roads were slick. She drove ten miles below the speed limit, anxiously clutching the steering wheel the entire way home. When she arrived at the apartment, she walked straight into the laundry room and hung her winter coat on a hook. Then she headed into the kitchen, swung open her fridge door, and inspected a carton of half-eaten take-out food that was probably no longer safe to consume.

Diana sighed, her gaze wandering to the empty wine rack on her counter. She didn't have any merlot either. She'd drained the last of her supply last night while watching the one and only Christmas movie she could stomach this year: *Christmas with the Kranks.* The Krank family had nothing on her lack of Christmas spirit.

Settling for a glass of water, she gulped it down and then stripped off her scrubs as she walked down the hall to her bedroom. She wanted to feel close to Linus tonight so she veered in the direction of his closet for an old T-shirt and oversize pair of sweatpants. If this was as close as she could get to him right now, she'd take it.

His Snow Haven High School shirt was lying on the floor where he'd last left it. He'd come to Snow Haven his senior year, which had been her freshman year. They'd attended the same school for only a few months, and Diana's first year of high school had been rough. She barely remembered anything from that time, least of all an awkward boy with messy hair and glasses. Apparently, he remembered her, though. He'd told her he recognized her as soon as she'd stepped into the toy store that first day they met. He'd known exactly who she was and he'd wanted to know her better.

Diana picked up the Snow Haven High shirt and held it close to her nose, taking in a deep whiff. She'd turned into one of those people who smelled random things and tried to catch nostalgia. Pulling the shirt over her head, she turned and bumped against his curtain of ties. She stared at the goofy ties for a long moment. What thirty-year-old man owned such a ridiculous collection? One who worked at a toy store, she guessed. Linus had an adorable way about him. He was equal parts nerdy and sexy, like a Clark Kent, and she was his Lois Lane.

Her gaze fell on the tie with a print of little dogs playing fetch. It was one he'd worn often. He'd even worn it on the day of his accident. She'd taken it to the dry cleaners the next week because it had gotten bloodstained and dirty in the collision. It was his favorite tie—he adored it—and she'd wanted him to have it when he woke up.

She lifted her hand to touch the silk fabric before noticing that the collection of ties was lying funny on their rack. It was as if they were leaning against something stashed behind them.

Reaching past the ties, her fingertips tapped against a box. *What is that?* She slid the ties aside and realized the cube-shaped box was gift-wrapped in shimmery paper with a large red bow on the top. Her name was printed in neat block letters on the tag that hung off the front.

For several seconds, Diana forgot to breathe. He got her a gift? Carrying the box to the bed, she carefully set it down in front of her. She considered shaking the package before opening it, but that had backfired on her once—a tiny ceramic figurine had lost an arm—and Grandma Denny had never let her hear the end of it. Diana's hand shook as she took her time breaking the tape seals on each side and then folding the paper neatly back. Who knew Linus was so meticulous with his wrapping?

When the paper was peeled away, she pulled in a breath before lifting the box's lid, peering down, and gasping. "A snow globe!"

Diana lifted it from the box and looked through the glass. Inside was a tiny replica of the downtown area of their small town of Snow Haven. Diana unexpectedly caught herself smiling as she admired the gift. She tipped the snow globe upside down and upright again, watching the glittery silver-and-blue snow flutter around the tiny buildings and trees. There was even a little Santa standing on the sidewalk, which just so happened to be true on her street as well. Their apartment building bordered the downtown area and the sidewalk Santa here never seemed to give his bell a rest.

"I love it," she whispered out loud, wondering if Linus could hear her. Then she rolled her eyes at herself. *He isn't a ghost, Diana. He's still alive.*

The doorbell rang at the front of the apartment and Diana startled, nearly dropping the snow globe. That would have been a tragedy. Not quite as big as the one where her fiancé was hit by a delivery truck, but tragic all the same. Hugging the snow globe to her side, she carried it out of the room and placed it on the table before going to answer the door. She was half expecting to see Linus's mother standing there. Instead, she found her lovable, slightly eccentric neighbor smiling back at her. Henrietta Guzman was pleasant, never stayed for long, and often brought her own snacks when she stopped by.

"Hello, Mrs. Guzman. How are you?"

"I'm well. I hope you are too," the older woman said. Mrs. Guzman had long silver-blond hair and striking green eyes that stood out against a backdrop of aged skin. She was barely five feet tall and always wore long dresses that made it look like she didn't have any feet. The prints were usually colorful in nature just like Mrs. Guzman's vivid personality.

"I'm fine," Diana lied. *F-word alert.* "Come in. It's freezing out there."

"*Brrr.* Yes, thank you, love." Mrs. Guzman stepped inside, her long dress sweeping the floor as she walked. "I just came over to bring you a Christmas gift." She held up a bottle of red wine.

Diana felt the heat of embarrassment climbing through her chest and neck. "Oh, you shouldn't have. I didn't do any shopping yet this year."

Mrs. Guzman waved a dismissive hand, showing off rings on every finger and at least a dozen gold bangles encircling her wrists. "Of course not, dear. You've had your hands full. A gift never needs to be reciprocated, though. That defeats the whole point."

Diana smiled and took the gift. "Well, thank you. That's very kind." *How did Mrs. Guzman know she'd needed wine?* "Let me just put this away." She carried the bottle into the kitchen and slid it into the empty rack on her countertop. This would come in handy later.

"You should pour yourself a glass tonight," Mrs. Guzman suggested as if reading her mind. "Unless you have something stronger, hmm?"

"Oh, I don't keep liquor," Diana said, turning back to her.

"That's not what I was talking about, dear." Mrs. Guzman winked.

What does that mean? Diana had heard the whisperings that the old lady read tea leaves and concocted potions of some sort. Hearsay was that she'd prepared Mr. Zitnik in apartment twelve a love potion a few weeks ago. Diana wondered how that was fairing for the middle-aged accountant.

Diana headed back toward Mrs. Guzman, who was now standing at the dining room table and marveling at the snow globe. "Oh, this is just gorgeous! Who gave this to you?" The older woman leaned forward, nearly pressing her nose into the glass globe.

"Linus, actually. Or he was going to give it to me. I found it in his closet. I guess he was hiding it until the big day."

"It's just lovely," Mrs. Guzman gushed. "You know about the magic of a snow globe, yes?"

Diana furrowed her brow. "Magic?"

"Mm. There's a whole world in there."

"Or a model of our town, at least," Diana said with a nervous laugh.

"Yes, that too." Mrs. Guzman placed her hand over the top of the glass globe and closed her eyes, showing off her sparkly purple eyeshadow.

"Um, are you okay, Mrs. Guzman?" Diana was starting to become concerned about her neighbor's mental state. Or maybe the older woman was about to pass out. Diana didn't want her to drop the last gift Linus had ever gotten her. She was about to take the snow globe from Mrs. Guzman's hands when the old woman began to whisper softly.

"One more day to love the lost. One more day to live. As the snow comes down, all around, make a wish. Love knows no bounds." Her eyes popped back open with such force that Diana took a step back. Then Mrs. Guzman shoved the snow globe into Diana's hands as quickly as she would a hot potato.

Diana hugged the globe against her midsection. "What was that?"

"An enchantment." Mrs. Guzman smiled back proudly.

Obviously, Diana's neighbor had already delved into her own supply of *something stronger* tonight. "You cast a spell on my snow globe?"

"I don't do spells, dear. I do enchantments. There's a difference. And when you're ready, shake the snow globe, think of the one you've loved and lost, and enjoy one last day together. That is my real gift to you."

Diana tempered her reaction. She'd known Mrs. Guzman was a little odd, but she hadn't realized the woman was unstable. Maybe Diana should call someone for her. Was she safe to be alone in her apartment? "I see."

"No, you don't. But you will." Mrs. Guzman's eyes were almost twinkling. The woman lifted a finger, her nails painted in a festive red. "But be warned, whatever happens on the day that you relive with your loved one, it doesn't change the future. It doesn't make a difference in the end."

"Noted." There was no part of Diana that thought her snow globe from Linus was magical in any way. The only thing special about it was that Linus had picked it out for her. "Thank you again for the wine. And, um, the enchantment."

"You're very welcome, dear. Merry Christmas." Mrs. Guzman patted Diana's hand, the bangle bracelets on her wrist clanging quietly against one another. Then she headed back toward the door.

"Merry Christmas," Diana called after her. Mrs. Guzman wasn't staggering so she must not have been too tipsy. Diana followed her and closed the door, barring the frigid air. Then she looked down at the snow globe that she was still holding. She believed in enchanted snow globes about as much as she believed in Santa Claus and tiny elves.

Her cell phone rang from the dining room table, making her jump and nearly drop the snow globe for the second time tonight. She quickly walked to the fireplace mantel and set the snow globe there next to a series of photographs of her and Linus. Then she hurried over to her phone. Joann Grant's name flashed on her screen. Diana was going to have to talk to Linus's mother at some point. Might as well be now.

She connected the call and held the phone to her ear. "Hello?"

"Diana. You answered," Linus's mother said, sounding surprised.

"Well, you called." Diana let out a nervous laugh, hoping she didn't sound curt. That wasn't her intention. "I'm sorry for not being available for the last couple of days," she said, trying to sound warmer. It wasn't that she was cold. Just that she felt awkward and nervous. Her instinct, when something bad happened, was to isolate herself. Linus's mother seemed to do the opposite. "It's been busy at work."

"Oh, I understand," Mrs. Grant said. "But even so, I hear that you stop by to see Linus every day. I'm sure he appreciates that."

Diana cleared her throat. "I hope he knows I'm there."

"Oh, he does. I'm sure of it," Mrs. Grant said with a confidence that Diana envied. "And if there's anyone who could pull him out of that coma, it's you."

How did Mrs. Grant have so much faith in Diana when she barely knew her?

"That man adores you," Mrs. Grant went on. "He has been so excited to marry you." Her voice cracked. "I'm not sure I've ever seen him so happy as he's been since you came into his life. It's like a light has lit up inside him."

Guilt whirled around in Diana's chest. She should have set a date with Linus. Instead, she'd let her anxiety build up walls around her heart. She'd pushed him away and prioritized her work. So much so that Linus had even wondered aloud if she regretted saying yes to his proposal. He'd even said he regretted proposing to her. "How are you doing, Mrs. Grant?"

"Please, call me Joann. We're practically family at this point, aren't we?" Joann said on a teary sounding laugh. "I'm hanging in there."

"Good. I'm glad to hear that."

"I won't deny that it's been hard. I miss him. Christmas just won't be Christmas without my Linus. Nothing will be." She sucked in an audible breath. "But he'll wake up. I know he will. Linus is as stubborn as he is quick-witted. He'll prove those odds wrong."

Diana wondered what odds Joann was referring to. Had the doctors told her something more than they'd shared with Diana? Diana wasn't officially family. The Grants had to sign paperwork to even allow Diana to be included on Linus's medical information.

"I just wanted to call and check on you. Can I help you with anything, dear?" Joann asked.

"No, thank you. I'm fine. I'm actually just putting the finishing touches on my tree," Diana lied. She hadn't even started the beginning touches on the tree. She wasn't sure why she felt the need to be untruthful. Maybe it was to prove to all who wondered that she didn't need their concern or fuss. Drawing attention to oneself was always something Grandma Denny frowned on.

"A Christmas tree? Oh, you got yourself one?" Joann sounded relieved. "I was worried you wouldn't."

Diana's gaze jumped to the corner of the room where the tree she and Linus had dragged home at the start of the month still sat, untrimmed, unlit, and undecorated. She had at least been watering it every morning while her coffee brewed.

Joann cleared her throat, signaling a change in conversation. "Well, have you considered my invitation to Christmas dinner?"

Diana hedged. "Um . . ."

"Linus wouldn't want you to be alone. He'd insist that I make sure you get a proper ham-and-turkey dinner, complete with eggnog."

Diana wasn't sure she could go to the Grants' home without Linus. For the last nine months, she'd shied away from the Grants' events even when he was right beside her. Going without him would be torture. "I'm, um, actually working tomorrow."

"Linus always said how committed you were to your job. He was so proud of you, Diana . . . You can spare an hour to eat and open gifts, though, can't you? Or how about I bring the gifts to you after you've gotten off shift?" Joann offered. "That way I can see your tree."

Diana looked at the barren tree once more. She had no intention of trimming or decorating it between now and then. "No, that's okay. I'll plan to stop by your place after seeing my patients."

"Oh, wonderful. That will be nice. I'll make your favorite, pecan pie."

"How . . . ?"

"Linus told us. He never stopped talking about you, Diana. We'll look forward to seeing you tomorrow, then," she said.

Diana had said maybe, and that was as good as a no in her world. She'd just have to find an excuse before then. Like a headache. "Okay."

"Have a good night, dear. We love you."

Diana froze, unsure of how to respond. "You too," she finally said, feeling awkward. "Bye." She disconnected the call and set her phone down on the dining room table, wishing she had handled that interaction a little more gracefully. Or maybe she shouldn't have answered the call at all.

A person didn't get to turn back time, though. If they could, Diana would shake that snow globe that Mrs. Guzman claimed to have enchanted, turn back the clock, and fix all her mistakes with Linus. She would have set a date to marry him instead of pulling away. She would have tried harder to fit into his world rather than insisting on staying on the outer edges of it. She would have been an Anna instead of an Elsa.

Diana swallowed past the rising lump in her throat making it hard to pull in a full breath. A magic snow globe was a fantasy. Her fiancé was in a coma, and he might never wake up. *That* was reality.

Chapter 5

All I Want for Christmas

Christmas Eve

Diana stirred in bed and reached out for Linus. She patted the mattress beside her with her eyes still closed, finding nothing. Then the memory came slamming back into her mind. Linus wasn't here. He may never lie beside her in their bed again. This happened the same way every single morning. The realization hit her like a Mack truck, rolling over her heart until it burst. She felt numb and breathless, broken and shattered. This, every single morning.

The sound of jingle bells tinged in the distance as Diana sat up and opened her eyes. She blinked the room into focus, her gaze landing at the empty space on Linus's side of the bed.

More jingles filled the air. It was the Santa on the corner outside her apartment building. Diana had given the bell ringer all her spare change this month. He was raising money for children, which was a cause that Diana could get behind. If she could do anything to ensure a child had more than she'd had growing up, she'd do it. Not to say Grandma Denny had been poor or stingy. At least not with material items.

Diana stood and dragged her feet down the hall, desperately seeking coffee. All she needed was enough to stave off a headache while she worked today. Christmas Eve or not, someone had to take care of her patients. Like the U.S. Postal Service, their ailments didn't halt for rain, sleet, or the holidays.

After downing a cup, she took a quick shower and changed into a pair of scrubs. She had ones with Christmas trees and gingerbread houses. She had Grinch scrubs and Hawaiian Santa ones. Since it didn't look like it was going to snow this year despite the local meteorologist's promises, she chose the Hawaiian Santa, who had a bead of sweat lining his sunburned brow. To complete the look, Diana opened her box of Christmas accessories and put on her traditional elf ears and lighted tree bulb necklace.

She felt ridiculous as she left her apartment, but hopefully her ridiculousness would bring a smile to her patients' faces today. If so, it was worth it. She locked up her door behind her and headed toward the parking lot, walking quickly in case she ran into Mrs. Guzman again. As she approached the shared parking lot for her apartment complex and downtown, she saw the Santa standing there with his pail for donations. She dug into her purse for some dollar bills, but she'd given them all away on the other times she passed him this week. All she had was a ten-dollar bill. She stuffed it inside the Santa's pail.

"Merry Christmas Eve!" he belted.

Diana steadied herself against the cheerful blast. "Not for everyone," she said quietly.

Sidewalk Santa's brow furrowed. "I'm sorry?"

Oops! She hadn't meant to say that out loud. *Hold it together, Di.* "God bless us, everyone," she said, channeling Tiny Tim from *A Christmas Carol.*

Sidewalk Santa seemed to accept that answer and his smile curled back to its previous jolly height. *What is wrong with me?* Christmas had never been her favorite holiday, mostly because it emphasized the things she didn't have but longed for. Like big, loving families. She wasn't a Grinch, though.

Diana hurried toward her car. As she drew closer, she clicked the key fob to unlock the driver's side door and got inside. She waited a few moments for the car to warm and then pulled onto Oakwood Drive. Maria Harris had canceled her appointment for this morning so Diana was heading to Addy's house first.

Diana fiddled with the radio as she drove, but only Christmas tunes were playing. She pushed the OFF button and instead listened to her blaring thoughts until she parked along the curb in front of the Pierces' home. After getting out of her car, Diana headed up the driveway to the porch. She pushed the doorbell and waited, feeling silly as she stood behind the front door in elf ears and a lighted necklace. Hopefully this would cheer Addy up. Maybe Diana wasn't as good with kids as Linus, but she liked them. Not that Addy was necessarily a child. At sixteen, the girl was closer to being an adult.

Mrs. Pierce opened the door and smiled brightly. "Merry Christmas, Ms. Diana. Addy's been waiting for you all morning. Oh, she'll love your accessories." Mrs. Pierce opened the door wider for Diana to enter the home which smelled of cinnamon and spices.

"How is she doing this morning?" Diana asked.

"Happy, I think. She's binging the Home Alone movies today. Ever since she was a little girl, those have always been her favorites."

"Her pain level?" Diana asked.

"She hasn't mentioned any pain today."

"Good." Diana glanced down the hall where Addy's room was. "I'll get started with our therapy, if that's okay."

"Of course, of course. I'm cooking nine different things in the kitchen. I need to monitor those. We're having the whole family here for Christmas dinner tomorrow so that Addy doesn't have to travel."

"Wow. You're going to be busy," Diana commented.

Mrs. Pierce's smile faded momentarily. "Being busy helps."

"I understand." All too well, but most of Diana's patients didn't know she was in a relationship with Linus. Everyone had heard about his accident, of course. This was a small town. The owner of Snow Haven's only toy store landing himself in a coma was big news. Their relationship was relatively new and a lot of folks just didn't realize that Linus and Diana were linked. That was for the best. She was here to focus on her patients' needs, not vice versa.

Diana gave Mrs. Pierce a small wave and turned, walking to the end of the hall and knocking on Addy's bedroom door.

"Come in!" the girl called from the other side.

Diana pushed the cracked door open. "Hey, Addy. How are you this morning?"

Addy removed her earbuds. She was pale, but smiling, which Diana took as a good sign. "Good. It's Christmas Eve after all."

"So I hear." Diana stepped into the room and closed the door behind her.

"I like your elf ears," Addy said with a tiny laugh.

Mission accomplished. Laughter was, in fact, the best medicine. "Thanks. And I like your antlers."

Addy was wearing reindeer antlers over a bandana that covered her thinning hair. She rolled her eyes slightly. "My mom kind of insisted I wear these. I'll probably have to wear them tomorrow too along with some ugly sweater." Addy gave Diana a conspiratorial look. "Unless you tell my mom that I might overheat in an ugly Christmas sweater and antlers. Then she'd have to listen and let me wear something cooler."

Diana tapped a finger to the side of her chin as she feigned a thoughtful look. "Yes, I think that's actually true. And the uglier the sweater, the hotter you would be while wearing it. That's not healthy."

"Exactly." Addy gave a wide grin. "And since you're being

so cool, I think you should tell my mom that I need to skip straight to dessert tomorrow because I get full a lot faster these days. I would hate to miss my Aunt Becky's ten-layer chocolate cake just because I was forced to eat Grandma Ann's Brussel Sprouts Casserole first." The girl wrinkled her nose, making Diana laugh. "I'm not a fan."

"Well, perhaps if you eat just a bite or two of the actual meal prior to dessert . . ." Diana pulled her blood pressure cuff from her bag. She just needed to check Addy's vitals and ask a few questions before getting on with therapy.

Addy stuck out her arm without Diana needing to ask. She knew the drill. "Have you seen *Home Alone*?" she asked.

"Of course. You know, Macaulay Culkin is older than I am now."

"Wow, that's old!" Addy said with a wide grin.

"Hey." Diana flicked her gaze away from her laptop for a moment. "I'll have you know, I'm only twenty-nine, and old is a state of mind." In which case, Diana was feeling like a senior citizen these days. She'd been turning in every night by nine and waking with the birds the way that Grandma Denny used to.

"Who did you watch the movie with last?" Addy wanted to know.

"My, um, fiancé." When Diana flicked her gaze up to meet Addy's again, the girl's eyes were narrowed.

"The one you're not marrying just yet?"

"I only have one fiancé," Diana said, hoping her sarcasm would deter the teen. No such luck.

"Oh, come on. Tell me something, at least. When is the wedding? Can I come? I can be the balding flower girl."

Diana ignored Addy's self-deprecating comments and focused on the blood pressure reading, which seemed to be having a hard time finding a pulse. "We still haven't set a date." That was Diana's fault. And maybe her resistance was the whole reason Linus was in a coma right now. It was probably irrational of her to think so, but grief had a way of making a person believe things that weren't exactly true—at least that's what Rochelle claimed. Perhaps if Diana and Linus hadn't fought the night before his accident, he would have allowed her to give him a ride to the toy store that morning. Then she would have had to pick him up later in the evening, and he wouldn't have been hit by a delivery truck.

"Is your fiancé one of those guys who proposes, but then freaks out because he's secretly afraid of commitment?" Addy asked, her pale brows lifting curiously.

Diana shook her head. That description was more fitting for Diana than Linus. "No. That's not him at all. We've just been busy. And how do you know about those kinds of guys anyway?"

Addy shrugged, making her collar bones jut out more prominently above her scoop neck tee. "My dad. He didn't freak out with marriage, but he freaked when I came along. Thus, the reason I'm being raised by a single parent."

Diana blinked Addy into view. That was Diana's story too. Diana's dad had left when she was just a colicky baby. Then her mom had decided that being a single mother interfered with her drinking habit too much, and she'd handed Diana over to Grandma Denny, who'd barely had two pennies to scrape together.

"It's complicated." Addy's blood pressure reading finally came through. Diana tapped her fingers along her keyboard and recorded the stats.

Addy sighed as the cuff deflated on her thin arm. "Too complicated for a teenager? My mom used to tell me that I could know and do all these off-limits things when I became an adult. She would tell me to be a kid for as long as I could. But I think chemo and radiation have earned me maturity points, don't you?" Her gaze was still narrowed. The girl was destined to be a reporter one day.

"I do think you're mature for your age, yes." Diana removed the cuff from Addy's arm. "But I'd still rather focus on you when I'm here. That's my job."

"Oh." Addy's gaze fell momentarily along with her smile. "That's kind of my problem, I guess. Everyone's always focused on me. That's not how life is supposed to be, though. I mean, I'm not dying anymore. I'm still living, aren't I?"

"Very much so." Diana smiled reassuringly.

Addy offered an exasperated sigh. "Well, tell that to my *ex*-boyfriend and *ex*-best friend, Sierra."

Diana placed her BP cuff back in the bag at her feet and sat upright. She remembered a couple weeks ago when Addy had mentioned her former boyfriend and best friend. Addy had burst into tears that day and hadn't talked about it since. The last thing Diana wanted was to make Addy cry again. Maybe Addy needed a session with Rochelle. Diana could suggest it to Mrs. Pierce later.

"Never mind," Addy muttered. "Forget I said anything."

Diana was tempted, but she could also tell the girl was hurting and from what Diana could tell, Addy didn't exactly have a lot of people to talk to. She had her mom, of course, but what teen girl wanted to talk about what was going on in her life with her mother? "I'm a good listener, you know."

Addy hesitated. She took a moment to inspect her nails as she seemed to contemplate whether to confide in Diana. "Once I got sick, they both completely forgot that I existed."

"Why would they disappear on you like that?"

"I don't know, maybe because I'm a weirdo now. I don't exist in their world anymore." Addy shrugged again, as if this was no big deal, but the circles under her eyes suddenly looked darker.

"I'm sorry," Diana said. "It's their loss. Do you want to talk about it?"

"Do you want to disclose information about *your* personal life?" Addy asked with a hopeful rise to her voice.

"No," Diana said flatly.

"Fine. Me either." Addy returned to looking at her chipped polish.

"Okay then, we'll just continue with your physical therapy." Diana turned to her company laptop. Before she even got started with her questions, Addy began rattling off her answers.

"I'm a five on the pain scale. I already went to the bathroom this morning. Number one, not two. I had some water and one boiled egg for breakfast. No nausea or vomiting." She grinned but Diana could see that whatever was going on with Addy's boyfriend and best friend was bothering her more than a little bit. "Do you think my exes are scared of me now? Because I had cancer?" she finally asked.

Diana looked up from her laptop as she recorded Addy's responses. "No, of course not. Maybe they're just uncomfortable because they don't understand what you're going through. Sometimes it's hard to talk to someone when you don't know what to say."

Addy fidgeted with her hands in her lap. "It doesn't matter what they say as long as they say something. Their silence is brutal."

Diana suddenly felt the urge to reach out and hug the girl. She suppressed it because it wasn't exactly professional, right? Therapists didn't embrace their patients. "This won't last forever, you know. And right now, your focus needs to be on getting stronger so that you can return to school and everyday life. Your true friends will be waiting for you when you get back."

Addy's eyes were shimmering with unshed tears. "Sure," she said after a moment. "Focus on getting better. So, what are we doing today? Let's do this," she said, forcing a smile.

After twenty minutes of exercise and therapeutic activity, Diana stepped out of Addy's room and talked to Mrs. Pierce in the kitchen. Mrs. Pierce extended an invitation to Christmas dinner tomorrow, which Diana politely declined. She was neither friend nor family to the Pierces. She was sure William would have no issue blurring the lines, but she wasn't William. Plus, she just didn't feel like celebrating this year.

"Unfortunately, I'll be at my future mother-in-law's house," Diana said, even though she had no intention of going to the Grants' place.

"I understand," Mrs. Pierce said. "A person should be with their family on Christmas."

Linus was Diana's family. And she did intend to spend the holiday with him at New Hope. At least for a couple hours.

Diana waved goodbye and then headed back to her car parked along the curb. The temperature felt ten degrees colder as she hurried to tuck herself behind the wheel. Then she proceeded to see three more patients before pulling into the parking lot for New Hope that evening. Her phone chirped with an incoming text message from Rochelle.

Rochelle: *You're not breaking the holiday drinks tradition. It'll be good for you. Plus, I miss my friend.*

This was in response to a message that Diana had sent her yesterday. Diana tapped off a quick reply.

Diana: *I miss you too. I guess I can hang for one drink.*
Rochelle: *Good.*
Diana: *I'll meet you there in half an hour?*

That would give Diana time to step inside New Hope and check on Linus.

Rochelle: *I'll be there with bells on. Literally.*

Diana shoved her phone back inside her purse and climbed out of her car. She hurried to the building, exhaling only after she was warmly inside.

"Merry Christmas Eve!" Ernest said as she entered. "Love the elf ears!"

"Oh. Thanks." She hadn't realized she was still wearing them. The light-up necklace too. All her patients had loved them today, which was the point. *See? My bedside manner is fine.* She stripped the headband and necklace off as she continued toward room fourteen, passing the nurses' station. The staff was huddled around something sweet that a patient's family had likely given them. Probably cookies. A lot of Diana's patients had given her baked goods as well. Baked goods but no Glow Cards, which were what she really wanted this year. That, and for Linus to wake up.

Ducking into room fourteen, she closed the door behind her and turned to face the bed in the room. Linus's eyes were closed. His body was lying in the same position as yesterday.

"Hey, sleepy man," she said, stepping toward him. She missed the way he'd always woken her up with nearly those same words. "Merry Christmas Eve." She leaned over him and carefully placed the elf ears headband on the crown of his head where his brown hair was disheveled and in need of a cut. "These ears look better on you." She took a moment to add more tinsel to the tree on his bedside table and then a couple of miniature ornaments from inside the bag she'd carried in yesterday. "Your tree is looking good," she told him. "You should open your eyes to see it."

She waited a moment, in case he did. Then she moved to the foot of the bed and took hold of his leg, gently lifting it up and bending it at the knee. She held it for a prolonged stretch and repeated on both sides as she talked, giving him physical therapy the way she would one of her patients.

"I'm meeting Rochelle tonight for drinks. Or one drink," she amended. "I don't really feel like going out—too cold— but you know Rochelle. She doesn't take no for an answer." Kind of like Joann Grant. Diana doubted Linus wanted to hear her complain about his mother right now. He also wouldn't be pleased to know Diana had been avoiding most of Joann's calls.

Diana lowered his leg to the bed and stepped over to the head of the bed. She took hold of his arm and lifted it up, giving it a decent stretch like she'd done every day since he'd arrived here. The movement was good for him, even if his muscles weren't the ones doing the heavy lifting. She didn't want him to be as stiff when he woke up. He'd want to get on his bike first thing. Not a day went by when he didn't ride it. As she stretched him, she watched his face, waiting to see any sign he knew she was here. There was nothing.

Beep. Beep.

The sound of the monitor beside him was at least proof that his heart was still beating. The ache in her chest, deep and painful, was proof that hers was too.

At 6:00 p.m., Diana pulled into the parking lot of Sparky's Tavern and cut the engine. As she was gathering her scarf and purse, someone knocked on her driver's-side window, making her nearly jump out of her skin.

Rochelle could be heard laughing hysterically outside. "C'mon! It's freezing out here!" she said in a muffled voice. "My tits are going to fall off!"

Diana rolled her eyes at her friend's crassness. She collected her bag beside her and then stepped out and, *whoa*, Rochelle wasn't kidding. The temperatures were dropping exponentially.

Rochelle wrapped Diana in a quick hug. "Now let's go in and get our drinks."

They hurried inside the hole-in-the-wall bar owned by a woman named Sparky. Both Diana and Rochelle had gone to school with Sparky, who'd been somewhat of an artsy loner growing up, despite being well liked. Now her bar was a town favorite decorated on the outside with artistic graffiti and on the inside with sketches and paintings from local artists.

Sparky waved from behind the crowded bar. It was a packed place tonight, but thankfully two men were getting up to leave just as Diana and Rochelle walked in. They bee-lined in that direction and took a seat.

"What'll you have?" Rochelle asked Diana. Tonight her dark, wavy hair was pulled back in a messy bun. "I'm buying."

"You don't have to," Diana protested, but Rochelle was already shaking her head.

"It's my gift to you."

"But I didn't get you anything," Diana said, just like she'd done with Mrs. Guzman last night. Where was her Christmas spirit?

Rochelle shrugged. "You showed up. That's gift enough for me."

Diana had never missed a single Christmas Eve outing with Rochelle since they were sixteen. Back then they'd gone for hot chocolates instead of alcohol.

Sparky stepped in front of them with an expectant look. "Hey, ladies. What can I get for you?"

"Two of your most festive drinks, please." Rochelle was wearing tiny Santa-face earrings tonight. She was also wear-ing a red long-sleeved top that shimmered under the bar's ac-cent lighting.

"The Jingle Bell Hopper is tonight's special," Sparky told them.

"Sounds perfect." Rochelle glanced at Diana. "Yes?"

Diana nodded. "Sounds good to me as well."

"You got it. Two Jingle Bell Hoppers coming right up," Sparky said. "Good to see you, ladies."

"Thanks." Rochelle turned to Diana once Sparky had moved on to prepare the drinks. "So, what's new with you?"

Diana cast her friend a look. "Really?"

Rochelle gave a rueful smile. "Yes, I know the obvious, but what about work? How's your new supervisor?"

Diana sighed. From one bitter topic to another. "William is on a major power trip. He keeps calling me into his office to check up on me, like he even cares."

"Maybe he does," Rochelle said.

"He doesn't. Then he assigns me work that he's supposed to be doing himself."

Rochelle lifted her brows. "What? Why?"

Diana shrugged. "He says he's too swamped with important stuff, but I think he just doesn't know what he's doing. It's pretty obvious he got the job solely based on his people skills, which I apparently lack."

"That's not true. You care about people more than anyone I've ever known. You just don't give people a chance to care for you. You're closed off."

"Closed off?" Diana gave Rochelle a look. She wasn't sure if that was better or worse than being called curt on her first ever Glow Card. "You mean I'm cold, like Elsa?"

Rochelle placed a quick hand on her forehead in mock disbelief. "I really can't believe your patient said that. And Linus agreed with her."

Diana shook her head. "He was just frustrated, and with good reason. The whole argument was my fault. He wanted to set a date. He was excited about getting married and I just pushed him off."

"I'm sorry." Rochelle gave her an apologetic look.

"Anyway, I guess it's good that I didn't get that promotion. With Linus's accident, I don't need added responsibilities. Even if I'm actually doing those added responsibilities for William anyway." She tapped her fingers along the bar. "I'm tired of talking about me. What's going on with you? Any new guys?"

Rochelle scoffed. "Well, the guy I was excited about last week turned out to be a complete jerk."

"What guy?" Diana asked.

Rochelle glanced over. "Sorry. I didn't get a chance to tell you about him."

Diana felt her shoulders slump forward. "I've been a little—"

"Preoccupied. It's completely understandable. My dating life, or lack thereof, is unimportant in comparison to your fiancé being in a coma."

Diana felt the sudden need to apologize. "Your dating life is important to me. I've been a horrible friend, haven't I?"

Before Rochelle could confirm or deny, Sparky slid two drinks in front of them.

"Here you two go! Enjoy!"

"Thank you," Diana and Rochelle said in unison.

"You're welcome." Sparky winked and quickly moved on to the next customer. The bar was bustling tonight. Excitement about what tomorrow would bring hung thick in the air.

"I wasn't thinking you were a horrible friend," Rochelle said quietly. She reached for the bright green-colored drink.

"No?" Diana molded her lips around the candy-cane design straw.

"Of course not. I was thinking you've been through hell and back this past month. I can't even imagine how hard this all is for you. I really think you should see someone, Diana. I can recommend one of my colleagues."

Diana side-eyed her. "A psychologist?"

"Or a counselor. Anyone, really, just as long as you're talking to someone. It can't be me, though. I'm too partial and you don't listen to me anyway."

Diana expelled a sigh. Maybe her fake cheer worked on acquaintances, but Rochelle could see through the forced smiles. "Or," she muttered, "I could just shake a snow globe and disappear into some fantasy land where I get to spend a whole day with Linus."

Rochelle furrowed her brow over her beverage. "Huh?"

"My neighbor paid me a visit last night. She picked up a snow globe of mine and"—Diana made air quotes—"she 'enchanted' it. She said I could shake the globe and spend one last day with someone I've lost."

"Sounds kinky," Rochelle said with an eyebrow waggle.

Diana chuckled dryly. "Mrs. Guzman is the one who needs a referral for a psychologist, not me."

Rochelle hummed on that thought. "I can refer you both. There's enough listening ears to go around. And elf ears too."

"I got a pair of those already, thank you very much. I gave them to Linus before coming here."

Rochelle grinned. "He's somewhere in the coma-verse cursing you right now for that," she said sarcastically.

"Doubtful. The man loves tacky things like that. You should see his array of ties." Diana thought about the gift he'd gotten for her. "The snow globe was actually a present from him. I found it hidden inside his closet last night."

Rochelle pulled away from her straw. "Wow. That's so sweet."

"It is," Diana agreed. Linus was ever thoughtful. It was one of the things she loved about him. He was always doing things for her and bringing home little trinkets. "It has a model of our town inside it."

"Snow Haven? In a snow globe?" Rochelle snorted out a laugh. "That's ironic considering that this is the town that never snows."

"They're saying maybe it will this year," Diana noted.

"Who's saying that?" Rochelle asked skeptically. "The same guy who predicted rain all last week when it was bright and sunshiny every day?"

Diana took another sip of her drink. "True enough . . . This is pretty tasty."

"You want a second one?" Rochelle asked. "My treat."

"No. One is enough for me. I have to get home in one piece tonight."

"Now that's the Christmas spirit," Rochelle said, offering a smile. "Are you going to Linus's parents' place tomorrow?"

Diana watched Sparky move from patron to patron behind the bar. She was a ball of energy. She reminded Diana of Linus in that way. When he was in his toy store, the man was practically one big kid. It was his happy place. And now he was stuck lying on a bed in some dimly lit room, day in and day out. "I told Mrs. Grant I might stop by for dinner and pecan pie."

"Why do I get the feeling that you won't?" Rochelle asked, finishing off her drink. "I know you won't agree to my invitation either, but I'm extending one anyway. Feel free to spend the day with me and my folks."

"Thank you. But my preference is to skip the day altogether."

Rochelle reached for Diana's hand and gave it a quick squeeze before pulling her hand back.

Diana swallowed back her emotions and reached for her pearl earring, giving it a twist as she breathed in and out. "I'm okay. Really."

"If you weren't, that would be okay too, you know?" Rochelle gave her an assessing look.

"I'm fine."

"F-word alert," Rochelle said quietly, bumping her elbow against Diana's. "You're about as bad as a drunken sailor, you know that?"

Diana laughed. Then she took one more sip of her drink and stood. "Time for me to get home."

"To do what?" Rochelle asked, still looking concerned.

Diana pulled her purse onto her shoulder and shrugged. "I don't know. Maybe I'll shake that snow globe after all and see what happens."

Chapter 6

There was a Christmas gift waiting in front of Diana's door when she got home. Maybe it was something more from Mrs. Guzman. Another spell maybe? Perhaps this one would suck Diana into the snow globe itself.

Diana picked up the package and then fiddled with her keys, poking the house key into the door's lock. Once inside, she carried the gift to the dining room table before heading down the hall to her bedroom. The first order of business was to change out of her Hawaiian Santa scrubs and into something fresh and clean.

Diana stepped into her closet and grabbed the first shirt and pajama shorts she could find. She carried them into the bathroom and changed, then stood at the sink, inspecting her reflection in the mirror. Her skin was ashen and she had dark circles under her eyes from sleepless nights. Even her dark blond hair was lifeless. No wonder Rochelle looked worried.

With a sigh, she walked back into her living room. There were no lights. No holiday decorations of any type except for the barren tree in the corner. The only hint of cheer in the whole apartment was the present she'd just found outside her door.

The wrapping paper on the gift had little elves dancing around with various kinds of toys. There was no card, no tag. She hesitated before ripping into the paper and letting it fall on the floor at her feet. Underneath the wrapping was a gold-colored box. She lifted the lid and peered inside at a silver picture frame. She pulled it out and looked at it. It held a picture of her and Linus from Thanksgiving at the Grants' house last month.

This was obviously from Linus's mother, Joann. In the photograph, Diana and Linus were both standing under a twig of mistletoe and Linus was about to kiss Diana's cheek.

What kind of gift was this? Diana didn't need a reminder of all she'd lost. She sucked in a steadying breath, waiting for herself to calm. *No tears, no tears, no tears.* If she started crying now, she might not be able to stop.

A tear finally slipped down her cheek. Then another. With a shaky hand, she walked over to her mantel and carefully set down the silver picture frame. She placed it right beside the snow globe and then stared at Linus's gift to her for a solid minute as more tears began to well. She couldn't seem to hold them back any longer. The dam was broken and the flood was inevitable.

All she wanted was one more day with Linus. Okay, she wanted more than one, but if she could have only twenty-four hours more with the one she'd loved and lost, she'd want it to be with him. If she could have anything for Christmas this year, that's what she would wish for.

She picked up the snow globe and stared down into the little town of Snow Haven, thinking of her dear, sweet, incredibly nerdy fiancé. She missed him more than there was air in her lungs.

She was angry at him too. *So* angry. For calling her distant and saying he almost regretted proposing. For rushing her into things she wasn't sure she was ready for. Things she may never be ready for. For not being here for her now when he'd promised he'd never leave. And being so careless on his bike that day three weeks ago. How hard was it to see a delivery truck coming straight at you?

She sucked in a breath, thought of Linus, and shook the snow globe just like Mrs. Guzman had instructed her. Glittery silver-and-blue snow bloomed around the tiny replica of her town, fluttering its way from the top to the bottom.

Nothing happened. *Of course* nothing happened. It was a silly little snow globe. There was nothing magical about it.

Even so, she shook it again, harder this time, as sobs rose in her throat. They rumbled through her, shaking her body as she jiggled and joggled the snow globe.

"One more day!" she cried, shaking the snow globe with everything she had and wishing with all her might. Then the globe slipped out of her grasp and crashed to the floor at her feet, shattering into a million little pieces just like her heart. "Damn it!" The water of the globe splashed onto her bare feet as tears ran down her cheeks. She was vaguely aware of a gut-wrenching noise she'd never heard before. Then she realized it was coming from her. She missed her fiancé. Her best friend. The man of her dreams and the person she was supposed to grow old with.

"You promised," she said, flicking her gaze to the framed picture of them at Thanksgiving. He was smiling. So was she. "You promised me forever." She took a few steps backward before collapsing onto her knees.

Kneeling there, she cried until there were no tears left. Then she picked herself up off the floor, took a few calming breaths, and turned to grab the broom and dustpan from the laundry room. Numbly, she swept up the glass shards and dumped them into the trash. After that, she grabbed a towel to sop up the glittery liquid on the floor. When she was done cleaning, she retreated to her room and fell into her bed, spent and exhausted. She didn't even have enough energy to change into her pajamas.

'Twas the night before Christmas and her life was a merryless mess.

The next morning, sunlight streamed through the blinds that Diana had failed to close last night. She stretched beneath her covers and cracked open an eye, groaning at the room's obnoxious brightness. "Ughhh." She started to reach for Linus, but stopped herself. *Right.* He wasn't there. On a yawn, she sat up in bed and draped her legs off the side, her eyes still refusing to open.

Merry Christmas to me.

She sat there a moment, considering the day ahead. She had two options: stay home alone and pretend like this day didn't exist. Or go to New Hope Long-Term Care Facility to see Linus.

Linus, it was. She opened her eyes, stood, and started shuffling toward the bathroom. The door was closed, which was odd. Why had she closed it? She twisted the knob and pushed it open, banging it against something solid that let out a soft grunt.

Diana stumbled backward and screamed. "Who's there?" Her heart pounded inside her chest. Someone had broken in and they were in her bathroom! On Christmas Day, at that. Seeing as she didn't believe in Santa anymore, this had to be a burglar.

On instinct, she reached for the door again and used her body weight to hold it shut. Whoever was in her bathroom was not coming out until she could call the police. Then again, her cell phone was on the other side of the room. How was she going to reach it?

Think, Diana, think.

As her mind raced, she felt the person on the other side

trying to pull the door open. It rattled and banged against the doorframe as she used every muscle in her body—even the ones in her eyelids—to keep it closed.

"Di, what are you doing?" The man's voice was deep and familiar.

Diana gasped and let go of the doorknob, nearly stumbling back onto her bottom. She knew that voice. She loved that voice. "L-Linus?" She pressed a hand to her chest, heart kicking against her palm as the bathroom door opened. There he was in the flesh. And a pair of snowflake design boxer shorts.

"Wh-what are you doing here?" She blinked several times just in case he was a hallucination. Hadn't Rochelle mentioned that sometimes grief made you imagine things that weren't true?

Linus's whole face scrunched up, looking at her like she was crazy. It was a look he liked to give her on the regular. "I live here."

She clutched her chest, struggling to pull in a full breath. "Did you . . . did you wake up last night? Did they discharge you?"

Linus's dark brown hair was sticking up in various directions, overgrown and in need of a cut. The elf ears she'd put on him last night were gone. He must have taken them off when he'd climbed out of bed. How was he standing? Walking? He hadn't used those muscles in weeks. She'd made sure he was getting stretched, but there was no way that being on his feet for so long wouldn't be pushing the outer limits of his endurance. "You need to get back in bed. What if you fall and hit your head a second time?" She could lose him all over again.

"A second time? Why are you acting like this? Did you have a bad dream or something?"

The last three weeks had felt like one big nightmare. But it had all been real. "Didn't they tell you? Linus, you were in a coma." She stepped toward him. "Why didn't New Hope call and let me know you were awake? Do your parents know? Are you feeling okay?" Her questions came in quick succession.

"A coma?" Linus chuckled wryly. He was still looking at her like she was talking gibberish. "Wow, that must have been some dream you were having. Maybe you dreamed about something happening to me because I kind of agreed with your patient about you being an Elsa last night."

"An Elsa?"

Linus cringed. "Please forgive me?"

"Forgive you?"

"Why are you repeating everything I say?" He shook his head. It was surreal to even see him move, to hear his voice. "I'm a bit worried about you. Perhaps *you're* the one who hit your head?" He stepped closer, his eyes searching hers. It'd been three weeks since she'd looked into those blue-gray eyes, the color of the ocean in a thunderstorm.

Diana reached for him, bracing his body between both of her hands. "No. You hit your head. In the accident. You fell off your bike." Her gaze jumped to the side of his head where there should have been a nasty scar. It wasn't there. Instead, the skin was smooth and perfect.

One corner of Linus's mouth hooked up. He looked slightly amused. "I haven't taken a spill from my bike since I was six. Last night, I came home and we had a bit of a squabble," he said, calmly. Patiently. "I mean, there's no real fighting with you, is there? You just shut down and go to bed. Maybe if you'd taken a moment to yell at me, you would have had a more restful sleep."

Diana knew the night he was referring to. How could she forget? She'd been replaying it in her mind and making herself miserable, ever since. "You suggested we get married this Christmas," she said quietly.

Linus nodded. "It was just a thought. I'm not trying to force things along. I'm just excited about marrying you, that's all. I wish you were as excited as me."

Guilt swirled at the center of her chest. "That discussion was . . . weeks ago. Is this some kind of Christmas miracle?" she asked, still looking for an answer. None of any of this made sense.

"A bit early for Christmas miracles, wouldn't you say?"

"What do you mean?"

"Well, the big day is still weeks away."

Linus had been unconscious for the last three weeks. It was no wonder he didn't know what day it was. "Today is December twenty-fifth."

Linus gave her a strange look. Then he stepped past her and walked over to the nightstand nearest his side of the bed.

How is he walking with such balance after lying motionless for nearly a month?

He grabbed his cell phone and walked it over, flashing the home screen in her direction. The screen's wallpaper behind the date and time was a picture of her. "See there? It's December fourth."

Diana straightened. "What? It can't be December fourth." Time had passed since then. Weeks had passed. She'd been dragging through recent days, numb and clinging to quickly draining hope that Linus would get better. "December fourth" she said again. "That's the day . . ."

"The day that what?" he asked, starting to get restless.

"The day you were hit by a delivery truck."

Linus laughed out loud. "Geesh, Diana. I know you're upset at me, but dreaming I got hit by a truck?"

She shook her head. "It wasn't a dream."

"Want me to call Rochelle?" he asked.

Diana stared at her fiancé, who shouldn't be here right now. He was supposed to be at New Hope Long-Term Care.

In his bed. In his coma that he was never going to wake from. It wasn't a dream. *This* was the dream. It had to be. That was the only explanation. Unless . . .

Diana clapped a hand to her mouth. "Oh."

"What?" he asked, the skin between his eyes pinching deeply.

"The snow globe. Mrs. Guzman placed a spell on it."

Linus's jaw went slack. "Have you been in my closet? Did you peek at the gift I got you?"

She shook her head. "No. I mean, yes, but I couldn't help it. You weren't here. You were . . ."

"Comatose?" Linus turned and headed into his closet. "I'd love to discuss what happens to impatient people who peek at their gifts early"—he cleared his throat—"but I really do need to get dressed."

"No! Don't go to work today. Stay home. With me." She practically chased him into the closet.

"I can't. This is the busiest time of year for the Toy Peddler. Plus, I have a meeting with the new distributor today, remember? And you need to get dressed for work too. You're going to be late, which isn't like you at all." He looked back, giving her an assessing glance.

Diana reached for his arm. "Just don't work late tonight, okay? Come straight home. And maybe don't ride your bike. Take your truck instead. There might be ice on the roads." She was talking quickly, her words spilling over each other. She still wasn't sure what was going on, but if this really was December 4th, then Linus's accident was tonight. Everything in Diana's world had come crashing down around her on this day.

She watched as Linus picked out a long-sleeved lavender shirt and a pair of pants. Then he walked past her, heading out of the closet. He pointed a finger as he passed by. "I'm on to you. The only reason you don't want me to ride my bike today is because you're scheming on buying *me* a Christmas present now. Probably some sort of bicycle accessory," he said. "The rule is twenty dollars or less. No cheating, Diana."

"But *you* cheated."

"I didn't. I'll have you know I traded something for that snow globe."

Diana followed him. "Let me drive you to the store today."

He turned back with a skeptical expression. "Why?"

"I just want to spend time with you. How about lunch? Can you spare an hour with me?" That would give him time to meet with his distributor. Then she could find an excuse to spend the rest of the day together. She didn't want to waste any of the time they were given.

Linus hedged. "We'll have to eat in the store. I'm not kidding when I say it's my busiest season. Santa Claus has nothing on me."

"I don't mind," Diana said quickly. She'd take whatever time she could have with him. She wasn't sure what was going on, but she was determined to find out. And the first person she was going to visit this morning would hopefully have the answers she was looking for.

Diana's gaze trailed after Linus for a moment. He'd refused her offer to drive him. Of course he had. The man was almost as devoted to his Schwinn as he was to her. Maybe if he didn't ride his bicycle home from work tonight, though, things would turn out differently.

Determined to find answers, she left her apartment to go see Mrs. Guzman. Her older neighbor was the only person who might have some inkling of what was going on because the past didn't skip like an old vinyl record, resetting to a day that had already happened. That's not how life worked. Time moved forward. It didn't even glance over its shoulder. It was merciless and took no prisoners, at least in Diana's experience.

Diana stood behind Henrietta Guzman's door, sucked in a breath, and knocked. She felt flustered and nervous as she waited. She was also excited. Linus was on his way to his toy store right now. He wasn't lying comatose in a hospital bed somewhere. This was good news.

Diana knocked again, harder this time. Mrs. Guzman was retired and as far as Diana knew, she didn't have any local family. All she had was her little Chihuahua named Leonardo.

The door opened and Mrs. Guzman smiled back at her. "Diana! What a pleasant surprise. Come in, come in."

Diana stepped past Mrs. Guzman and into her home. The place was crowded with two sofas and several recliners. There were stacks of books in every corner. "Today is December fourth," Diana said, turning back to her neighbor.

Mrs. Guzman's thick silver-colored brows furrowed. "Yes. I believe that's correct."

"But it's supposed to be Christmas Day. You came to my house Christmas Eve and you said these strange words over a gift someone gave me. And now it's December fourth again."

Mrs. Guzman looked bewildered. "Did I?"

"You don't remember?" Diana felt breathless and out of control. She pinned a hand to her chest, trying to inhale more deeply. "You put a spell on my snow globe."

Mrs. Guzman chuckled softly while shaking her head. "No, I don't do spells, dear," she corrected, a smile lining her fuchsia-colored lips. "I enchant things."

"Okay, you *enchanted* my snow globe to give me one more day with the one I love. With Linus."

Mrs. Guzman was watching her. "Why do you need one more day with Linus?"

The older woman really didn't know what was going on. She didn't remember because none of the past three weeks had happened yet. Somehow Diana had slipped back in time and landed on the worst possible day. Of all the days to repeat, why this one?

"Because Linus is in a coma. Or he was in a coma. Now he's riding his bike to the toy store as if his accident never happened. But it did—it does—today. He might die, or at least that's what the doctors said. Then you whispered these words over my snow globe and told me to shake it."

Mrs. Guzman pressed her hands together at her midline. "Well, if that's true, then today is a gift, my dear. What are you doing standing in my living room with me? Make the most of this time."

"How?" Diana asked, throwing out her arms. She needed answers and she needed them now.

"That's not for me to decide. What would you tell Linus if you knew you'd never get to talk to him again? What would you do for him? With him? We don't often get a second chance in life," Mrs. Guzman said, her face beaming. "And if we did, we'd usually find a way to mess it up. It's human nature."

Diana thought for a moment. "I would use this day to keep him from getting into that accident."

Mrs. Guzman held up a finger. "No. I might not remember what you're talking about, but I do know that the past can't be altered, no matter what kind of enchantment I performed on that snow globe of yours. Don't waste your time trying."

"But how do you know it can't be changed?" Diana asked. "Have you done this before?"

Mrs. Guzman shook her head slightly. "Well, no, not exactly, but . . ."

"Then maybe it's possible. This whole day was one big fumble. With Linus and my boss. And even Rochelle." Diana was talking quickly as the events of this day ran through her mind. "If this is the day that I returned to, it has to be for a reason, right? I get a do-over. I can fix everything."

"Oh, I'm not sure that's a good idea." Mrs. Guzman shook her head. "Things happen for a reason, dear. Always. When you change one thing, it alters everything else. Just spend the day with the one you love." Mrs. Guzman bent to pick up Leonardo as he whined at her feet.

"Linus is working. It's his busiest time of year, and I have patients to see," Diana said, talking more to herself than the old woman. "And I have a meeting with my boss this afternoon. It's for a promotion I'm up for." If she could change the outcome of that meeting with Mr. Powell, she could keep from being stuck with William as a supervisor. This whole day could go differently, and her life could be put back in order—the way it was supposed to be.

Mrs. Guzman smiled at her. "I trust you'll figure it all out, dear. And then I guess we'll wake up tomorrow and it'll be Christmas. In which case, I better put up my tree. What did I gift you for the holiday?" Mrs. Guzman asked.

"A bottle of wine," Diana told her.

"Hmm. Always a good choice." She walked Diana to the door and opened it. "Good luck. Every moment is like a fragile snowflake. None are exactly the same, but once they hit the ground, they become what they were always meant to be. Part of the larger picture."

Diana didn't speak her neighbor's quirky language. It didn't make a lick of sense, and she was no wiser for stopping here. She needed to leave. There was no time in this day to waste. "Thank you, Mrs. Guzman. I have to go."

"Yes, you do. Good luck."

Diana was going to need it. She headed out of the apartment building and passed the jingling Santa on the sidewalk. She pulled a five-dollar bill from her purse to stuff inside his pail. "Merry Christmas!" she called in a merrier mood than she'd been all month.

"And to you!" He jingled his bell a little more forcefully.

Diana hurried through the parking lot and got inside her car. She cranked the engine, taking a moment to let the motor warm. It was freezing outside. And inside as well. Her breaths came out in white clouds in front of her. Then something caught her eye. At first, she thought it was rain hitting her windshield, but it made a certain sound. It was heavier than rain. *Sleet?* It was sleeting? It hadn't sleeted yet this year. She was sure of it.

Another drop of sleet hit her windshield. And another. That was new, and maybe, at the risk of sounding too wishful, it was a sign that even if the day was repeating, the events of the day didn't have to. Maybe she could change history after all. She had to try.

Chapter 7

At five minutes after nine, Diana dipped inside her car. Her cell phone buzzed from inside her purse. Without thinking, she pulled it out and checked the screen. It was Maria Harris, her first patient of the day. And according to the time, Diana was already five minutes late.

Diana quickly tapped the screen to answer. "Hello, Ms. Harris."

"Diana? Are you okay?" the older woman asked. "You're late. I was starting to worry."

"No need to worry. I apologize. I'll be there in just a few minutes." Diana suddenly remembered what had happened on the first December 4th. "Oh, wait. Ms. Harris?"

"Yes?"

"Please don't try to get your Christmas decorations down before I get there."

Maria chuckled. "How did you know I was about to do that?"

"Lucky guess. You shouldn't do that on your own. You could break something, like oh, I don't know, your ankle."

Diana put the car in DRIVE as she talked. She would prefer to drive to the toy store and see Linus right now. He had an important meeting, though, and she had responsibilities too.

Her patients were depending on her, and Diana wasn't one to shirk her duties, especially since she was up for a promotion. She'd lost it last time, but that wouldn't be the case today. There was no room for error, which meant she needed to see Maria and keep her from breaking her ankle.

"I'm perfectly capable of pulling down my Christmas tree and the boxes of ornaments, you know?" Maria said. "The stroke may have slowed me down, but it didn't ruin me."

"I understand that you want to be independent, but please don't do it on your own, Ms. Harris," Diana pleaded. "I'll help you when I get there. Just wait for me, okay?"

Maria hesitated. "You'll help me?"

"Of course. It won't take long." And it would save Maria a lot of future suffering with a broken limb.

"Fine. That's very nice of you to offer," Maria said. "I'll see you soon."

Diana exhaled softly and disconnected the call. Then she drove to the west side of town as fast as the speed limit would allow. Ten minutes later, she pulled into Maria's driveway and cut the engine. The sleet had stopped, leaving the ground a soft mush that sank beneath her boots as she cut across the lawn and headed toward the older patient's front porch.

When Maria opened the door, she greeted Diana with a weak smile. "There you are. I was just about to give up on you coming and go ahead and climb into my attic."

"Well, I'm glad you waited." Diana stepped into Ms. Harris's home. "Sorry, I'm late. I'm having a bit of a strange morning." That was an understatement. She shut the front door behind her and followed Maria into the living room where they normally worked together.

Maria moved slowly. Her stroke had affected the whole right side of her body, which made her right arm hang flaccidly at her side and her leg drag just a touch as she moved. Diana had taught her to use her left arm to support the right when she walked, which the older woman was thankfully doing. "It's no problem. It happens to the best of us," Maria slurred, another effect of her stroke.

Earlier this week, when Diana had seen Maria, the slur had been barely noticeable. Now that time had reversed three weeks, however, there it was again.

"How are you today, Ms. Harris?" Diana looked around the living room, her gaze falling on the box of Christmas decorations near the wall. "I thought I told you to wait for me."

"I did. I had already gotten that little box down when we spoke. There are three more boxes I wanted to get. I waited on those since you were so adamant on the phone."

Diana inwardly cringed. Maria had been less than five minutes away from breaking her ankle again. She hadn't, though. Diana had changed fate, and if she could do that for Maria, she could do it for every horrible aspect of this day, including Linus's accident.

"Good. Thank you for waiting. I'll just get those boxes once we're done with our therapy." Because therapy came first. That was Diana's job and Diana did it well. She was more than a qualified physical therapist and she wasn't curt, despite what her anonymous patient had written on a Glow Card.

Maria reached for her right shoulder and grimaced. "Ow. This arm is so stiff today. Must be the weather. It's been so cold this past month. I could hardly stand to come out from under the covers this morning."

"I've heard it might snow," Diana said, knowing good and well it wouldn't, no matter what the weatherman on her local television station said. Diana gestured for Maria to lie on the twin-size bed, which had been moved to the far corner of Maria's living room last month. Right after her stroke, Maria was unable to safely climb the stairs to get to her bedroom so everything had been moved to the ground floor of her home. She was taking the stairs better these days, but that would all change if she broke her ankle while pulling boxes from her attic.

Diana pulled up a chair and took hold of Maria's right arm, gently guiding it up and past her head until she couldn't easily move it any further. Then Diana held the position for a deep stretch, lowered Maria's arm back to her side, and eased her through several repetitions. Diana passively stretched all the joints of Maria's arm including her shoulder, elbow, wrist, and finger joints, swollen from limited use.

She had been seeing stroke patients like Maria for so many years that she could practically do this type of therapy in her sleep. She bet William couldn't say the same. When William had been hired, Diana had gone with him to several clients' homes and she'd taught him the basics of good patient care. Of course, William had invested more time in talking to those patients than listening. He'd later said he was building rapport, but Diana suspected he was just making up for a lack of knowledge.

Not that being inexperienced was a crime. All therapists started out that way. But William shouldn't be her supervisor. And he wouldn't be after today. This afternoon, Diana was going to walk into Mr. Powell's office and walk out as the facility's newest supervisor.

After stretching Maria's arm, Diana helped her patient sit up on the edge of the bed. They ran through basic strengthening exercises in a seated position because Maria's balance was affected—all the more reason the older woman shouldn't be climbing up and down a ladder with heavy boxes.

"Okay, let me get those other boxes for you," Diana finally said. "Where are they? In the attic?"

Maria nodded. "That's right. Thank you so much for offering to help me. To tell you the truth, I was a little worried I might hurt myself."

Diana turned back to her patient. "If that's the case, why didn't you call to ask someone for help?"

Maria lowered her gaze a moment. "Because I don't have anyone to call."

Diana remembered seeing framed pictures on Maria's mantel. "No family?"

"Just a daughter, but she doesn't speak to me. We had a falling out many years ago."

"Oh, I'm sorry." Diana knew exactly how hurtful it was to have family that didn't want to see you.

Maria forced a wobbly smile, but Diana could see the sadness in the woman's eyes. "It's okay. It was my fault, and I understand why she doesn't want to speak to me. To be honest, my stroke has been good for me because it brings you to my home. I guess one might say I'm a bit of a shut-in. I used to know most of the people in this town, but now, well, I'm afraid I don't keep up with many of the locals."

Diana was speechless. She was Maria's only visitor? In all these weeks coming here, Diana hadn't even taken the time to learn that Maria didn't have any family who visited. Diana hadn't wanted to cross a professional boundary. She was here to treat Maria's symptoms after all, not to pry into her personal life. "I'm sorry, Maria," she finally said.

"For what?" Maria chuckled softly. "For being my angel?"

Some angel.

"I'll go ahead and get those boxes for you." Diana climbed the stairs to the second-floor hallway, where the attic ladder was already pulled down. "If you're ever worried you might hurt yourself doing something, that's a sign you should call in backup. You can always call me."

"Oh, you're such a sweet lady," Maria said as Diana climbed the narrow steps and poked her head inside the attic.

She spotted three boxes that read CHRISTMAS DECORATIONS in black Sharpie handwriting. "Found them!" she called down. They were big boxes. No way Ms. Harris would have been getting these on her own without hurting herself.

Diana pulled one to her with a grunt, nearly dropping it as

she climbed back down the steps. Once that box was on the ground floor, she climbed back up and grabbed another, repeating the process until all three boxes were on the floor of the living room. "There." Her scrubs were dusty and she was breathing heavily, but at least Maria wasn't going to break her ankle today. Not on Diana's watch.

"Thank you so much." Maria beamed at her. "Putting these things out will take all day. Would you like to stay and help me with that as well?" she asked hopefully. "I've got tea and cookies."

Diana hated to disappoint her patient, but that wasn't how she was going to spend her second-chance day. "I wish I could, but unfortunately I have another patient to see." Diana headed toward the front door.

"The young girl?" Maria asked.

Due to patient confidentiality, Diana hadn't shared who the girl was or the specific details of what Addy was dealing with. All Maria knew was that Diana saw a sixteen-year-old female after she left Maria's home most days. "That's right."

"Please tell her hello from me." Maria shuffled behind Diana toward the door.

"I will."

Maria stepped over to a table beside the door and picked up a piece of fruitcake wrapped in cellophane. "Here, this is for you. And a slice for your fiancé as well. You can have it for dessert tonight."

Diana took the fruitcake, surprised by how heavy it was. What was in this thing? "Thank you. Linus has a sweet tooth. He'll love this." *If he makes it home tonight . . .*

No. Diana silently reprimanded herself. There was no place for doubt. The weather had changed, Maria's ankle wasn't broken, and no matter what it took to change his fate, Linus wouldn't be having an accident tonight.

Chapter 8

Diana stepped back out into the cold morning. The sleety rain had stopped, and now the air felt cold and wet. When she arrived at Addy's home fifteen minutes later, Cecilia Pierce answered the door with a worried look.

"Hi, Diana. I'm so glad you're here."

"Why? Is something wrong?" Diana stepped into the Pierces' home. Once again it smelled of cinnamon and spices. If home had a smell, she imagined this is what it would be. Grandma Denny's home had smelled of bleach and cigarette smoke, which wasn't necessarily the worst aroma. Sometimes when Diana entered a patient's house, she caught the same combination of smells and a wave of nostalgia crashed over her.

"Oh, Addy is just in one of her teenage moods," Mrs. Pierce said. "There's some sort of drama going on, but I'm her mother and she won't tell me anything."

"Oh, that's right." Diana gave a knowing nod as Mrs. Pierce closed the door behind her.

"What do you mean?" Mrs. Pierce asked.

Oops. Had Diana said that out loud? She remembered Addy being in a funk over a boy and her best friend on this day. Since Addy's immune system was compromised, she couldn't go to school, and she completed her work online.

"N-nothing." Diana shook her head as she peeled off her winter coat and hung it on the rack by the door. She left her boots on the mat as well. "I just mean, sixteen-year-olds are always going through some sort of teenage tragedy, aren't they? Maybe she'll talk to me."

Mrs. Pierce's pinched brow relaxed. "I would love for you to talk to her. Thank you so much. I'll be in the kitchen cooking for this evening. There'll be more than enough food if you want to come back later." Mrs. Pierce was always offering Diana a meal, and Diana was always finding a polite excuse to turn her down. Polite, but never curt.

"Thank you for the invitation, but I'm afraid I can't today. It's my best friend's birthday. I'm meeting her somewhere for a little celebration this afternoon." At least that was the initial plan, but Diana couldn't be at Sparky's Tavern with Rochelle when Linus needed her most. Diana needed to be close to him and stop him from riding his bike home.

"A rain check, then." Mrs. Pierce pointed down the hall. "Addy is in her room. Fingers crossed you can work your magic on her."

"I'll do my best." Diana headed down a hallway that veered off the main living room, walking back to the last door on the left. Diana already knew that Addy had been upset about her ex-boyfriend and former friend for a while. The teen had been through a lot and was rightfully sulky.

Diana knocked on the girl's bedroom door and waited.

"Come in!"

When Diana entered, Addy didn't even look over from where she lay across her bed, staring up at her ceiling. Her thin arms were folded behind her head.

"Hey, Addy. You doing okay?" Diana asked as she stepped inside.

"No. My life is over," the teenager huffed.

Diana shut the door behind her and stepped over to sit on the girl's bedside. "Boys come and go. It'll be okay."

Addy slid her gaze over with interest. "How did you know this was about a guy?"

"Oh. Well . . . Isn't it always?" Even Diana's troubles were about a guy these days. Not that Linus would ever intentionally break her heart. He was the kindest, sweetest man Diana had ever known. She was the one who'd broken his heart by dodging the wedding talk and making him think she regretted saying yes to his proposal.

"What would you know about guy troubles? I bet your life is perfect. So perfect that you never have any problems." There was more than a hint of sarcasm in her voice. She sat up and breathed a sigh, her slender body folding over her knees.

Diana looked at the teen for a long moment. Addy had been hounding Diana about her personal life since the day Diana had walked in the front door of her home. Diana didn't mind sharing about the simple things, like what she enjoyed watching on TV or her favorite food, but Addy was like a journalist with a lead. She liked to ask invasive questions like how Diana and Linus met. Was it love at first sight? What was the wedding theme going to be? Where was Diana's family and why didn't she talk about them?

"Okay," Diana said. "If you want to talk about what's bothering you, we can, *but* we have to do it during your physical therapy. That's why I'm here after all." Addy was weak after her last round of chemotherapy. She could barely stand at the bathroom sink for ten consecutive minutes to fix her thinning hair and put on the little bit of makeup that she wore. Diana was working on helping her build endurance and teaching her energy conservation techniques so she didn't wear out so quickly.

Addy blew out another exasperated breath as she sat on the edge of her bed. "Fine. We'll talk while I moisturize. Or you can talk because that means I'll be expending less energy, right?"

"Glad to know you've been listening to me at least a little bit," Diana said.

"We can trade stories. Like real friends."

No way was Diana going to get into what had happened with the snow globe or how time was repeating itself with a sixteen-year-old. Although Addy might be the most likely to believe her.

Diana angled her body toward Addy's. "Go ahead and stand. I'll walk with you."

Addy rolled her eyes. "You don't have to worry that I'll fall. I can walk to the bathroom, you know?"

"Then do it," Diana challenged.

Addy stood and headed toward her personal restroom, talking to Diana at her back. She might know how to conserve energy, but she wasn't doing it. "All my friends have stopped calling. It's like they've completely forgotten about me. You're the closest thing I have." She stopped in front of the sink and looked at Diana through the mirror, her breathing already heavy. Her chest was rising and falling rapidly.

Diana pulled up a chair that she'd placed in the bathroom for Addy. "Sit."

"I'm not an old lady," Addy protested. "I don't need a chair to brush my hair."

"No, you're a stubborn teenager." Diana pressed her hands down on Addy's shoulders, guiding her to take a seat. "This is part of energy conservation."

Addy rolled her eyes. Then she took the brush that Diana handed her. She hesitated as she looked in the mirror, lifting the brush to one side of her head.

Diana could see the sudden, unmistakable look of vulnerability in the girl's expression.

Addy's hand trembled as she looked at herself. Then she lowered her brush and dropped it down in the sink. "My hair is fine like this. It doesn't need brushing."

Diana reached into the sink, picked up the brush, and

handed it back to Addy. "It's part of your therapy. We lift the brush versus lifting weights in the gym," she said, trying to make the girl smile.

Addy wasn't smiling, though. Instead, she had a thick sheen of tears in her blue eyes.

Crap. Diana suddenly remembered this visit. How could she have forgotten? She'd unintentionally made Addy cry the first time she'd gone through this day. And she was thoughtlessly doing so again.

Addy snatched the brush from Diana's hand and ran it through her thinning hair as tears streamed down her face. Then she lifted the strands that fell out for Diana to see.

"This is why my friends don't care about me anymore. It's why Jay is more interested in Sierra than me too." She threw the brush back down in the sink with a loud *clink*.

Diana's lips parted for a moment. "I-I'm so sorry, Addy." Addy hadn't told Diana about Sierra until yesterday, which was Christmas Eve. Somehow Diana had gotten her to tell her sooner in this new timeline, though. That was something else that had changed.

Mrs. Guzman was wrong. Diana could use this day to alter what would happen, but right now she was only making things worse.

"Sierra is supposed to be my best friend, but she's stealing my boyfriend while I'm stuck in my bedroom prison going bald. I hate my life!" Addy lowered her face in her palms and her body shook as she cried.

Diana placed a hand on the girl's back. "That's not true. Your life is better than you think, and you'll be back at school before you know it."

"That's not the point." Addy looked up. Her cheeks had a ruddy hue now. "Old people are always talking about the future. Don't you get that I'm stuck in today and today sucks?"

"Yeah. I get it." Diana was quiet for a moment, scared to say anything more and make matters worse.

"Prove it," Addy sniffled. "Tell me one thing about your life that sucks."

Diana could choose from a mile-long list. Her fiancé was in a coma. They'd fought before his accident because Diana wasn't ready to get married yet. She'd been pushing off the planning because of a promotion at work she didn't even get. Instead, it had gone to the least experienced and most obnoxious person on the company's payroll. Oh, and one of her patients had called her curt on the one and only Glow Card she'd ever received.

Diana met Addy's gaze in the mirror. "The heater in my apartment is on the fritz." At least it was true. The thermostat reading never got over sixty no matter how high Diana set it for.

"Oh." Addy seemed to deflate, her body shrinking smaller somehow. "For a moment, I thought you were actually going to be real with me. Whatever."

Diana's mouth fell open. "What's that supposed to mean?"

"You know, I thought you were going to drop the whole ice-queen thing."

"I'm your physical therapist, Addy. Not your friend."

Addy's face scrunched up again. "Burn," she mumbled.

"I didn't mean it that way, okay?" Diana hoped Addy wasn't about to start crying again.

"Sure, you did. No one wants to be my friend because my hair is falling out and soon I'll be bald, and my former best friend will be dating my ex-boyfriend." She stood on wobbly legs, pushing the chair out and knocking it into Diana's midsection. Then she turned and headed toward her bed.

Diana followed close behind in case she fell. "Addy, I'm sorry. I just meant that I'm not here to share my life story with you. I'm here for you, not me. I'm a professional."

Addy plopped onto her bed facedown. "Get your stupid heater fixed, but I doubt that'll warm you up. You need a heart to be warm, *Elsa*."

"Addy . . ." Diana sat on the bed next to the girl. Teenage years were hard without the added stress of a cancer diagnosis and chemotherapy. At Addy's age, Diana had thought life pretty much sucked too. She was living with Grandma Denny and waiting for her mom to come by for the holidays because that was the only time Jackie Merriman seemed to remember that Diana existed. Her mom had forgotten the year that Diana was sixteen, though. It had been tough, and Grandma Denny's only comforting words were to *suck it up* and *dry your eyes.*

"I'm sorry about your hair," Diana said gently. "And your friend, who doesn't sound like a great friend at all if she's making a play for your crush."

Addy rolled onto her back and looked up at the ceiling again. "Jay was more than a crush. He was my boyfriend."

"He broke up with you?" Diana asked, treading lightly.

"No. He's just ghosting me. And so is Sierra. Rebecca told me that she saw Sierra eating lunch with Jay yesterday, so . . ." A tear streamed down Addy's cheek.

Diana resisted wiping the girl's tear away. "What does your mom say?"

Addy rolled her eyes, dislodging another tear that she quickly swiped away with the back of her hand. "My mom is so focused on my cancer. It's all she can think about. She says she doesn't want to hear me complain about"—Addy's voice changed to a deeper version as she mocked her mom's words—"something as superficial as hair when my life is hanging in the balance." Addy blew out a breath. "It's like, suddenly, all I am is a girl with cancer."

Diana reached out and touched Addy's arm. "You're more than that."

Addy sniffled quietly. "You say that now, but you're just like everyone else. All I am to you is your patient. That's why you don't tell me about yourself. We're not friends. This is all business for you."

"That's hardly fair," Diana said, even though the truth punched her in the gut. She did care about Addy, but her actions weren't showing that. Maybe she really was a curt therapist.

Addy blew up a breath to dry her eyes. "Well, in my experience, nothing in life is fair."

"Ouch!" Rochelle said on the phone as Diana left Addy's home and recapped what the girl had said. "Being called an ice queen is harsh. But not completely out of line."

"I thought you were on my side," Diana lamented.

"I am. And I'm looking forward to birthday drinks tonight to celebrate another year of me," Rochelle said with an excited rise to her voice.

"About that." Guilt knotted Diana's stomach. Rochelle had been less than pleased the first time Diana had canceled on their birthday drink tradition. What could she do, though? There was no room for alcoholic beverages today.

"About what?" Rochelle's voice was now tinged with dread.

"Well, happy birthday for one," Diana said, forcing a cheerful voice. "That should have been the first thing out of my mouth."

"You normally text me as soon as you wake up, but you didn't this morning. I'm trying not to take it personally. I understand you have a life, and while I wake up alone most days, you do not."

"Most days?" Diana asked.

Rochelle chuckled. "Well, Shadow is sometimes curled on top of my head when I awake. She counts as a bed fellow."

Shadow was Rochelle's black cat.

Diana gave a small laugh. It was more nerves than humor. "So, I need to bring Linus to your birthday bash tonight."

"What?" Rochelle said.

"I know we have that whole *chicks before Nicks*, or Linuses, but this is kind of necessary." Diana hoped Rochelle would understand. It was the only way that Diana could think to save Linus and not disappoint her best friend on her birthday. Pleasing everyone wasn't easy.

"It's necessary for you to bring your fiancé to a ladies-only birthday for me because . . . ?" Rochelle trailed off. She was perpetually single, and Diana knew she didn't like being a third wheel. That's why Diana always left Linus at home.

"It's complicated."

"Everyone's life is complicated, Diana." Rochelle didn't bother to hide the irritation in her voice. "I'm a counselor. I know that firsthand. But just because it is doesn't mean you can bail on your relationships. Plural because I suspect it's not just me you've been bailing on."

Diana drew back from her phone for a moment. Then she returned it to her ear. "What's that supposed to mean?"

"It doesn't matter. What matters is that it's my birthday and we have a rule."

"Linus can sit there and not say anything," Diana promised. "Or I can make him sit on the opposite side of the bar."

"Then what's the point of him even being there?" Rochelle asked. "Other than to ruin my birthday. You know I love Linus to death, but I never get to spend any real time with you anymore. Call me possessive or jealous or whatever, but I miss you."

"I'll make it up to you," Diana promised. "We can have one-on-one drinks next week. Or tomorrow, even." After Diana had saved Linus from being hit by a delivery truck. After she'd adjusted fate.

"You know what? Just forget it," Rochelle huffed into the phone's receiver.

"What? No. I want to see you. We always have a drink on your birthday."

"Not tonight. Spend time with your fiancé." Rochelle's words were tense, lined with frustration and maybe a hint of anger. She wasn't shy about telling people how she felt. Being a clinical counselor, Rochelle was of the mind that emotions should never be stuffed down in the places where Diana locked hers away. "I'll find someone else to celebrate with."

Diana clutched the phone to her ear. She was about to apologize, but the line went dead and a soft buzz hummed quietly in her ear. She lowered her cell phone and looked at the screen. The connection was gone.

Rochelle was pissed and history had just repeated itself. At least she'd kept Maria from breaking her ankle. That was proof that there was hope for Linus.

Diana checked the time on her dash. Half the day was already gone, and the small slice of it that Linus had agreed to spend with her was within her grasp. Time to get back to Linus's toy store. She wanted to stare into his eyes and tell him all the things she hadn't been able to over these last three weeks. And come hell or high water, or sleet, she needed to convince him to avoid riding his bike home tonight.

Chapter 9

On the way to Linus's toy store, Diana stopped at Buddy's Best Sandwiches for lunch. She purchased two bacon–cheddar cheeses on rye with a pickle on the side. It was Linus's weakness and she knew all the tension from last night would melt away as soon as he saw this peace offering.

She and Linus hadn't had lunch on the first go-round of December 4th. Instead, she'd gone home and freshened up prior to her meeting with Mr. Powell. She'd assumed that she and Linus would have time together that night, but, of course, she'd been wrong.

Forever is a myth. All we have is this moment. Linus hadn't known how right his grandfather was.

The bell above the toy store's entrance jingled as Diana pushed her way inside, bumping into a little boy as he left in a hurry.

"Sorry," he said, clutching a lump under his coat. For a moment, Diana wondered if he was stealing something, but he was just a child. He struck her as looking familiar. Where had she seen him? Before she could figure it out, he was gone. She let the door close behind her and turned to look around the store. Christmas music filled the air but it wasn't the classic, soothing-to-the ears kind. No. Alvin and the Chipmunks were obnoxiously crooning through the speakers. Did kids these days even know who the Chipmunks were?

Diana spotted Linus helping a young child beat *Pac-Man* on an old arcade game in the back of the store. The Toy Peddler had belonged to Linus's father before Linus had taken it over earlier this year. Diana wouldn't guess that running a toy store was stressful but earlier this year Mr. Grant had had a heart attack. That's when he'd retired and Linus had become the store's official owner.

Linus turned from the arcade game and spotted Diana standing near the door. He waved her over. "Hey, you," he said when she was standing in front of him. "I somewhat thought you'd cancel on me."

Diana bunched her brow as she looked at him in question. "O, ye of little faith."

"Well, it's the big day of your interview with the boss, right? I thought you'd want to go home and brush your hair."

Diana narrowed her eyes. "You think my hair needs brushing?"

"No, your hair is beautiful." He reached up and smoothed a piece and then another.

"I can brush my hair in the car, you know. And apply lipstick too."

To this, Linus bunched his own brow. "Why are you applying lipstick? Are you planning to kiss your boss?"

With an eye roll that would make Addy proud, Diana held up the bags from Buddy's Best Sandwiches.

Linus's jaw dropped. "A woman after my own heart. Is it—?"

"A bacon–cheddar cheese with a pickle on the side? Why, yes, it is," Diana confirmed proudly.

"Mmm. If we weren't already engaged, I'd drop to my knees and propose right now." He nodded a hello to a man standing nearby—no doubt the *Pac-Man* player's father—then led her behind the register and pulled up a stool for her to sit. "Sorry, we'll have to eat here. Jean called out with vertigo so it's just me." He glanced around. "I believe I have the father and son and one other customer lurking around somewhere. A little boy."

"No, I don't think so. He was leaving as I was coming in," Diana said. "He was in a bit of a hurry. And shouldn't he be in school right now?"

Linus chuckled. "That's Dustin. He skips school on the regular and borrows things from the store."

"Borrows?" Diana asked.

Linus sighed. "A nice way of putting it. His foster mother isn't such a lovely woman so I cut the kid a little slack and give him odd jobs to earn what he takes. On the occasion that I actually catch him."

Diana sat down and laid her wrapped sandwich on the counter in front of her. "You're so good with kids. Whereas my younger patients compare me to Elsa."

Linus took a seat beside her. Then he leaned in and gave her a quick kiss on the cheek. "Di, I really am sorry about last night."

She slid her gaze over and laughed quietly.

"What?" he asked.

"It's just kind of funny now. We were fighting over some cartoon character."

"Maybe that's how it started, but it turned into more than that," he said quietly. "I shouldn't have pressured you about the wedding."

"No, you were right. I *have* been dragging my feet. And once this promotion is past us, I promise we can focus on the wedding plans. I meant what I said this morning. We can set the date tonight." A date that would not be as early as this Christmas.

Linus went quiet. "You know, if you regret saying yes to me, you can tell me. Don't let the lavender shirt and dog tie fool you. I'm stronger than I look."

Diana hated that she made him second-guess her love for him. "Why would you think I have regrets about saying yes to you?"

"Well, I popped the question this summer. It's been months and you haven't wanted to make any plans. Not even one. One might assume you don't really want to marry a bloke like me."

Diana's lips parted. "No, that's not it. I love you."

"I don't doubt that. I doubt that you want to commit your life to me. Maybe marrying a guy who owns a toy store isn't how you see your dream life." There was a sudden vulnerability in his eyes.

Diana swallowed past a tight throat. "You're not just a guy who owns a toy store, Linus. You're sexy and you have a heart of gold. You make me laugh more than anyone ever has. You're good for me. Really good."

Linus waggled his brows. "You think I'm sexy, huh?"

"You *would* focus on that detail." She shoved his arm softly. "Yes, you're sexy and not at all full of yourself." Tipping her head at his bacon-cheddar on rye, she said, "I brought you your favorite sandwich because I'm sorry for being so distant and dragging my feet on the wedding planning."

"Stop right there. We can't make up yet." He finally began to unwrap his own sandwich.

Diana didn't pick hers back up just yet. "Why not?"

"Because we need to save that for tonight." He picked up his sandwich, braced it between his hands, and took a healthy bite.

Diana watched as he chewed. "You want to talk things out some more?"

He picked up his napkin and swiped it below his mouth. "No, I don't want to talk. I mean I do, but . . ." There was a twinkle in his blue-gray eyes as he looked at her.

"Oh," Diana said, understanding. "You want to make up, make up?"

"They say it's better after an argument. Not that we argued much, but maybe we could try again. I could call you Elsa and you could call me a beast."

Diana shoved his shoulder in jest. "You're mixing your Disney movies."

"We can argue about that as well." Linus leaned over to kiss her. "And then we can make up even more."

She kissed him back, hoping there weren't any child eyes watching in the toy store. "I like the sound of that, Mr. Grant. It's a date."

He straightened on his stool and steadied his sandwich, preparing to take another bite. "Are you nervous about your meeting with Mr. Powell?" he asked before doing so.

Diana sucked in a breath. "Yeah, I guess so. I really want this promotion." Even more so after losing it to William last time.

"Well, you're a shoo-in for it, aren't you?"

"I thought I was." Diana picked up her sandwich and nibbled off a tiny bite. "I've been at Powell Rehabilitation the longest. I pull the longest hours."

"See? The promotion's in the bag."

"I don't know. Maybe Mr. Powell is looking for more than just a steady employee. Maybe he wants someone with charisma."

"You have charisma," Linus said. She loved that he would say so.

Diana nibbled another bite from her sandwich, barely tasting her food. "Maybe Mr. Powell wants someone who patients rave about."

"Your patients love you," Linus said.

"They like me, and I do a good job with helping them in their recovery. But maybe I'm not someone my patients feel like they can talk to. Maybe I'm too curt," she finally said.

Linus set his sandwich down and looked at her. "You *are* someone that others can talk to. You just need to go in and show that to Mr. Powell. Leave him with no doubt that you are the perfect woman for the job."

Diana sucked in a tiny breath that didn't seem to fill up her lungs. She gave a small nod and then looked at her watch. "Oh, geez. Mr. Powell won't think I'm a worthy candidate if I show up late."

Linus glanced at her sandwich. "But you haven't even eaten your lunch yet."

"I'll eat it afterward. I need to go." She didn't move to leave, though. "Let me pick you up after work. Don't ride your bike home."

Linus reached for his soda and took a swallow. "Why is that?"

"Because it'll be cold and icy this evening. It's not safe."

"It's perfectly safe. The exercise will be good for me."

"Please." She clutched her sandwich bag, silently pleading with her eyes.

"Don't worry about me. Just go to that interview and knock Mr. Powell's socks off. Just his socks, though. And no kissing. That's where I draw the line."

Diana laughed despite her nerves. "Thanks for the pep talk."

"Anytime."

"I'll call you afterward?" she asked.

"Counting on it."

And then she'd convince Linus to let her drive him home.

* * *

Diana pulled into the parking lot of Powell Rehabilitation Center and parked in the spot closest to the building. That was perhaps the luckiest thing that had happened to her today, aside from seeing Linus this morning.

She grabbed her purse, took a breath, and stepped out of her car. Mr. Powell liked punctuality. He liked order and hard workers. Diana was all those things on her best day, which the first December 4th was not. This one would be different, though. It could only go up from here.

Ducking into the building, she headed toward Leann Dixon, the company's receptionist, who sat behind a large counter in the center of the room.

"Hi. I have an appointment with Mr. Powell at two o'clock."

Leann's small spectacle-style glasses slid down her nose a notch. "It's two o'clock now," she said pointedly, eyebrows lifting high on her forehead. Despite the exaggerated brow lift, Leann's forehead didn't wrinkle. She was a walking advertisement for Botox. Even so, her frown lines seemed to persist.

"Sorry. The weather is bad," Diana explained. "But I'm right on time." Just as she said it, the digital clock on the wall behind Leann turned to one minute after the hour.

"Hmm. I'll let Mr. Powell know you're here." Leann forced what was obviously an insincere smile. Then she picked up the phone's receiver on her desk and held it to her ear.

Diana walked toward the waiting room and took a seat in one of the cushy chairs provided. She pulled out her cell phone, willing Linus to say something more. She couldn't get enough of him now that he was awake. She wanted to spend every waking moment together, but this meeting was important too. It would give them better footing for when they finally did get married. Marriage was hard even without financial struggles. Diana's parents hadn't made it. Neither had her grandparents. Didn't it make sense to have a firm financial foundation before tying the knot?

"Ms. Merriman?" Leann called from the counter.

Diana looked up from her phone. "Yes?"

"Mr. Powell is ready to see you now."

Diana's chest tightened as she stood. "Thank you." Following Leann, Diana remembered when she'd made this walk three weeks earlier. She'd taken the time beforehand to brush her hair, put on lipstick, and powder her face before the meeting. She was going in for a promotion after all. She wanted to put her best foot forward.

This time, however, she must look a mess from the sleet and all that the day had already brought. She'd gone to see Linus instead of primping, and she wasn't sorry. William didn't have to fix his hair or put on makeup to win Mr. Powell's approval, so why should she?

Mr. Powell looked up from his laptop as she walked into his office. "Hi, Diana," he said in a deep voice that seemed to fill the room.

"Good afternoon, Mr. Powell." Diana stepped over to his desk to shake his hand. His grip was firm and his eye gaze was direct. She'd always liked the owner of the company. Mr. Powell's father had owned it before him. It was a business that catered to all avenues of patient rehabilitation, including physical, occupational, and speech therapies.

"Please, call me Todd. I believe I've been telling you that for years now, haven't I?"

"Right. Todd." Even though Todd was only a couple years older than Diana, it was hard to address her boss so casually. William Davis probably didn't have that hang-up. She removed her hand from his and stood there nervously, her head bobbling up and down in a nod. Rochelle had given Diana a few pointers on how to calm her nerves during situations like this, but she always shut her friend down when she stepped into her counselor role. Rochelle was her friend when they were together, not a counselor. Even so, Diana wished she had listened to Rochelle's tips on navigating important interviews. Diana wanted this promotion so badly she could taste it.

"The weather is a mess out there, isn't it?" Mr. Powell's gaze lifted to her hair.

"It is. Yes. That's why I am also a mess right now. Bad-hair days are a hazard of working in home health." She giggled out loud and then felt the burn of her cheeks because giggling wasn't professional. She was trying to be more personable, like Mr. Powell apparently wanted, but she just felt foolish. *Confidence, Diana. You deserve this promotion. It's rightfully yours.*

"Well, please have a seat. Would you like a cup of coffee?" Mr. Powell gestured to a Keurig machine that sat on a tiny table against the wall of his office.

Diana shook her head as she sat down, not wanting to inconvenience him.

Mr. Powell began to sit as well. "Okay, then let's—"

"Actually, yes!" Diana blurted, interrupting her boss. Because maybe sharing a cup of coffee would contribute to a more casual meeting. Friends shared coffee, right? And Mr. Powell valued a friends and family environment. "A cup of coffee sounds wonderful."

Mr. Powell blinked politely. "Of course." He stood and walked to the machine on the counter.

"Sorry, I barely got to taste my first cup of coffee this morning. It's just been one of those days," she explained, feeling less and less at ease. The first time she'd had this meeting, she'd felt so confident. At least until things had begun to go wrong.

"I understand." Mr. Powell talked to Diana over his shoulder. "That's one thing I like about you. It doesn't matter what kind of day you're having, you're always at the job. Some employees would call out for breaking a nail. Men included." He grabbed a mug from where it sat upside down against his counter and placed it under the coffee machine. Then he grabbed a pod and popped it into the top of the machine.

Diana nervously listened to the machine rev under the tap of his fingers. "I love my job, Mr. Powell—um, Todd."

"Well, it shows, Diana." A moment later, he carried her mug of coffee over.

She didn't meet his gaze. Instead, she grasped the mug tightly, remembering the first time she'd gone through this day. Mr. Powell had already decided to give the promotion to William. He had just wanted to break the news to her in person. She needed to change his mind. But how?

Mr. Powell held out his palm with sugar and creamer condiments. "Pick your pleasure."

"No, it's okay. I'll drink it black," she said, mind spinning. Her breathing felt rapid too. And her palms were slick.

"That's how I take mine as well." He placed the condiments on the edge of his desk and then propped himself there versus returning to his chair. It was an intimate position, and the close proximity made her feel even more anxious.

"So, let's talk about why you're here." Mr. Powell clasped his hands in front of him.

Diana smiled over her coffee mug as she took a sip. "Okay."

"You're a valued employee here at Powell Rehabilitation, Diana. You rarely miss a day of work, and your documentation is so precise. Quite simply, you do your job well, and it doesn't go unnoticed." He hesitated for a moment as if weighing what was on his mind. "I must admit, I was surprised you applied for the management position, though."

"Thank you, sir. Todd. Well, I enjoy working with my patients, but I would love to share my expertise and knowledge with the staff here as well. In fact, I'm already doing that," she pointed out, mentally patting her own back. "I've been the one who has mentored many of the new hires, including William Davis."

At the mention of her coworker's name, she inwardly cringed. That was suspicious, right? Not that Mr. Powell would suspect that she'd gone back in time after he'd already given William the position.

"That's right, you did," Mr. Powell said. "I must have forgotten about that."

Diana nodded. "William had no idea what he was doing when he was first hired. I taught him everything he knows, which still isn't what a seasoned staff member here knows." She couldn't believe what she was saying. Yes, she was irritated about William's promotion from last December 4th, but she would never talk about a coworker like this. It wasn't professional. It wasn't her. *What am I doing?*

Mr. Powell's smile began to slip.

"We learn as we go, of course," Diana said, backtracking. "I'm just saying that I'm very comfortable assisting others. Taking on a management position really wouldn't be much of a stretch for me." She tried to smile, but it felt wobbly and nervous.

"Diana, you recently lost a patient of yours, didn't you? Betty Krick?" Mr. Powell asked.

Diana swallowed. Mr. Powell hadn't brought that up the last time they'd interviewed. Betty Krick had been an elderly patient of hers who'd died in her sleep in November. Diana had already been treating the patient for two months at that point, and Betty was improving. "That's correct, I did."

"You wouldn't be applying for this position because of her, would you? It's hard to lose someone who you work closely with. Some therapists might decide to retreat into a safer position. Unfortunately, losing patients comes with the job when you're out in the field."

Diana's lips parted. She shook her head vigorously and then stopped when her coffee swished over the rim of her cup onto her lap, creating a stain in a less than desirable spot. *Geesh.* She clutched her mug more tightly. "I assure you, Mr. Powell—Todd—that I keep a professional relationship with all of my patients. I was sad to know about Betty's passing, but her death hasn't affected my role at this company whatsoever."

Mr. Powell gave a thoughtful look. "Losing a patient *should* affect us, though, shouldn't it?"

Diana froze. "I'm sorry?"

"I mean, we're not robots. We have hearts and feelings. If you're hoping a desk job will shield you from those two things, you're applying for the wrong reasons."

Why would he think that? "That's not what I'm hoping, Todd." She shook her head again and more coffee spilled over her mug's rim. *Ouch!* "I have a heart and feelings, but my job is to help my patients make progress in their therapy. In order to do that, sometimes I have to put my feelings aside." She blew out a frustrated breath. "William crosses that line, in my opinion. He's *too* involved if you ask me."

Mr. Powell gave her a confused look. "Diana, why do you keep talking about William?"

"Because we both know that's who you want to promote. Because I'm too professional and not attached enough to my patients, right? But if I was too emotional, you'd write me off for being too much of a woman. Whereas William can do no wrong. His patients love him and leave him Glow Cards, which I'm pretty sure he helps them fill out himself."

Mr. Powell stared at her a moment and then cleared his throat. "Well, Diana, thank you for coming in. Rest assured, you will be considered along with all of the other applicants."

Diana bit the inside of her cheek to hold her emotions at

bay. "I have worked hard, Todd. And I'm devoted." She stood quickly from her chair, the emotion pushing her upward. Then the coffee in her mug swished over the rim one last time and splashed onto the front of Todd's shirt. Her hand flew to her mouth. "Oh, my gosh! I am so sorry!"

Mr. Powell held his arms out to his sides as he looked down at his crisp white, now coffee-stained, shirt.

"That was an accident." She swallowed as hot tears pressed behind her eyes. *Don't cry. Try to smile.*

"It's all right. I have a clean shirt in my desk drawer." He finally looked up. "I come prepared for employees who toss coffee at me," he said, teasingly.

Diana reached past him and placed her coffee mug down on his desk. She took a breath and forced a small smile. "Thank you for your consideration, Mr. Powell . . . um, Toad, *er*, Todd. Have a good afternoon." She turned and walked briskly out of his office. Her legs trembled as she hurried past Leann at the receptionist's desk and headed into the parking lot. She waited to breathe until she was sitting behind her steering wheel. She waited to let the tears reach her eyes until then too.

She didn't think it was even possible for her meeting to go worse than it had the first December 4th, but it had. And now she felt like she needed to call William and apologize profusely for what she'd just said to Mr. Powell. Jealousy and resentment made a person do awful things. And *ugh*. Had she accidentally called her boss a *toad*?

She turned the key in her ignition and was about to pull out of the parking lot when her phone began to ring.

Please don't let it be Todd telling me I'm fired. She needed her job. But after that debacle, there was no way she still had it.

Instead, her phone read JOANN GRANT.

Diana hesitated. She needed someone to talk to, but her future mother-in-law was the last person she wanted to have a conversation with right now. They didn't have that type of relationship, which was primarily Diana's fault. The person Diana needed most right now was Linus.

She checked the time on her cell phone. It was just after three o'clock. Jean had gone home sick, and it was just him at the toy store. Since Diana was probably fired, she should go see him. Then she could drive him home after closing. Or keep him in the store's backroom and they could make love all night until they both woke up tomorrow. Safe. Healthy. Happy. And in love. Albeit, she probably wouldn't be employed.

Chapter 10

Diana reached to grab her umbrella from the glove depart-ment, preparing to head into the drizzling sleet that had been coming down off and on throughout the day. Nervous antic-ipation made fluttery feelings around her heart. She couldn't wait to go inside the toy store and see her fiancé, awake and alive. She still couldn't believe this day was really happening—again. She had a second chance. She and Linus both did. And maybe she'd made a debacle in Mr. Powell's office, but that wouldn't happen here.

She pushed her car door open and popped her umbrella overhead. The beady sound of tiny ice pellets tapped above her. Avoiding a puddle, Diana hopped onto the sidewalk and stepped under the small awning that led into the store. She closed her umbrella and then left it beside the entrance as she pulled open the door.

Christmas music greeted her as she dipped inside. Thank-fully, it wasn't Alvin and the Chipmunks this time. At first, she didn't see Linus. Her gaze bounced around to several cus-tomers. Then Linus appeared from the back room and stopped walking when he saw her. His face lit up for a moment, and Diana couldn't stop herself. She rushed over and threw her arms around his neck, pressing her cheek against his chest.

She wished she could hear his heartbeat over the tune stream-
ing through the speakers.

Linus grabbed hold of her shoulders and gently peeled her
back. "What are you doing here?"

"I came to see you. Again." Her heart skipped as she met
his eyes. Open. Bright.

"But you were just here a couple hours ago. Don't you
have work?" He wasn't exactly smiling at her. Instead, his
forehead was pinched with worry. "How did your meeting
with your boss go?"

Diana grimaced as the memory of coffee drenching the
front of Mr. Powell's shirt flashed across her memory. "Not
very well." She briefly looked at her feet. Her shoes were
soggy and wet from a puddle outside. "It went horribly, actually." She looked back up at him and forced a smile. "But
that's not why I'm here. I wanted to see you. I thought, since
Jean went home sick, I'd help you at the store."

Linus's eyes seemed to search her face. He was always
doing that, as if trying to read her like one of the books he
read before bed. "What about your patients?"

She glanced around, noticing that Linus had a couple of
customers browsing along the aisles. "I canceled the rest of
my afternoon. I wanted to focus solely on my interview. Be-
sides, I think my meeting with Mr. Powell went so poorly
that I no longer get to see my patients. I'm pretty sure I'll be
fired. At the very least, I think I've been demoted instead of
promoted."

"What?" Concern continued to rise along his brow line.
"What happened? How do you go into a meeting when
you're up for a promotion and walk away without a job?"

Diana stepped back a little. She was aware that one of the
mothers in the store was looking at them. Lowering her
voice, Diana said, "I don't really want to discuss the meeting
right now."

Linus ran a hand through his overgrown waves of hair and let out an exasperated breath. "Of course you don't."

"What?"

Linus was supposed to be happy she was here offering her help. He adored his toy store, and he'd always wanted to tell her about it. He was always wishing out loud that she could make time to come see some toy he'd put together or some display he'd created. Well, here she was.

"That's just like you, Di," he said in a low voice.

"What is just like me?"

"You only want to discuss things when *you're* ready. And only the ones *you* want to discuss. Forget what anyone else wants."

"That's not true." *Is it?*

"This promotion is the whole reason you've been dodging wedding plans. At least that's what you've been saying. Today is a big day—not just for you, but for both of us. Because after today's meeting, you promised you'd be ready to start planning our marriage. We were going to set a date tonight."

"I know." Diana glanced around at the store's patrons again, feeling flustered and guilty. He was right.

"Some part of me thinks that your job was just an excuse." Linus seemed to visibly deflate. "You know what? I love you and I love spending time with you, but now is not the right time for this conversation. You're here because you're upset. But you won't let me comfort you. You won't even tell me what happened, so what's the point? Go home, Di. We can discuss it tonight. Or not. It's up to you, as always."

"Linus, this isn't fair."

He chuckled humorlessly. "No, it isn't. See you once you're home from Rochelle's birthday outing."

Diana flinched. "Actually, I told Rochelle I couldn't make

it. I want to be with you. I thought we needed to spend some time together."

His lips stretched into a thin line. "See? Everything is funneled through you and your feelings. And how you do your best to avoid feeling them."

Diana was about to argue when a customer rang the bell at the front counter.

Linus reached for Diana's hand and gave it a squeeze. "Go out with Rochelle. I'll be here working a bit late anyway." Linus let go of her hand, and it was all she could do not to snatch it back and hold onto it forever. Instead, she watched as he turned and walked away, leaving her standing there, heart pounding in her chest and Mariah Carey crooning "All I Want for Christmas Is You" in her ears. She didn't want to leave, but she couldn't just stay where she wasn't wanted either. Especially after Linus had accused her of always doing that exact thing.

Her feet were heavy as she turned and left the store. She grabbed her umbrella on the way to her car, but didn't bother to open it or shelter herself from the sleet this time. She let the precipitation hit her skin as she walked past Linus's bike on the rack. Turning back, she looked at it.

He can't ride home without his bike, now can he?

Without giving herself time to second-guess, she jogged over, lugged the bicycle off the rack, and wheeled it to the back of her vehicle. Then she heaved it up on the rack she had for when she and Linus went out of town. He never left without his precious bike.

There! Linus wouldn't get hit by a delivery truck tonight. And he wouldn't land himself in a coma either. *Problem solved.*

Diana quickly strapped the bike onto the rack and then hurried to the driver's seat, closing the door behind her. She took deep breaths while contemplating where to go next. She had no scheduled patients and Linus didn't want her helping him here at the store.

Her phone buzzed from her purse. She pulled it out and checked the screen. It was Linus's mom. Again. Diana started to drop her phone back into her purse, but at the last second, fueled mostly by guilt, she connected the call.

"Diana?" Joann said. "There you are. I was getting worried. You haven't been returning my calls."

"Sorry. I've been a little busy."

"Well, the holidays get that way, I guess. I know you're at work right now, so I was expecting to get your voice mail. I just wanted to see if you and Linus would come over this weekend. I can cook and we can plan that wedding of yours."

Diana watched as a car parked beside her. A couple got out to go inside Linus's store. No doubt they were playing Santa Claus for their child this month. She thought they looked excited as they held hands and hurried through the cold drizzle. For a moment, Diana pondered having a family of her own. Linus would, of course, be a natural with their children. Diana would love to be a mother, but what if Grandma Denny's influence was too much and she was one of those cold, standoffish caretakers?

Joann cleared her throat and continued talking. "So, you and Linus discuss if you can spare an hour or two this weekend, okay?"

"Right. I'll talk to him." Why hadn't Joann just called Linus? "It's his busy season, though."

"Trust me, I remember. When Linus's father ran the shop, I barely saw him during the month of December. I used to carry our meals to the store." She laughed quietly. "If Linus can't make it this weekend, maybe you still can. We can have a bit of girl time. I always wanted a girl, you know?"

Diana didn't make any promises. She wasn't sure what to even do with all of Joann's attention. "I'll let you know," she said noncommittally.

"Yes, please do. Okay, well, I know you're busy. I'll let you go," Joann said. "Call me."

"Mm-hmm."

Diana disconnected the call and watched through her windshield as more customers headed inside Linus's store. Joann seemed to be trying harder to connect with Diana since Thanksgiving. For some reason, she thought she was getting a daughter out of this engagement, but Diana felt differently. She didn't even really know how to be a daughter, no thanks to Jackie Merriman.

Diana turned on the windshield wipers and looked out at the shop in front of her. As long as Linus was inside selling toys, she didn't have to worry that he was in immediate danger. And since it was Rochelle's birthday, she knew her best friend would be taking an extended lunch. She always did on this date.

Diana pulled up Rochelle's contact and tapped both thumbs along her screen in quick succession.

Diana: *Where are you?*
Rochelle: *Are we on speaking terms again?*
Diana: *I'm sorry. I need you.*

Rochelle texted an eye-rolling emoji.

Rochelle: *I'm at the tavern having a quick bite.*
Diana: *Alone?*
Rochelle: *Yes, I am confident enough to eat alone in public.*

Another eye-rolling emoji came through.

Diana: *Great. I'll be there in five.*
Rochelle: *Fine. But, just so you know, I'm still upset.*
Diana: *I know. I'll buy your food to make it up to you.*

* * *

Diana stepped inside Sparky's Tavern and scanned the room, spotting Rochelle at one of the tables in the back. She headed that way. "Hey," she said, pulling out a chair and plopping down.

Rochelle swirled a French fry in a dollop of ketchup and looked up. "Hey." Her gaze hung heavy on Diana, traveling from the top of her head to the front of her shirt, damp and sticking to her. Thankfully the table blocked the lower half of Diana's outfit, which was coffee-stained in unfortunate places. "Ever heard of an umbrella?" Rochelle finally asked.

Diana could see her hair curling in her peripheral vision. But she had bigger issues than a bad-hair day. "Happy birthday. I'm sorry. I'm a horrible friend," she rattled off in quick succession.

Rochelle nodded in agreement to all. "Thank you. Apology considered, but not yet accepted. And your ability as a friend is subjective," she said in reply. Then her expression softened. "It's not like you to say you need me. What's up?"

Diana reached for one of Rochelle's fries and took a bite. "Well, I wish I would have listened to your advice on calming my nerves before the meeting with Mr. Powell. I bombed it again."

"Again?" Rochelle looked up from her basket of fries and narrowed her eyes.

"No. Not again. I only bombed it once." Diana took another bite of her fry. She kept forgetting that no one else was reliving this horrible day. Just her.

"Come on, it couldn't have gone that bad. What happened?" Rochelle asked.

Diana nibbled at her lower lip for a second. "Well, I told Mr. Powell that he was going to promote William instead of me because he's a man."

Rochelle's mouth dropped. "You accused your boss of being sexist?"

"I didn't mean to. But it's true, he *is* going to promote William instead of me. William, who doesn't even have half my years of experience."

"And you know he's promoting William how?" Rochelle reached for her drink.

"I just know. But I was still determined to go into that meeting and convince Mr. Powell to change his mind. Then he brought up Ms. Krick—"

"Your patient who died last month?" Rochelle asked with a touch of sympathy in her voice.

Diana swallowed. "I guess he expected that I'd be torn up about it because I'm a woman, whereas William is a man."

"Hmm." Rochelle hummed as she bit into another fry.

Diana knew that sound. It meant that Rochelle was avoiding saying whatever was really on her mind. "Just say what you're thinking."

Rochelle looked at her across the table. "Maybe he didn't think you'd be upset because you're a woman, but because your patient was your patient. Anyone would be affected by that, Diana. I've lost a patient before. I couldn't get out of bed for two whole days afterward. I was devastated."

Diana focused on the fry in her hand. "Of course I'm sad and I miss her. I'm not going to break down in the middle of a meeting with Mr. Powell, though. Life goes on." Even if Diana had felt like staying in bed for two days afterward herself.

"So what did you do when your boss mentioned your patient?" Rochelle asked.

"I spilled coffee all over myself and then on him. Accidentally."

"Hmm," Rochelle said again.

Diana didn't want to know what Rochelle was avoiding saying this time so she didn't ask. "Needless to say, I'm not getting that promotion. Mr. Powell probably never wants to see me again. And maybe I'll be job searching in the near future. I wonder if Sparky is hiring here at the tavern."

Rochelle chuckled at this. "You'd make a good bartender. People could rattle off their sob stories and it wouldn't get to you at all. Meanwhile, I listen to my patients' stories all day and I have a slew of things I do at night just so I can get some sleep." She lifted a brow. "How do you sleep at night?"

"Stop being a therapist. You're my best friend."

"Yes, I am. And it happens to be your best friend's birthday," Rochelle pointed out.

Diana stood, walked around the table, and gave Rochelle a hug. "Happy birthday. I love you."

"And I still hate you for ditching the girls' night later. But I love you too. And since love is an unconditional thing, we can still be friends."

Diana smiled and returned to her chair. "Glad to hear it."

"Since you don't want counseling from me, you can call the receptionist at my workplace tomorrow and get an appointment with one of my colleagues."

Diana didn't respond to that. She didn't need someone to talk to. She was just desperate to get her life back on track. She'd blown her chance at fixing her career, but she wasn't about to blow the rest of this day. She reached for another fry off Rochelle's plate, but this time Rochelle swatted her hand.

"We can still be friends, but this friend isn't sharing her birthday fries with you anymore today."

Chapter 11

The sun was down and it was dark outside as Diana sat in her car outside Linus's store that evening. She had this feeling she was doing something criminal even though she was only waiting for her fiancé. She had dropped his bicycle off at home to ensure he didn't refuse her ride and opt to pedal instead. That would be just like him, wanting to get those extra miles in. *Not tonight. Sorry, Linus.*

Diana stiffened as she saw him step out of his store. He turned to lock up behind him and then headed forward, noticing her after a few steps. His brow wrinkled. He must think she's losing her mind today. This was her third time being here, which was more than she usually stopped by in a month.

He glanced over to his bike rack on the sidewalk where his bike was no longer waiting for him. Then he hurried to the passenger side of her vehicle and dipped inside.

"Di," he said after closing the door behind him, "I've lost count of how many times I've asked you today, but what is going on? Why are you here? And where is my bike?"

"Surprise." She offered a wobbly smile. "It's cold and dark and icy. You shouldn't be traveling on a night like this. So, being a loving fiancé, I came to pick you up."

Linus narrowed his eyes. "You've never cared about cold, dark, or icy before. And neither do I. I like to ride my bike, regardless of the weather. I mean, perhaps a hurricane might deter me, but not this." He gestured all around him.

"It's not safe." Diana shrugged. "And, I don't know, I thought you and I could use the extra time together."

"It's a ten-minute drive to our home," Linus said flatly.

"Not if we take the long way." She gestured at his seat belt. "Please buckle up."

"For a ten-minute drive?"

"It's the law and accidents happen." Even though she was changing up all the contributing factors for Linus's last accident, it couldn't hurt to be as safe as possible. Perhaps she should have kept his bicycle helmet handy for him to wear in the car with her. He really would have balked at that.

Linus expelled a breath and pulled his seat belt across his chest. "You're acting peculiar. Is this about last night's spat? Or about what happened with your boss?"

She reversed out of the parking spot and drove up to the mouth of the lot, waiting for the slight traffic to clear before turning right.

"Our home is to the left," Linus said.

"I'm taking the long way, remember? And yes, maybe this is about last night's argument. I don't like it when we're mad at each other."

"I'm not mad at you, Di. I love you. I just . . ." He sighed beside her. "I wish we were *us* again."

"Us?" She looked away from the road for a moment and then screeched as her vehicle hit a patch of ice. Her fingers reflexively curled around the steering wheel as she righted back in her lane and blew out a heavy breath.

"You okay?" he asked.

She wasn't. She was trembling from head to toe. Her eyes welled with tears, which was so unlike her. She was usually so in control of her emotions that the tears never surfaced.

They'd already surfaced several times today, though. "What do you mean by wanting to be *us* again?"

In her peripheral vision, she saw Linus shrug. "You know. The way we used to be before I proposed. We were just . . . us. We'd take bike rides together and lay in bed talking for hours. I miss that. We don't sleep in on the weekends the way we used to."

Her fingers gripped the steering wheel as she listened. Instead of sleeping in, she'd been reading books on leadership, preparing for her new management role. "I'm sorry, Linus. Truly."

He reached for her hand and squeezed. "Are you also sorry about stealing my bike?"

She laughed out loud. "No. I will not apologize about that because maybe I'm jealous of Byron," she said, bringing up the time he gave his Schwinn bicycle a name. Of all the names to give, why that one? At least he hadn't preceded it with *Lord*.

"Growing old with you is going to be murder, isn't it?" he asked, teasing her and slapping a palm against his forehead.

"Careful," Diana said. "That's my very attractive fiancé you're hitting. And I happen to want to spend time kissing that face once we're home."

"Yeah?" He lowered his hand.

"Unless you think I've lost my mind, and you've decided to run as far and as fast as you can once you step foot out of this car."

"I don't run. I bike," he said with his quick wit that she'd been missing these last three weeks. She'd missed hearing his voice and the way he made her laugh unexpectedly all the time. Growing old with him would be more than she ever dreamed she could have.

"Hardy-har," she teased back.

"I think for Christmas I will get one of those two-seater bikes for us. What do you think?"

"We have a strict twenty-dollar-gift rule, remember?" She glanced over for a brief second.

"Well, it wouldn't be a gift," he said. "It's transportation. A necessity, if you will."

Diana laughed again. *Ah, yes.* This was what he meant by *us*. This was the banter that made her heartbeat quicken. The feeling of *us* came with an easy smile and a stolen breath. A disbelief that she would be so lucky to have this man in her life. *Us* felt like magic. Like seeing a shooting star. Or watching the first winter snowflakes float on the crisp cold air.

"Back to your comment about running fast and far from you, I would never leave you, Di," Linus said. "I'm being serious."

He had, though. He'd left her over the last three weeks. Those weeks had given her a glimpse at a life without him, and it was like *A Christmas Carol*'s Ghost of Christmas Future had come to visit her. A life without Linus, without *us*, was frightening. "I would never leave you either." She squeezed his hand back.

"Almost home. Maybe we can seal that promise with a make-up kiss. And more," he said in that low bedroom voice he got sometimes. He hadn't used it in a while, though. That was her fault. She'd been subtly pushing him away, protesting that she needed to catch up on notes for work. Or saying she was too tired. Was she lying to him? To herself too?

They were approximately three minutes from home. She and Linus had almost made it. And once she was parked in their spot, safe and sound, Linus would be okay. They would make love until it was morning. Would it be December 5th? Or would she skip to Christmas morning since yesterday— her yesterday—was Christmas Eve? She didn't know the ins and outs of whatever was happening. All she knew was, if Linus was with her, it didn't matter what day it was.

Diana looked over and smiled. "I love you so much."

"Warts and all?" he asked.

She couldn't look away. He was so handsome. The first time she'd ever seen him, something inside her had shifted. She'd known then and there that he was special. "You don't have any warts, but yes, I love everything about you."

Linus leaned in to kiss her cheek as she turned her eyes back to the road. Then she screamed as headlights blinded her. She swerved left to dodge the oncoming vehicle, but it was too late. Metal screeched and Linus's hand let go of hers as the truck hit his side of the car.

No. Don't let go. I'm marrying you.

Her eyes shuttered closed and the world disappeared as one last thought ran through her mind: *We haven't even set the date yet.*

Chapter 12

Play It Again, Sam

Diana opened her eyes and blinked the world into view. She was in her bedroom and sunlight streamed through the blinds to her right.

No. *No, no, no.* Her one day with Linus was over and now it was Christmas. She'd ruined her chance at saving him. He was gone. Or actually, he was back at New Hope Long-Term Care, lying lifeless like he had before she'd shaken that silly snow globe.

Diana sat up in bed. Her body felt heavy, weighed down with every terrible, horrible, no good, very bad emotion that ever existed. She just wanted to disappear back under the covers and return to sleeping, but her bladder was full. Groggily, she stood and shuffled toward the bathroom, stopping short when she heard a noise beyond the closed door. Her eyes opened fully and she stared ahead, her breaths coming out shallowly.

Why was the bathroom door closed? She was the only one here. Unless she was in the bathroom, the door would be left open.

Linus's faint hum played on the air. Was she hearing things? The melody was a Christmas tune. Diana listened, trying to pick it out. "Rudolph the Red-Nosed Reindeer"? Linus was the only thirty-year-old man she knew who would hum a song about a red-nosed reindeer.

Diana's eyes stung as she stood there frozen, wondering if she were still dreaming somehow. Then the bathroom door opened and Linus took a step before noticing her standing there in her pinstriped pajama pants and soft pink tank. When had she put these on? Last she remembered, she'd been wearing the pants she'd spilled coffee on during her interview.

He stopped humming and looked at her. "Well hello, sleepy girl."

"You're here," she said, letting out a small laugh. "We did it! We made it!" Relief poured over her as she threw herself in his direction. His arms encased her and she breathed in his minty scent. Pulling back, she shook her head in disbelief. Were her eyes deceiving her? "It's Christmas and you're here! I can't believe it! You're awake!" Perhaps the accident they'd been in hadn't been so bad after all. She wasn't sure how they'd gotten here afterward, but there must be some reasonable explanation.

"Christmas?" His head flinched back slightly. "What are you talking about?"

Diana swallowed as her heart sank like an anchor in the ocean. "It's not Christmas?"

The look on Linus's face confirmed that it wasn't.

But it had to be. Mrs. Guzman had said one more day. That was all Diana got with the one she'd loved and lost. "It's December fourth?" she asked.

"That's correct. Why are you acting so bizarre?" His brows furrowed.

Diana felt like crying. "Um, well, I . . . I have to pee," she said quickly.

"Of course. That explains everything." Linus stepped to the side and gestured for her to go into the bathroom. "The loo is all yours," he said with exaggerated politeness. He got this way when they were upset with one another. He wasn't the type to fight back. Not usually at least. Instead, he got overly civil.

Diana didn't budge. "I'm sorry about last night, Linus." Her last night was when they'd been driving home to make love. Linus's was December 3rd when he'd suggested they get married three weeks from now. His family would all be in town, and it would be perfect. Diana rolled her lips together, choosing her words wisely. "Maybe we can, I don't know, spend the day together. You can call out sick and I'll do the same. We can lie in bed like we used to. We can be *us* again," she said, remembering their car ride from last night.

"Us?" Linus didn't seem to know what she was talking about. He was the one who'd penned the term about them, though. "What does *us* mean?"

Diana swallowed thickly. "You know. When we finished each other's sentences and stayed up late talking all night long. When we slept in on the weekends. We've been so stressed lately. We've barely spent any time together."

"*You've* been stressed. And I've tried to spend time together. It's you who's been too busy," he pointed out, continuing with his exaggerated politeness. He hadn't accepted her apology yet, she realized. Yesterday he'd let the whole conversation from the night before roll off his shoulders, but today his demeanor seemed different.

"Well, I'm not busy right now. Let's just blow off the whole day and stay here, where it's safe and warm."

This made Linus chuckle. "Safe? We live in Snow Haven. We're as safe as it gets. And today is your big meeting with Mr. Powell, remember? You're up for that promotion you've been talking nonstop about for the past month. The one that you've been using as an excuse to not plan our wedding."

"It's not an excuse. It's a reason." And it was a good one. Diana wanted the promotion. It was the next goal on her upward path. Shouldn't Linus want her to follow her dreams and succeed?

"You deserve that promotion, Di," Linus said. "You've worked hard for it. And you're a shoo-in. Let's just get through this day, and then we can talk some more tonight."

She stood there, looking at him and trying to memorize every freckle on his face. Then she moved toward him to give him a hug, but Linus stepped away. Diana swallowed. "Oh. Okay."

He scratched absently at the side of his face. "I, uh, have to get ready for work. I'm meeting with a new distributor this morning. And you have to pee, remember?" He smiled sheepishly.

She'd said she was sorry, but he still looked hurt. "Right," she whispered. Then she continued toward the bathroom and closed the door behind her, trying not to cry. *Don't cry. Don't cry.* What was the point of a second chance—*er,* third chance— if Linus didn't want to be with her?

She used the bathroom and then stood in front of the mirror, washing her hands. She took an extra moment to run a brush through her hair. After that, she splashed some cold water on her face while her mind raced. She was only supposed to get one more day, but she'd gotten two. Why? What was she supposed to do differently?

She stepped out of the bathroom and watched Linus as he pulled on a pair of khaki pants and looped the belt around his narrow waist. "Can we at least have lunch today?"

He glanced up, but didn't meet her eyes. He was obviously still harboring hurt feelings. Maybe he was wondering again if she regretted accepting his proposal. Maybe he was still re- gretting proposing like he'd said on the very first December 4th. "It's okay, Di. It's not like we've never argued before. We'll talk tonight after you get home from Rochelle's birth- day drinks."

"I'll skip drinks with Rochelle."

Linus stopped what he was doing and looked up. "She's your best friend. You've been blowing her off a lot lately."

Diana's lips parted. "No, I haven't. I just saw her a couple nights ago." But that was Christmas Eve in Diana's reality, not the one she wasn't currently living.

"Go to your meeting with Mr. Powell. Have drinks with Rochelle. We'll see each other tonight," he reiterated as he completed the last button on his lavender-colored shirt. She'd just picked that shirt up from the dry cleaner right before his accident. He loved freshly pressed clothing, and those goofy ties of his. The one he was currently looping around his neck had little dogs on it, just like yesterday.

What could she say right now? Telling Linus she'd rather be with him than her best friend made her look like a jerk. "I'm just sorry if I've made you feel unimportant in my life lately. I've been a lousy fiancée and I know that. I love you, though. I want to do better."

Linus stepped toward her, leaned in, and kissed her cheek. It was brief, but she closed her eyes and soaked up the sensation of his lips on her skin. "I love you too. We'll talk tonight, okay?"

She nodded numbly, wanting to reach for him and pull him back toward her. What if she didn't see him tonight? What if he didn't make it home? A dozen thoughts ran through her brain, but before she could say or do anything else, Linus was gone. He left the room and grabbed his keys on the way out the front door.

Diana startled as it shut loudly down the hall. Then she scrambled to find some clothes of her own to wear. She'd gone to see Mrs. Guzman yesterday after Linus left. She guessed she'd start her day there once again even though the older woman didn't remember coming to see Diana the day before Christmas Eve. At least she believed what Diana was telling her. Diana seriously doubted anyone else would.

After brushing her teeth and putting on her shoes, Diana

grabbed her keys and purse and headed out the door. The temperature was frigid as she hurried across the apartment complex's courtyard. She stopped behind Mrs. Guzman's door, took a breath, and knocked.

A moment later, the older woman opened the door. "There you are, dear. Come in, come in." Her neighbor reached for her arm and practically yanked her inside.

"What do you mean, 'there you are'? Did you know I was coming?" Diana asked, hope swelling around her heart. Maybe Mrs. Guzman remembered what was going on this time?

"Well, you were the first person I thought of when I woke up this morning, so I figured I'd be seeing you sometime soon." Mrs. Guzman said this as if it made complete sense. "Some tea?" she offered.

"What kind of tea?" Diana was leery because maybe Mrs. Guzman put spells on her teas too. The enchantment she'd done on the snow globe was an incredible gift, but Diana wasn't sure she needed anything else to add to her confusion.

"Peppermint. It'll warm you up. Snow is coming. Not today, of course. It's still too cold to snow." She gave Diana a conspiratorial look and then turned toward the kitchen where a hot kettle sat on the counter as if Mrs. Guzman really was waiting for company. The old woman flipped the kettle on and opened the cabinet to grab a mug.

"So," Diana began, "you aren't going to remember this, but the day before yesterday, you came to see me at my apartment and you brought me a gift. It was December twenty-third. The day before Christmas Eve." Mrs. Guzman didn't react to that so Diana continued. "I invited you inside, and you admired the snow globe Linus had given me." Diana was talking fast, trying to get all the information out. She didn't want to waste a second of this new day.

Mrs. Guzman nodded as she listened. She opened a tin full

of tea bags and dropped one into the mug. "A snow globe is a magical thing."

"That's what you said the first time. Do you remember any of this?"

"No." Mrs. Guzman turned to look at her.

Diana felt her body fold forward, her shoulders rounding. Of course she didn't. Diana needed someone to be in on the secret, though. She was scared and alone in a day she'd already lived before—twice. "Okay, hypothetically, if you put an enchantment on my snow globe and made it to where I got a chance to spend one more day with someone I've lost . . ."

"Mm-hmm." Mrs. Guzman poured the hot water over the tea bag. She stirred in some honey and walked it over to Diana.

Diana waited to speak again until Mrs. Guzman met her gaze. "What would I do with that new day?"

"Another day is a gift," Mrs. Guzman said just like she'd done yesterday. "Hypothetically, you would use it to be with the person you lost."

"But can I use the day to change what happens? Can I stop something bad from taking place? So that the one I miss isn't lost anymore?"

Mrs. Guzman seemed to think about that response. "The snow globe's magic doesn't bring people back from the dead, if that's what you're asking."

"He's not dead, though," Diana said.

Mrs. Guzman lifted a brow. "Well, then, *hypothetically*, if he's not dead, you haven't lost him, have you? In that case, I would guess you could, possibly, save him."

"But how?" Diana took a sip of her tea. She barely tasted it because she was so nervous. "I mean, I tried yesterday. I took his bike. I drove him home a different way. The accident still happened."

"And now you're repeating the same day again?" Mrs. Guzman asked. The whole hypothetical pretense was out the door, but Diana didn't think her neighbor had ever bought it anyway. "It sounds like you're in what is referred to as a time loop, dear."

Diana nibbled on her lower lip as she considered the idea. "A time loop? Like in *Groundhog Day*?"

Mrs. Guzman scrunched her white-blond brows. "What?"

"It's a movie. The main character keeps reliving Groundhog Day." Diana gave her head a slight shake. "But things like that don't happen in real life."

"No? Then why are you panicking in my kitchen right now?" Mrs. Guzman waited a beat and then nodded. "I would say life is offering you a lesson that you must learn. Until then, you're stuck."

As long as Linus was in this day, Diana didn't mind being trapped in December 4th. She just wanted to make sure he came out of it with her. Intact. "What is the lesson? And who's teaching it?"

Mrs. Guzman chuckled. "I can't answer those questions for you."

"Can't you read your tea leaves or something?" Diana asked, glancing past the older woman to the tins of tea lined up on her counter. "I don't have time to make mistakes. What if this is the last day in the time loop? I need to get it right this time." *Forever is a myth. All we have is this moment.*

Mrs. Guzman gave her a gentle smile. "There is always time for tea and mistakes. That's my philosophy. This predicament is for you to figure out. I just wish you would have chosen a summer day to repeat instead of a freezing cold one."

"I didn't pick this day." Diana never would have chosen one of the worst days of her life.

Mrs. Guzman narrowed her wide blue eyes. "Oh, yes, you did."

*   *   *

After drinking her hot peppermint tea, Diana said goodbye to Mrs. Guzman and walked past the jingling Santa on the sidewalk, dropping some change into his pail.

"Merry Christmas!" he called after her.

"Thank you!" Diana called behind her, walking fast. She was on a mission. The best plan she had was to go about her morning as scheduled because if this was the day that stuck in the real timeline, she needed her job. She had patients to see and a promotion to win. Plus, Linus's accident wasn't until tonight. There'd be plenty of time to get to him, make up, and keep him from riding his bicycle into a delivery truck.

First stop was Maria Harris's house. *Crap!* Diana had nearly forgotten about Maria's broken ankle. She hoped it wasn't too late to save her. Diana dialed Maria's number and waited.

"Hello?" Maria sounded slightly out of breath when she answered.

"Ms. Harris? You're not trying to pull your Christmas decorations from the attic, are you?"

Maria coughed slightly. "I am, and it's a bit dusty up there."

"Stop what you're doing. That's not safe." Diana cranked the car and waited for the engine to warm, watching the frosty vapors rise from the hood. "I'll help you as soon as I'm done stretching your arm. Promise me you'll wait."

"Well, I'm perfectly capable—" Maria began to protest.

"I'm sure you are, but I want to help."

Maria reluctantly agreed. Diana exhaled softly, feeling like she'd dodged a bullet. Then she drove over and knocked on her patient's door.

"Diana, I'm so glad you're here," Maria said in greeting.

"Hi, Ms. Harris. How are you feeling today?" Diana stepped into the home and looked around, spotting one box of decorations from where Maria had already begun dragging them from the attic before Diana's call.

Maria rubbed her right arm as she flinched slightly. "The shoulder is stiff, but I'm alive, so that's a blessing, isn't it? And you are here with me." She offered a wide smile.

Diana was glad that Maria valued her visits and she felt pressured, in a good way, to connect on a deeper level with the older woman. Maria seemed lonely. "Let's get started, shall we?"

Maria slowly headed over to the bed in the corner of her living room and laid down with her right arm facing out for Diana to stretch. She closed her eyes like she often did and let Diana work.

"Your daughter is missing out by not having a relationship with you," Diana broached as she lifted Maria's arm above her, pushing it to the point of stiffness and holding the position for a beat.

Maria's eyes popped open and focused on Diana. "How did you know I have a daughter who lives nearby?"

Right. Yesterday had only happened in Diana's world. "Oh, um, I think you mentioned her once. Didn't you?"

"Hmm. That would be strange. I don't speak of my daughter often, but I guess I must have. I don't think my daughter would agree that she's missing out by not having a relationship with me though. I'm sure she's a busy woman anyway. She always was a busy body."

"Like someone else I know," Diana teased.

Maria smiled. "My daughter has a daughter of her own. My granddaughter is a beautiful teenager these days. I only know this because of a nice neighbor who cyberstalked her for me once." Maria looked down, not meeting Diana's gaze for a moment. "Allowing him to do that for me felt wrong. If my girl wanted me to know how she was doing, she would tell me herself. So, I've never looked her up again."

"It must be hard, not knowing." Diana finished stretching the shoulder and moved on to Maria's elbow and wrist.

"It's my burden to carry."

When Diana was finished stretching Maria's arm, she helped the older woman sit up on the bed's edge. Maria laid a hand over Diana's and gave her a meaningful look. "Thank you for letting me talk about my daughter. It helps. Maybe one of these days you'll tell me about your life too. You've been coming here for weeks, and I barely know a thing about you."

Diana shook her head just slightly. "That's because these sessions are for you, Maria. Not me." And Diana was private. "My life is pretty boring anyway."

"You're engaged, aren't you? Romance is anything but boring."

That wasn't necessarily true. Diana and Linus's relationship had gotten a bit mundane lately. Diana's fault, of course. She would do better once she rescued him from the delivery truck tonight. "Okay, let me get those boxes for you." She stood and headed for the second floor to reach Maria's attic. The ladder was already down and secured on the floor. Again, Diana didn't just retrieve the boxes for Maria, she also carried them into the living room and set them down at the exact spot where Maria needed them to be. Turning back to Maria, she pointed at the largest carton. "Leave the tree in the box. I will help you set it up tomorrow."

"But tomorrow isn't your day to come see me," Maria objected, eyes going wide.

"I know, but I want to help." And she wanted to make sure Maria didn't get hurt doing something that she had no business doing on her own. Not with her current limitations. "Promise me?"

Maria laughed softly. "Fine, fine. I'll look forward to having you come for a visit as something other than my physical therapist," she said. "That's very kind of you."

Guilt swirled around in Diana's stomach because she wasn't

actually intending to come over at all. Tomorrow would be Christmas Day if she had it her way.

Diana walked toward the front door, talking over her shoulder. "I'm on my way to see my next patient."

"The sixteen-year-old?" Maria asked.

"That's right."

"Here, give her this from me." Maria stepped over to a table beside the door and handed Diana pieces of fruitcake wrapped in plastic. "And here is one for you, and one for your fiancé."

"Thank you. We can have it tonight after dinner," Diana said, feeling a strange sense of déjà vu. She hadn't actually gotten to eat that piece of fruitcake last night. Instead, she'd gotten in an accident and had woken up back in December 4th. "See you tomorrow, Maria."

"I'll look forward to it."

The cold air rushed through Diana as she stepped outside and hurried inside her car. She set the fruitcake slices on the passenger seat and took a moment to check her phone. She had one missed call from Linus's mother. She'd return it later. Maybe.

Setting the phone back in her center console, Diana drove to Addy's home and parked along the curb. She grabbed the slice of fruitcake and got out to brave the cold once more, hurrying toward the front door. It was decorated with a large cedar wreath accented with holly berries. Diana shifted back and forth on her booted feet as she waited for Mrs. Pierce to finally answer.

"Ms. Diana. Addy's been waiting for you all morning." Mrs. Pierce opened the door wider, allowing Diana to enter the home.

"How is she doing?" Diana asked, getting straight to business as always.

"Good, I think. It's normal for a teenage girl to be moody and not want to talk to her mother, right?" There was a hint of worry in Mrs. Pierce's voice. "I believe I might have been the same way, even without cancer."

"I think it's normal, yes," Diana agreed, even though she hadn't had any personal experience to speak from. Her mother hadn't been around long enough to ignore.

"Oh, good. It's been so long since I was sixteen." Mrs. Pierce's smile wobbled nervously. "Anyway, I'm sure Addy will be happy to see you. Anyone but her mom is on the invitation list into her bedroom."

Diana offered up the slice of fruitcake. "For you and Addy."

"You shouldn't have," Mrs. Pierce said warmly.

"I didn't. It's from my last patient. She's very generous."

"Oh, how sweet." Mrs. Pierce nodded. "Thank you for bringing it over."

Diana gestured down the hall. "I'll go ahead in to see Addy, if that's okay."

"Of course. Let me know if you need anything," Mrs. Pierce called behind her.

Diana walked down the dimly lit hall and knocked on Addy's bedroom door.

"Come in," Addy called.

Diana twisted the knob and stepped inside the world of purple paint and teen heartthrob posters. "Hey."

Addy had a tie-dye scarf on her head today to hide her thinning hair. She pulled out her earbuds, giving Diana a pensive expression.

"Something wrong?" Diana already knew the answer.

"Oh, you know. I still have cancer, this house is still my germ-free prison, and I can't even sneeze without sounding the alarms and having my mom run in here to make sure I'm still breathing."

Diana closed the bedroom door behind her. "Sounds tough."

"Understatement," Addy said, sarcastically.

Diana sat on the chair beside her bed. "You know it won't always be this way, right?"

Addy gave her an eye roll. "It feels like I'm stuck in the same day, over and over."

Diana blinked and momentarily wondered if Addy was also experiencing a time loop. She wasn't, though. Diana was the only one reliving December 4th. "Yeah. I can relate to that a little bit."

Addy gave her an assessing look. "You have thick, healthy hair, though. So at least if you were stuck in the same day, it'd be a good-hair day."

Diana pointed at her head. "Have you seen this mop top? The weather has already gotten a hold of this do and had its way."

Addy's gaze flicked up to Diana's hair. "You're not wrong," she said, cracking a small smile.

Diana nibbled her lower lip and broached the subject just like yesterday. "This isn't about hair, though. It's about a guy, right?"

Addy lowered her brow. "What makes you say that?"

"Because it's always about a guy. How about you tell me all about it while we do your physical therapy?"

Addy blew out another breath. "Why should I?"

"Because talking to me is better than keeping what's bothering you bottled up inside." Somehow Diana felt hypocritical for saying so. Keeping bottled emotions was Diana's MO and she resented anyone, namely Linus and Rochelle, for trying to nudge her feelings to the surface.

"Fine." Addy stood and walked to the bathroom.

Diana followed close behind in case she fell. The teen hadn't fallen the first December 4th, or the second, but Diana wasn't taking any chances. Diana pulled a chair in front of the sink and Addy sat down in front of the mirror without protests this time.

"I was seeing Jay for a couple months before I got sick,"

Addy said, looking at Diana through the mirror. "We started hanging out over the summer. And sometimes my best friend, Sierra, hung out with us too, but she always complained about being the third wheel."

"And now?" Diana avoided the brush today, knowing that would upset Addy. There were perks to repeating a day. Instead, Diana handed Addy the facial moisturizer from her bag on the counter. That wasn't likely to lead Addy to tears.

Addy twisted off the lid and dipped the tips of two fingers inside. "Now, they're still hanging out without me. Because I'm sick and I'm not at school." She swiped the moisturizer along her well-defined cheekbones.

"They've ghosted you?" Diana asked, feeling anger on Addy's behalf.

"Not exactly. Jay was calling for a while, but I wasn't answering. Who wants to talk to a depressed girl? I'm not much fun to be around, not even on FaceTime."

"That's not true, Addy. I love being with you."

Addy rolled her eyes as she looked at Diana through the mirror. "You get paid to hang out with me."

"That doesn't mean I don't enjoy it. So, you were the one who ghosted him?" This was new information.

Addy used both hands to rub the moisturizer in. When she was done, she seemed depleted just from that simple task. "Yeah, but Jay wasn't supposed to use that opportunity to go after my best friend. That's so rude."

Diana couldn't disagree. "You're sure that's what's going on? How do you know he's doing more than just talking to your friend?"

"Because my friend Rebecca DM'd me. She's seen them together," Addy said.

"Like kissing?" Diana asked.

Addy glared at Diana through the mirror. Then she stood up, pushing the chair back into Diana's midsection just like she had yesterday. She sniffled a little and Diana wondered if she was crying again, even though Diana had avoided the hairbrush. "You're not helping at all," Addy called behind her as she made her way to her bed and plopped down. "Now I'm envisioning my boyfriend and best friend kissing. Thanks a lot, Diana."

After leaving Addy's house, Diana got inside her car and checked her cell phone, noticing another missed call from Linus's mom. Joann was a lovely woman, but the fact that she was a mother put her in the category of people who couldn't be trusted or depended on. Diana didn't want to feel that way, but she did.

She tapped the screen and listened to the voice mail.

"Hi, Diana. This is Joann. I was just walking downtown and passed a bridal shop and thought of you. I would love to come dress shopping with you sometime soon. Wouldn't that be lovely? Anyway, call me when you have time. Bye."

The voice mail ended.

Diana released a breath as if she were relieved, but she wasn't sure why. Had she expected Joann to deliver some sort of bad news? Diana didn't have time to return that call right now. There were too many other things to take care of today. Like texting Rochelle and wishing her a happy birthday.

Diana had let Rochelle down in a big way yesterday. But when your fiancé's life was in the balance, having birthday drinks with your best friend wasn't on the list of priorities. Maybe Diana could smooth things over with Rochelle by sending flowers. *Yeah.* Rochelle loved flowers, and since she wasn't dating anyone these days, she never got any.

Diana tapped the local florist's information into her cell phone and pressed DIAL.

A cheery voice answered on the other end of the line. "How can I help you today?"

"Yes, hi. I would like to order my best friend some birthday flowers," Diana said, feeling proud of herself. Today was going to go much better than yesterday. She could feel it to her core. Third time on December 4th was a charm.

Ten minutes later, Diana had completed the order. Moving on! Her interview with Mr. Powell wasn't until two. She wanted to see Linus, but that could wait until after she secured her promotion. If this was the day that stuck, Diana needed to ace this meeting with her boss. Yesterday had gone about as disastrously as it possibly could. But today was a new day, and she was bound and determined to do it right.

Diana drove home, parked, and quickly passed by the jingling Santa on the sidewalk as she hurried to her apartment. She was going to take the time to change, brush her hair, and apply some lipstick. This time she needed to dress the part when she went in for her interview.

Once inside her apartment, Diana stepped inside her closet and grabbed a pair of black slacks and a long-sleeve button-down top. She also grabbed a cardigan and slipped her feet into some dress shoes that she would never wear to see her patients. She stepped inside the bathroom, ran a comb through her hair, and applied some plum-colored lipstick. It had been a long time since she'd worn makeup. Makeup was reserved for special occasions or for dates.

Something achy resonated in Diana's chest right above her heart. If she had known her time was limited with Linus, she would've made more of an effort. She would've applied lipstick and gone on more dates. And after she saved Linus, she *would* do those things. After she got this promotion she'd been working toward, she'd be able to relax a little. No more overtime. Everything would be the way it should be.

With one last glance in the mirror, Diana hurried back out of her apartment, nearly bowling down Mrs. Guzman. "Oh, hi, Mrs. Guzman. What are you doing here?"

Mrs. Guzman smiled back at her. "Well, I saw you return to your apartment, and I wanted to see how your time loop was going."

Diana looked around to make sure no one else was in hearing range. Gossip spread fast in this apartment complex. Folks were already whispering about Mr. Zitnik's love potion from Mrs. Guzman. Diana didn't want to be the focus of another rumor. "It's going well so far, but I don't have time to talk right now. I'm heading to a meeting with my boss. For a promotion," Diana said.

"Oh, isn't that nice?" Mrs. Guzman clung to Leonardo's leash as he sniffed Diana's dress shoes. "Well, I won't take up much of your time, then. I just wanted to mention that I was thinking about your time loop and your question about what you should do differently."

"Yes?" Diana asked.

"I wanted to add that priorities shift like ocean sand when you realize there isn't unlimited time. Those are the moments when you lead with your heart instead of your mind."

Did that rhyme? Was Mrs. Guzman somehow working another enchantment on Diana without her knowing it? Maybe Diana was being paranoid, but she took a step backward. "Thanks for the tip, Mrs. Guzman. I've got to run. See you tomorrow," she called behind her, wondering what tomorrow would bring. A new day or the old one again?

Diana skipped past jingling Santa, dropped some change in his tin, and hurried to her car in the lot beside the complex. She plopped into the driver's seat and shut the door, barring the winter wind. Then she drove toward Powell Rehabilitation Center.

She used her hands to smooth the wrinkles out of her clothing as she stepped from her car. She wanted to make a good impression on her boss. Usually when she ran into him she was either too quiet or too chatty. Those weren't management qualities. Then again, Diana had never thought she'd wanted to be in management until this past summer when she'd heard that her supervisor was retiring. Diana had suddenly felt like maybe some strand of success was what was missing in her life.

Linus didn't understand her new goal, of course. But he owned his own toy store. He was an entrepreneur, and she was just someone else's employee.

"Success doesn't buy you happiness," Linus had said once when Diana had worked overtime to cover one of her coworker's missed hours.

"No, but it does afford you nice things," she'd retorted. "And a wedding costs money."

Linus negated that comment. "I don't need fancy things or a flashy wedding. All I need is you," he'd said, sweetly wrapping his arms around her.

Diana wished she could feel his embrace again. She almost had last night. She still wasn't sure what had happened. One moment they were laughing and racing home. He was leaning in to kiss her. The next moment, everything had gone black.

Not tonight.

Her phone buzzed with a text message as she walked toward the rehabilitation center. She stopped and pulled her phone out of her bag to see who it was from.

Rochelle: *You sent me flowers? Why?*
Diana: *Because it's your birthday, silly.*

Instead of waiting for a response, Diana placed her cell phone back inside her purse. She needed to mentally prepare to go into this interview. Rochelle had flowers and when Diana was done with her interview, she would call Ro and say whatever was necessary to make her best friend understand why she couldn't go out tonight.

When time was limited, priorities shifted. That's what Mrs. Guzman had said, and it was true. Diana pulled open the door of Powell Rehabilitation and stepped inside.

Leann looked up from behind her desk as Diana approached. "Can I help you?"

"Yes, I have a meeting with Mr. Powell this afternoon." Diana shook her hands out by her side, willing her nerves to calm down. She could do this. She could convince her boss that she was confident and personable. That she would make a great manager. A much better one than William.

Leann looked at the schedule on her desk and nodded. "Yes, there you are. Two o'clock?"

"That's me," Diana said, forcing a smile.

"Wonderful. Have a seat and I'll call you when he's ready."

Diana had sat down for no more than a minute before Leann stood and called her name. "Ms. Merriman? Mr. Powell is ready to see you now."

Diana's legs felt shaky as she followed Leann down the hall toward Mr. Powell's office. She mentally rehearsed how she would greet him, deciding she would offer her hand and shake his firmly. And she absolutely would not throw William under the bus during this interview. This meeting was about proving she was a well-rounded therapist who genuinely cared about her patients and coworkers. Because she did.

Mr. Powell looked up as soon as Diana walked into his office, flashing his winning smile. Even if she didn't know him, she would definitely assume he was a leader of some sort. He had the confident vibe that all her leadership books talked about.

Diana tried to replicate that vibe as she stepped toward him and shook his hand. "Hello, Todd. Thank you for meeting with me today." She'd only just walked in and her heart felt like it was going to beat out of her chest. She had never been good in these types of situations. She preferred easy, friendly interactions with her patients and coworkers. But seeking a management position was the right next step in her career.

"Of course," Mr. Powell said. "Please have a seat. Would you like a cup of coffee?"

Diana nodded. "A cup of coffee would be lovely. Thank you."

"Of course." Mr. Powell headed over to his counter where he had a Keurig set up along with a tray of coffee condiments. "Do you take cream or sugar?"

"I drink mine black," she told him, just like yesterday.

"My kind of woman." Mr. Powell prepared her mug of coffee and then walked over and handed it to her. Diana reached up to take it with shaking hands. When her fingers touched the warm mug, she pulled back. Mr. Powell had already released the mug, though, and it dropped through Diana's fingers and onto her lap.

Diana squealed as the hot liquid burned her skin through her dress pants. She shot up, knocking her head directly under Mr. Powell's chin. She audibly heard his jaw clink against his teeth. "Oh, no! Are you okay?"

Mr. Powell had a dazed look about him. His polished smile drooped as he clutched the side of his face. His gaze also held a hint of irritation that slipped past his refined demeanor. He quickly blinked the look away and forced a faint smile that looked kind of painful to Diana.

"Are *you* okay?" He looked down at the dark brown coffee stains all over her thighs.

Her skin burned beneath the fabric, but she had forgotten about the pain when she realized what she'd done to Mr. Powell. Five minutes in and she'd already blown this interview. She took a step backward to give him space and tried to pull in a breath so that she didn't start hyperventilating. She felt like she needed a brown paper bag to breathe into right about now. What was the point of having a day to do over if she did it worse every time?

Mr. Powell cleared his throat. "Would you like me to get you another cup of coffee?"

Diana shook her head quickly. "No, that's okay."

"All right, then." He walked around the other side of his desk where he was probably safer. Then he sat down and rested his elbows on the wooden surface and looked at her. He blew out an exasperated breath. "So, tell me why you want this promotion."

Diana opened her mouth to speak but no words came out. She'd mentally rehearsed what she'd say to Mr. Powell, but now she felt rattled. All the composure she'd built on the drive over was obliterated. "Why do I want this promotion?" she repeated, looking for her rehearsed answers. Why *did* she want this promotion? She'd never considered herself a leader. She didn't like ordering people around. She didn't mind training others. Sharing her knowledge was something she actually enjoyed.

Across the desk, Diana could see the redness of Mr. Powell's face from where she'd bumped his jaw. Guilt swam through her, along with discomfort and a touch of embarrassment. "Well," she began, "you see, I've been a physical therapist for a long time. I've been working in the field for nearly ten years now, and it feels like this is the right next step in my career."

Mr. Powell reached for a pen and jotted that down in a notebook. "Management isn't for everyone, though. The right next step for one person isn't always the same for the next. It's like a marriage. Sometimes couples date for ten years before tying the knot. Sometimes they date for one month. And sometimes they don't get married at all."

Why was he talking about marriage? This was a job interview. And now Diana's mind was on Linus and their engagement. Why had she been dragging her feet on setting a date? The truth was, she was a little scared—more than a little.

Marriage was a big step. What if she wasn't what Linus needed? What if she turned out to be a failure of a wife and ruined his life? What if, like everyone else in Diana's life, he left?

"I know," Diana said, returning her thoughts to the interview, "but I think I could be good as management."

"Do you feel like you're a good leader?" Mr. Powell asked.

Diana rolled her lips together, moistening them as she thought on her answer. "Yes."

"Can you give me some examples of times you've been a leader in your current role?"

Diana took a breath and looked at Mr. Powell. "I lead my patients every day. They open their doors to me with the expectation that I'm going to help them get well. They put their trust in me. They look to me for leadership and that's what I provide them," she said, feeling good about that answer. *Okay, okay,* she was turning things around and getting back on track. Maybe there was hope for her after all—even though her pants were drenched in coffee.

Mr. Powell nodded as his smile drew up higher. That was a good sign. "Your patients have never filed a complaint."

But they hadn't filed many Glow Cards either—one to be exact. And William's patients had.

"I love working with my patients. But I would also love mentoring upcoming therapists," she added. "The best of both worlds." She let out a nervous laugh, very aware of the red marks on Mr. Powell's jawline. "Most of my patients have physical disabilities that prevent them from completing Glow Cards."

Mr. Powell looked at her strangely.

"I just mean, I know that some therapists here get lots of Glow Cards. But my lack of Glow Cards isn't a reflection on how good of a therapist I am."

"Of course not." He offered his winning smile again.

"Well, Diana, I'll look over your employee file and consider you for the promotion," he said noncommittally. "I just want to shoot straight with you. There are several folks here who are interested in the position."

"Of course." Diana felt herself deflate. She wasn't getting this promotion. She could feel it in her bones. The job was going to everyone's pal, William. "Thank you for your time." She stood and reached over his desk to offer her hand. In doing so, she knocked the picture frame off his desk. *Again?* The crystal frame crashed to the ground and Diana flinched at the sound of breaking glass at her feet.

Mr. Powell's entire face turned red now. Even so, he kept his smile firmly pinned in place.

"Oh, I am so sorry!" Diana said for the second time this interview. "I'll replace the frame." She looked at the photograph buried under broken glass. It was of a younger Mr. and Mrs. Powell. Diana had met Mr. Powell's wife many times before at company parties and picnics.

"Natasha and I chose the marriage-after-one-month route. She gave me that frame for our eighth wedding anniversary."

Diana wanted to shrink out of the room. She wanted to disappear into thin air. *Poof. Gone.* She realized her hand was still extended to Mr. Powell. He wasn't reaching for it, though. She slowly withdrew her hand and took a few retreating steps toward the door. "Thank you again for your consideration, Todd. I, um, will just be leaving now." She turned and hurried out of his office. Diana did her best not to cry as she passed Leann in the lobby and headed outside toward the parking lot.

She quickly got inside her car and held the steering wheel as her body shook. Again? Why couldn't she fix this meeting and nail her promotion?

Her phone buzzed from inside her purse. She took a breath, already knowing who it was.

"Hello?" she answered.

"Diana? There you are. I was getting worried," Joann said. "You haven't been returning my calls."

"Sorry. I've been a little busy." Trying to save her fiancé from a delivery-truck coma while also winning the promotion that her heart was set on.

"Well, the holidays get that way, I guess. I know you're at work right now, so I was expecting to receive your voice mail. I just wanted to see if you and Linus would come over this weekend? I can cook and perhaps we can plan that wedding of yours. What do you think?"

Diana watched a soft drizzle of rain fall on her windshield. She'd had this conversation in Linus's parking lot yesterday. There were slight changes about the day, but not enough to make a difference.

Joann cleared her throat, reminding Diana that she still hadn't answered.

"I'm sorry. What was the question?" Diana's emotions were threadbare. As long as she saved Linus tonight, everything would be okay, she reminded herself.

"I asked if you and Linus could spare an hour or two this weekend to come see us? Discuss it amongst yourselves, okay?" Joann asked.

"I'll talk to him." Why hadn't Joann just called Linus? She was *his* mother after all. "It's his busy season, though."

"Trust me, I remember. When Linus's father ran the shop, I barely saw him during the month of December. I used to carry our meals to the store," she said, just like she had yesterday, laughing quietly to herself. "If Linus can't make it this weekend, maybe you still can. We can have a little girl time. I always wanted a girl, you know?"

Diana swallowed. Something about that statement pricked at her emotions. "I'll let you know, Joann," she said. If she saved Linus tonight, they'd go to the Grants' house this weekend, Diana promised herself. She'd do a lot of stuff differently. She just needed to get past this one day.

"Yes, please do. Okay, well I know you're busy-busy. I'll let you go," Joann said. "Talk soon."

"Okay. Bye." Diana disconnected the call and sighed. What was next on her day of repeats? Ah, yes. Sparky's Tavern to toast Rochelle a happy birthday. At least Diana could do that right today. She hoped.

Chapter 13

When Diana walked into Sparky's Tavern at a quarter after three, she spotted Rochelle seated at a table in the bar. It was the same seat she'd occupied yesterday.

"Uh-oh," Rochelle said, noting Diana's expression as she walked up. "What happened?"

Diana pulled out a chair and plopped down, her body feeling like lead. "If I was the only applicant for the job, I still wouldn't get the promotion. That's how bad the meeting went this time."

"This time?" Rochelle lifted a brow.

A waitress set two drinks down on the table.

"Thanks," Diana told the waitress. Then she looked at Rochelle, ignoring her slipup and changing the subject. "How did you know I'd want one of these?" She gestured at the fruity drink. Diana was the one repeating this day and privy to information ahead of time, not Rochelle.

Rochelle shrugged as she molded her lips around her own straw. "Just a guess. It works for celebrating—or commiserating," she said before sucking some of the red-colored drink into her mouth.

Diana laughed even though she didn't feel even a tiny

ounce of joy. On the contrary, she felt miserable. "I have to drive when I leave here, so I shouldn't have more than a couple sips."

"Oh, come on," Rochelle chided. "It's my birthday. By the time you leave here, the alcohol will have worn off."

Diana didn't plan to stay that long, but she didn't want to disappoint her friend just yet. She'd done that on the first two rounds of this day. At least Maria wasn't breaking her ankle in this time loop. That was a success, albeit not one that would keep Diana warm at night for the next fifty years. "Happy birthday, by the way," Diana told Rochelle. "I hope your day is going better than mine."

Rochelle's cheeks flushed subtly as she bit into her lower lip for a beat. "It is, as a matter of fact. I met someone."

"You met someone? Like a guy someone?" Diana asked, spirits lifting. This was new. This hadn't happened on either of the first two December 4ths.

"Mm-hmm. He works in the office next to mine. He usually picks up our deliveries and brings them inside. Today he walked into my office, though, and brought me a tiny bouquet of flowers. For my birthday." Rochelle's grin spread through her cheeks. "I mean, it could just be a nice gesture. He saw the flowers you sent when he dropped off our mail. Thank you, by the way. After that, he walked down the way to the florist and got me some more flowers."

"That's great, Rochelle." Diana actually did feel happy right now. And intrigued. The do-over day was working out well for Rochelle too. Diana was positive this hadn't happened before because Rochelle had lamented both times about being single.

Rochelle shrugged. "The birthday gods have smiled down on me, I guess. A handsome lawyer is exactly what I would have asked for on my birthday if I thought there was a possibility of getting such a thing."

"What did the card say?" Diana asked.

" 'Thank you for being you.' " Rochelle brought her drink to her mouth and took a sip.

"Aww. That's sweet."

"Isn't it?" Rochelle smiled to herself.

"Maybe I should have sent Linus flowers today too," Diana said.

"*He* should be the one sending *you* flowers. Why would you send him some?" Rochelle asked.

Diana still hadn't sipped her drink. She wanted it, but she needed to have a clear mind to get through the rest of this day. Maybe her day would take a turn for the better too. "We've been fighting a bit."

Rochelle's voice dropped an octave as she leaned in toward Diana. "I'm sorry. Want to talk about it?"

"It depends. Are you being a counselor right now or a friend?" Diana asked.

Rochelle shrugged. "Whatever you need."

Diana took a tiny sip of her drink. She wasn't going to tell Rochelle what was really going on with this day. Her best friend would think she'd completely lost it. "Linus thinks I'm choosing work over him. He says I'm always too busy these days, and he's upset that I haven't nailed down a date for our wedding. He's worried I have regrets about saying yes."

"Do you?" Rochelle lifted a brow as she pursed her lips around her straw and drank.

"Of course not. He's the one for me. I was just trying to get the management job at work."

"Which will mean longer hours and a higher workload for you. Are you sure that's what you really want?" Rochelle asked.

Diana didn't appreciate her friend's doubt. "I've been seeing patients for nearly a decade. It's time for me to move up the ladder."

"Says who?" Rochelle asked.

Diana narrowed her eyes. "Says me."

Rochelle leaned back in her chair. Diana could practically see the wheels spinning in her head. "Sometimes when people are afraid, they hyper focus on something to channel all of their energy and attention toward. To avoid the things they're most afraid of."

Diana couldn't resist. If she was going to be subjected to therapy, she was going to take another sip of her drink. "I'm not afraid."

"Linus proposed this summer. Setting a date by now isn't an unreasonable expectation. Your parents divorced. Your grandmother was a single mom. It would make sense that commitment might be a scary thing for you."

Diana shifted restlessly. "No more counseling. I want my best friend back."

Rochelle leaned forward as she narrowed her gaze. "I *am* being your best friend, and I'm telling things the way I see them. Also . . ." She nibbled at her lower lip.

"What?" Diana asked, a pinch of worry in her chest.

"Maybe you don't truly want this promotion."

"Of course I want it!" Diana nearly shouted. "Why wouldn't I want it?"

Rochelle shrugged. "You're a caregiver. You love working with your patients. I'm not sure I can see you stuck in some office telling others what to do. It's not your style."

"I would make a great manager," Diana objected.

"I'm not saying you wouldn't. But would it make you happy? That's all I'm asking. I wonder . . ." Rochelle seemed to hesitate.

"Go ahead."

"I just wonder if you're investing so much energy into your work suddenly because you're avoiding taking the next step with Linus. He wants to build something with you, and, well, I wonder if that scares the ever-loving crap out of you."

"I'm not scared. And I'm not pushing Linus away."

"I just want you to be happy, Diana. But you can't be if you shut everyone out. That promotion to management won't fill the void."

Diana pushed back from the table and stood. "Thanks for whatever this was. Send me a bill."

"Diana?" Rochelle called after her.

Diana looked back at her friend before walking out. She couldn't sit and listen to any more of this. Were Rochelle's insights about her true? If so, it meant she'd wasted so much time this year when she could have been spending it with Linus. "What?"

"What would happen if you stopped pretending everything was fine? If you told Linus exactly how you felt? Me? Yourself?"

Diana shook her head. "You want to know how I feel? I feel ganged up on right now."

Diana turned and continued walking. She was shaking as she exited the bar and stood in the cold afternoon. It wasn't sleeting today, but the air was thick with moisture. Diana hurried to her car and got inside, taking deep breaths. *What was that?* Diana wasn't running scared from her life. She was living her life, trying to achieve success by going for a management position. Why couldn't everyone see that?

Diana checked the time on her cell phone. It was already late afternoon. Linus would be closing the store in an hour and a half. The rest of her schedule was clear. There was nothing stopping her from going to the Toy Peddler and spending as much time with Linus as she could before driving him home safe and sound.

Diana drove in that direction. Christmas was in full effect in Snow Haven. There were little wreaths on all the light posts. She drove past the huge Christmas tree in the town square. Then she arrived at Linus's store. As she got out, the air felt even colder than before. The sun wasn't even visible through the thick clouds that were hanging low and promising a blanket of the white stuff sometime soon. Diana had already lived through most of this month, though. There wouldn't be any snow falling. No chance of a white Christmas here.

She locked up her car and headed inside. The tiny bell jingled overhead and Linus looked up from his register where he was helping a man with his purchases.

Linus's brows hung heavily as he looked at her. No doubt he wondered what Diana was doing here. Linus had a passion for kids and toys but, with the exception of the time she'd come here looking for a toy for her coworker, she had tried to avoid places like this. When she was young, she'd always wanted to go into the toy stores, but Grandma Denny had told her toys from such places were too expensive. Diana's toys were mostly hand-me-downs or they'd been purchased from yard sales. That was one reason Diana always gave to the sidewalk Santa. Every kid deserved a new toy at Christmas. Every child should also have a loving home.

Diana headed down one of the aisles, knowing Linus would find her once he was done handling his customers. Baby dolls lined the shelves that she passed. There were all sorts of dolls that cried, peed, ate, and burped. Several of the ones with less savory traits were what Linus had suggested to her the first time she'd come in.

She smiled as she continued to peruse. There was doll clothing and shoes, strollers and diapers. Diana looked at them all, fascinated by the options. Then she overheard a woman and a small boy a little ways down the aisle.

"You'll have to wait until Christmas," the woman told the boy.

"What if Santa doesn't bring me anything? What if I've been too bad?" he asked.

Diana could hear that the boy was near tears. She doubted such a sweet child could have done anything wrong enough to warrant not receiving gifts. Then again, neither had Diana and she'd had many a sparse Christmas.

Diana pretended to study the dolls as she listened to the woman and the child. Then she turned and headed down another aisle to look at whatever was there. Legos maybe?

"Hi," a tiny voice said.

Diana turned and looked at the little boy, who was suddenly standing next to her. She recognized him from the day he'd rushed past her when she was bringing Linus lunch. He'd run into her that day, with something obviously stuffed beneath his coat. At close range, she noticed that he had freckles on his face that perfectly matched the rust color of his overgrown hair. "Well, hello there."

"Who are you?" the boy asked.

"Diana. What's your name?"

The child appeared to be around eight years old. He was wearing a T-shirt with superheroes under his open coat, but Diana couldn't name any of them. She didn't know any of the characters that children liked. She knew practically nothing about children. The youngest of her patients were usually teenagers, like Addy. "I'm Dustin," he said, revealing a missing canine tooth as he smiled.

Diana stuck out her hand for the child to shake. "Nice to meet you, Dustin."

He placed his hand in hers and gave it an energetic jerk that took Diana by surprise and made her laugh.

Then the boy leaned in and lowered his voice. "Hey, you know tomorrow is really Christmas, right?"

Diana blinked. "What? What do you mean by that?"

"It's supposed to be Christmas tomorrow," he repeated in a secretive voice. "But no one else believes me. I keep telling my foster mom, but she thinks I'm lying." He lowered his eyes for a moment.

Diana bent to hear him better. "Are you reliving a day too?"

The boy's eyes lit up as he looked at her again. "You believe me?"

"Dustin?" The woman from before turned the corner and

glared at Diana as she approached. "Who are you talking to, Dustin?" she asked in an irritated tone.

"This is Diana. She believes me about tomorrow being Christmas Day."

The lady gave Diana a disapproving look as well. Maybe she was just frustrated with the entire world. What was her excuse? Was her fiancé in a coma too? "I told you that's not true," the lady bit out. "Christmas is a couple weeks away. You'll be very disappointed when you wake up tomorrow if you believe it'll be the big day." She grabbed Dustin's arm and tugged him along, offering Diana a less than sincere smile from over her shoulder.

Diana wanted to stop them and pull the woman's grip off the boy's. She somehow suspected that wouldn't help him in any way, and Dustin might actually get in more trouble with the woman if Diana did that.

"Hey?"

Diana turned toward Linus's voice.

"What was that about?" He gestured down the aisle where the lady and Dustin had turned to go onto the next.

Diana fidgeted with her hands. "Oh. Hi. I didn't know you were there. Um . . ." She tried to think of a good way to explain what that had been, but she didn't even know. Was that little boy in a time loop just like her? Was that even possible? Then again, was any of this possible?

"You're telling kids that tomorrow is Christmas?" Linus's brows lifted high on his forehead.

"No." Diana shook her head quickly. "Of course not. He told *me* tomorrow was Christmas. I just kind of agreed with him."

Linus frowned. "Why would you do that?"

She shook her head. "It doesn't matter. You know I don't know how to talk to children. I've always told you that."

Linus reached for her hand. "It just takes spending a little time with them, that's all. It's an acquired talent. Don't worry. There are loads of kids in my extended family. You can practice on them. Then one day we'll have children of our own. I hope," he said softly.

Diana was slightly taken off guard. Of course he'd brought up the subject of having kids before, but he'd never referred to *them* having children together.

"You know," he continued, "lately I've even considered that it might be nice to foster a kid or two before trying to have one of our own. There are lots of kids who need someone to love them."

An ache settled over Diana's heart. She'd needed someone to love her when she was younger. A man who would say what Linus just did was a man she could love forever. She reached for his hand. "You'd be great at that."

"At loving kids?" he asked.

She nodded. "Yeah."

"Well, so would you. You just don't know it yet." He leaned over and kissed her cheek. "One day. We have all the time in the world."

She tilted her head. "I thought you said forever was a myth."

His brow furrowed slightly. "When did I say that?"

"Last night."

"Hmm. My grandfather used to say that." He grinned lopsidedly at her. "Forever might be a myth to some, but not us."

Warmness oozed over her. "That sounds even more poetic."

They both turned to the sound of the little boy crying on the next aisle. He was no doubt upset that tomorrow wasn't really Christmas. Or maybe his foster mom had hurt him. She'd had a death grip on his little arm a few minutes ago.

"You never did tell me why you're here. Is everything okay?" Linus pulled her attention back to him.

"Yeah. I just had drinks with Rochelle and since I had time, I decided to stop in."

"You've been drinking and driving?" Linus asked, brows dipping over suddenly concerned eyes.

"No. I didn't even finish one drink. I'm fine. Good enough to drive you home." She forced a smile, hoping he'd agree.

"That's not necessary. I have my bicycle."

"I know, but it's not safe." Diana was beginning to feel like a broken record.

Linus laughed. "Since when?"

"Since it's cold and icy and it'll be dark when you close," she explained. Why couldn't he just take her word for it this time?

Linus shook his head. "You're acting quite strangely today. Are you sure you only had one drink with Rochelle?"

"Less than that. I'm fine."

The bell at the counter rang and he turned his attention toward the register. "I've got customers. Go home and I'll be there in a little bit. We can discuss how today went for you. I want to hear all about it."

"I'm not leaving. I'll stay," Diana told him as he walked away.

He glanced over his shoulder. "Suit yourself." He lowered his voice. "You can practice talking to the kids some more. It's an acquired talent," he said with a wink.

Diana actually did want to talk some more to Dustin. She wandered around the store, looking for him again, but he and the woman had already gone. She perused the aisles, willing time to tick by. Mr. Powell had been right on that first December 4th when he'd said that time was relative. It was true. Diana felt like she was always either wishing it away or begging it to slow down.

When she grew tired of looking at the latest toys, she wandered into the back room and plopped down on a stool. She and Linus had made out in here once when they were first dating. She'd fallen so hard and so fast for him, and no one was more taken off guard than she was. She was most surprised at the fact that he was as into her as she was him.

They'd moved into an apartment together after just seven weeks of dating, and it had all felt like a whirlwind romance. This past summer he'd proposed. She'd met his parents, of course, but somehow Diana had managed to dodge his huge extended family until a couple weeks ago at Thanksgiving, when Linus had insisted on bringing her to his parents' home.

"We don't want everyone to meet you for the first time at our wedding," he'd teased.

She'd agreed because he was right, but she'd had no idea what she was walking into that Thursday afternoon. Linus had told her he had a "good-sized" family, but his family was so large that they had to eat in three different rooms of his parents' house. There were aunts and uncles, cousins, nieces, and nephews. Diana's Thanksgivings had always been just her and Grandma Denny eating turkey sandwiches and watching reruns of Denny's favorite westerns.

Diana's mind had been spinning after she'd gone home to the apartment she and Linus shared that night.

"My family loved you," he'd said, clueless that she was having a silent panic attack. It wasn't his fault. She didn't tell him how freaked out she was inside. Something about the engagement hadn't felt real until Thanksgiving with the entire Grant gang. His family would be her family. All those people would have the potential to let her down in a huge way. What was she thinking? She didn't know how to exist in Linus's world. The tiny world they'd made together, yes, but not his other world—the one with thirty people all talking at once and wanting Diana to hug them at every turn.

Thanksgiving weekend was when Linus had started pressing the wedding date issue. *"Why wait? It doesn't have to be big,"* he'd said. But he hadn't thought that Thanksgiving at his home was big either.

Diana had avoided the subject as much as possible saying,

"I can't think of wedding planning right now, Linus. I'm up for the big promotion at work." He'd let the subject go for a couple days, and then he'd brought it up again. And again. And Diana had dug in harder with her work promotion excuse, slowly pulling away from him, little by little.

"Hey." Linus stepped into the back room now. "There you are. I thought perhaps you'd left and went home."

"Not a chance. I'm just sitting back here thinking about things."

Linus leaned against the doorframe and folded his arms over his chest. "What things?"

"You. Me. Us. Is the store closed?"

"Yeah. I just turned the sign. You ready to leave?"

Diana's chest constricted. It felt like she was climbing aboard a roller-coaster ride and she had no idea where it was going. It could very well go off the track—again. She wasn't at all prepared. "Yes. Ready."

Linus stepped over to her and reached out his hand. She took it, feeling warm from the inside out. From the moment she'd first taken his hand, she'd felt safe and at home. These last three weeks, she'd been lost without him. She needed him more than she even knew. She had to fix this time loop tonight and keep him with her. Now that she knew what life felt like being loved, she didn't want to experience how it felt without that love ever again.

They walked outside and Diana clicked her key fob as Linus put his bike on her rack. Then they both climbed into the car and she cranked the engine. Once again, she turned right out of the lot and drove the long way home.

"How was your meeting with Mr. Powell?" Linus asked as he rode alongside her in the passenger seat.

"Don't ask," Diana groaned.

"That bad, huh? I'm sure it went better than you think."

Diana was hypervigilant as she drove, going five miles under the speed limit, her gaze darting from side to side looking for some hidden monster—a delivery truck, a dog, a deer—waiting to run out in front of her. Inside she was panicking. She had to do things right this time. There was no room for error. "Well, I poured hot coffee all over myself, cursed like a sailor, and stammered through Mr. Powell's questions."

"You're kidding me, right?" Linus said.

Diana blew out a breath. "I wish I were."

Linus reached over and touched her arm. His touch had anchored her from the moment they'd met. "Well, that's okay. Maybe you're not meant to be in management anyway. You're a good physical therapist. Your patients need you, Di."

"That's what Rochelle said too. I know she was trying to be positive, so why does it feel like you two are criticizing me when you say things like that? You don't think I can be a good leader?" Diana turned to look at Linus and then jerked her gaze back to the road. *No looking away.* They were making it home tonight. Linus was going to be fine, and tomorrow, it really would be Christmas Day.

Linus released her arm. "It's not that. I'm sure you would. You'd be wonderful at anything you do."

Diana swallowed, missing the feel of his hand. It was a necessary comfort right now. "Then why are you questioning this for me?"

"Maybe it's selfish on my part. Perhaps I'm just concerned that a promotion would mean you have less time for me."

Diana glanced over again, her mouth falling open. "What?"

Linus pointed at the road. "Eyes forward, please. I want to get home in one piece tonight."

"Right." She jerked her head forward again. "What do you mean by what you just said?"

"I know it probably sounds horrible, but you never have time for us anymore. You're always working, studying, reading. It's like we were on the moon when we first got engaged, and then you just slowly started pulling back. You've shut down, and you aren't talking to me as much as you once did. You used to tell me everything, and now I feel like there's something you're holding back. I'm worried about you, Di," Linus said gently, laying a hand on her forearm again.

Her eyes burned. She tried to remember to breathe. "Just because I'm reaching for a goal?"

"No, because it feels like you're reaching for anything that pulls you farther away from everything. From us."

Diana swallowed past a tight throat, her fingers curling around the steering wheel. Then she pulled her hand from Linus's.

"See?" he muttered. "Just like that."

Diana glanced over to meet his gaze and then she saw his eyes go wide as he looked out the windshield.

Damn it! Not again.

Metal clashed like thunder in the night. Diana yanked the steering wheel as hard as she could and then everything, once more, went dark.

Chapter 14

Fourth Time's the Charm

Diana stirred in bed. Morning already? She didn't want to wake up just yet. She felt like she'd run a marathon yesterday.

Or like she'd gotten hit by a delivery truck for the second night in a row. Diana's eyes popped open and she rolled over to look at the other side of her bed where Linus was lying beside her. Diana stared at him for a long moment and then reached over to touch his face and confirm that he was real.

He stirred at her touch and then his eyes popped open too. He blinked sleepily and then shot up in bed, uttering a choice word. "I overslept." Stumbling over his feet, he launched himself toward his closet.

Was today Christmas Day or a repeat of December 4th? She was afraid to know.

"What day is it?" she asked warily.

"December fourth. You need to get out of bed too," he said, stopping long enough to look at her. "I have a meeting with a distributor and you have that big meeting with your boss today."

"Not again." Diana groaned and covered her face with her hands. The thought of going through the same sequence of events one more time was exhausting.

Linus absently scratched at the side of his unshaven cheek. "You okay? Why aren't you getting up?"

She sighed and sat up in bed, draping her legs off the edge. "I am. Eventually."

"Are you still mad about yesterday?" He walked over and sat on the bed beside her. "I tossed and turned all night because I felt bad for what I said. If you don't want to marry me this year, we'll marry next year. Or the year after. I'm sorry. Forgive me?"

Diana leaned in and kissed his lips, savoring the moment. If there was one good thing that had come out of repeating this day, it was that she could kiss him again. She could see his smile and feel the warmth of his breath against her cheek. "There's nothing to forgive. I'm just glad you're here."

He wrinkled his brow. "Versus where? Did you think that one silly exchange would make me pack up and leave?"

"No." But maybe she'd wondered that on the first December 3rd.

"Good. Because you're stuck with me." He stood and headed toward the bathroom where he'd been the other two mornings when she'd woken. She dressed as she waited for him to reappear. "Want me to take you to work this morning?" she offered as he stepped out.

He gave her a strange look as she handed him the tie with the silly dog pattern. "How'd you know this is the tie I wanted to wear today?"

"Good guess, I suppose. A ride?" she asked again.

"No, thanks. I can drive myself."

"I think you said your truck was low on gas, though," she offered.

"Did I? I don't remember that." He grabbed his keys and kissed the side of her cheek. "See you tonight."

Diana nodded. "Tonight." There was no use in arguing with him about meeting for lunch or skipping the day and spending it together. "See you then."

"Good luck with your big meeting," he called behind him.

"Thanks." Diana watched him leave and waited before stepping out to see him get back out of his truck.

"It won't start," he said with a perplexed look on his face. "How did you know that?"

"You told me. So would you like a ride after all? I don't mind driving you."

Linus thought for a moment and then shook his head. "That's all right. I'll just take my bike. Exercise will be good. It'll be fine. And I don't want you to be late for your patients. Which you will be if you don't get going."

"Right. I love you."

"Love you too." He gave her an assessing look. "Everything okay with you this morning?"

"Mm-hmm. Just tired." She forced a yawn for show. "I'm also a little nervous about the meeting with Mr. Powell."

"No need to worry. You'll be amazing. You've worked hard for this promotion. You deserve it," he said, being the ever-supportive fiancé he was. After last night's argument in the car, however, she knew he didn't believe she actually wanted the job. And neither did Rochelle.

Linus rolled his bicycle out of the apartment where he kept it against the wall. He hopped on and waved before pedaling out onto the main street. Here went a repeat of the same awful day. Diana released a heavy sigh. Why was this happening? Why couldn't she save Linus in the end?

"Good morning, Diana."

Diana turned toward Mrs. Guzman out walking Leonardo. "Morning," she said, wondering if her neighbor had any recollection of yesterday or the day before. Of course she wouldn't. She was the one who'd started this whole mess and she couldn't even recall what she'd done.

"Chilly out here, isn't it?" Mrs. Guzman commented.

Diana took note of the weather. Cold, like yesterday, but maybe a degree or two warmer. At least it wasn't sleeting.

"Perhaps we'll have a white Christmas after all," Mrs. Guzman commented.

"Christmas? That's still three weeks away, isn't it?" Linus had already confirmed the date for her, but Diana wanted to gauge Mrs. Guzman's reaction.

"Plenty of time to get you a gift. Do you like wine?" the older lady asked.

Diana deflated a touch. Mrs. Guzman didn't remember putting a spell on the snow globe or her discussion with Diana yesterday. "Yes, I love wine. I need to get off to work. It's a big day. I'm interviewing for a promotion."

"Well, isn't that wonderful? I hope you get it. If you want it, that is."

Diana found that to be a peculiar comment. "I wouldn't interview for a position I didn't want—would I?"

Mrs. Guzman shrugged. "Sometimes we don't know our heart's true desires. Sometimes we just chase things because we think we should. That's why Leonardo here tries to go after the squirrels every day. If he ever caught one, he wouldn't know what to do with it—because he doesn't really want it." Mrs. Guzman chuckled dryly. "See you later, dear."

Diana stood there thoughtfully and then remembered Maria. *Oh, crap!* She picked up her cell phone and dialed her patient, impatiently waiting as the phone rang in her ear. "Pick up, pick up, pick up."

Maria didn't answer so Diana dialed a second time.

"Hello?" Maria finally said, sounding out of breath.

"Maria! It's Diana. Are you pulling things down from your attic?"

Maria coughed lightly. "How would you know that?"

"Hunch. Please stop, Maria. I will help you just as soon as I get there this morning."

"Oh, no, you don't have to—" Maria started to argue.

"Maria," Diana said sternly, "no pulling stuff down from the attic. You'll break your ankle."

This time Maria huffed. "Fine, fine. I have no idea how you knew what I was doing, but I'll wait for you to help when you come over this morning."

"Good." Diana exhaled as she headed back inside to finish getting ready. Afterward, she left her apartment and dropped a dollar in the sidewalk Santa's pail as she hurried toward her car in the parking lot. Then she drove to Maria's home, keeping to her schedule like the committed physical therapist she was.

"Come in, come in," Maria said when she opened the door. "You must be frozen solid standing out there."

Diana stepped into her patient's home and turned to face Maria. No broken ankle. Why was she successfully changing fate for Maria and not for Linus? It didn't make sense and it wasn't fair. "How's your arm today?" Diana asked as she normally would.

"Oh, it's stiff. Must be the weather."

Diana gestured toward the bed. "How about I stretch it for you and then I can pull down those boxes from the attic?"

"You are such a sweet girl." Maria shuffled toward the bed in the corner of the room and laid back. She closed her eyes while Diana lifted her arm and held it for a count of ten.

As Diana led the woman through a series of stretches, Maria chatted more than usual. Diana only halfway listened, though. Her mind was on the next steps in the therapy session and the day. How was she going to get that promotion at work? What was she going to do to keep Linus from landing himself in the ER tonight?

"I'm sorry I'm talking so much. I just don't get a lot of visitors," Maria finally said.

Diana remembered that Maria had said that yesterday as well. Maria had family nearby, but she never saw them. "I don't mind. I love hearing about your life. I'd love to hear more." Diana hedged. She wasn't a counselor like Rochelle. Her job was to work with the body, that was it. "Your daughter must be very busy not to stop in regularly," she broached.

"How did you know I have a daughter who lives nearby?"

Right. "I think you mentioned her once."

"Hmm. I imagine she is busy. She has a daughter of her own, you know. I'm a grandmother. My granddaughter plays basketball. I only know this because of a nice neighbor who cyberstalked my daughter's social media for me once."

Diana remembered this story. "I'm not trying to pry, but why would your daughter turn her back on a mom like you?"

Maria slowly sat up on the side of the bed. "There are some mistakes you can't take back." The older woman hesitated and then, after a long sigh, she continued talking. "After my daughter was married to her husband for about two years, they were at my home for the holidays and her husband, Blaine, upset me. It was no secret that I didn't like him, but he was my daughter's choice so I never said anything. That day, though . . ." Maria shook her head, regret spilling over in her expression. The folds of her wrinkles deepened on her forehead and around her eyes. "I just couldn't hold my tongue any longer. I was like this volcano primed to erupt."

"What happened?" Diana asked.

"I told my daughter she didn't have to let Blaine speak to her the way he did. That he was disrespectful, spoiled, and a child in a grown man's body. I told her that she could do better for herself than a man like him, and that I disapproved."

"Ouch," Diana said quietly. "I'm guessing that didn't go over very well."

"Not at all. It wasn't my finest moment." Maria looked down at her folded hands. "Anyway, Blaine heard everything. My daughter was obviously upset. Her husband made her feel like she needed to choose between the man she loved and me. They had a child together. What could she do? So, she cut me off. It's been twelve years now since we've spoken." She shrugged. "Love will make you do crazy things, I guess."

"I'm so sorry, Maria." Diana laid a hand over her patient's hand. "Twelve years is a long time. You should reach out to her."

"I have. Many times." Maria shrugged, her shoulders rising asymmetrically. The strong one rose two inches higher than the weak. "She's not interested in reconnecting with me. I understand."

"But you're her mother. She loves you. She must," Diana insisted. It wasn't as if Maria had chosen to leave her daughter like Jackie Merriman had. Maria was a present mom who'd let her emotions spill over one time. She was human. "That's not okay."

"It is what it is," Maria said glumly.

"No." Diana shook her head. "What's your daughter's name? I'll look her up and contact her myself." That was something Diana would never normally do. Not the pre–December 4th Diana, at least. She believed in professionalism and this was crossing a line.

Maria's jaw dropped. "No, you won't contact her. I appreciate that you're trying to help, but this is my situation. I'm honoring Cecilia's wishes by staying out of her and my granddaughter's lives. I haven't even seen my Addy since she was a little girl."

"Addy?" Diana repeated. The world seemed to slow just enough for Diana to piece together the puzzle. "Cecilia Pierce? Mrs. Pierce is your daughter?"

Maria's brow pinched softly, her brown eyes searching Diana's. "Do you know her?"

Diana could barely process what was happening. This was a small town, yes, but how could she have a mother and granddaughter as her patients, back-to-back on the same day, and not realize it? "Yes. Addy is my patient." Diana flinched and then covered a hand to her mouth. "But I wasn't

supposed to tell you that because of patient confidentiality."
Diana had never broken confidentiality before. It was a huge
no-no. She could be fired or even lose her license for doing
so. "Forget I told you that."

"Addy is a patient of yours?" Maria brought her left hand
to her chest, her lips parted slightly. "Why would a young
girl need you? You're a therapist for people who can't leave
their homes, aren't you?"

Diana couldn't believe how royally she'd messed up this
new day already. She felt so disoriented that none of what
was happening even felt real anymore. She'd already lived
this day—three times. Maybe she was stuck in a dream. Or
perhaps she was literally stuck in that silly snow globe that
Linus had gotten her. "I'm sorry, Maria. I can't tell you anything more. I can't believe I even let that slip."

Maria reached for her. "Is she okay? Is Cecilia okay?
Please. I need to know."

Diana didn't want to say too much, but Maria's gaze was
pleading and desperate. How could Diana turn her down?
"They're fine. It's difficult for them right now, but they'll be
okay eventually."

Maria seemed to wait for more.

"Mr. Pierce isn't in the picture. I've never met him, and
they've never mentioned him."

Maria's lips parted. "Cecilia is going through this alone?
Whatever *this* is?"

"I don't know." Diana shrugged. "But you're going
through your condition alone as well. You shouldn't be. Not
when you have each other." As soon as Diana said those
words, she felt like a hypocrite. These last three weeks after
Linus's accident, she'd dragged herself through on her own.
Rochelle, the Grant family, and even her new supervisor,
William Davis, had tried to be there for her and she'd pushed
them all away, holding in her emotions like Grandma Denny
would have insisted she do.

Diana stood. "I better get those boxes from the attic for you."

Maria shuffled behind her. "I still don't know how you knew that's what I wanted to do this morning, but I appreciate your help. Thank you."

"I'm glad to be of assistance." Diana went through the motions of pulling down the attic ladder, climbing up, and carrying one box down after another. Then she brought the boxes into the living room to ensure that Maria had no way to break her ankle.

"I need to go," Diana finally said when she was done.

"To Cecilia and Addy's?" Maria asked, her brown eyes lighting up to the color of bronze.

Regret washed over Diana once more. Her only saving grace was that Maria would forget all this tomorrow. Unless Diana broke the time loop. Then Maria might remember, and that might be a huge problem. Reliving a day for a better outcome was one thing. Making things worse for herself and everyone around her was another.

"Can you tell them . . . ?" Maria trailed off. "No. Cecilia doesn't want to hear from me. I don't want to add to her burdens."

"You shouldn't be a burden to her," Diana said. "One mistake shouldn't cost you your relationship."

"It's never just one mistake," Maria said wisely. "It's just one that tips the balance. Thank you for caring for my family." She took her time heading over to open the front door for Diana. "I don't keep up with the goings-on in town like I should. Maybe if I did, I would have known my granddaughter was sick." She looked at Diana. "It's just . . . keeping up with people in town means they'll ask how Cecilia is, and I'll have to admit that I don't know. Or they'll tell me something about her and I'll feel this deep regret because I don't know her anymore. I don't know my own daughter. It's almost unbearable." She shook her head, her face scrunching painfully.

"Anyway, I've cost them enough. I won't keep you here a moment longer. Please let me know if there's something I can do for them. I'll do it, and Cecilia wouldn't need to know."

"I'll let you know. Don't work too hard today. If you like, I'll come by tomorrow to put up your tree and help you decorate."

"Tomorrow isn't your day, though," Maria said, just like she'd done yesterday.

"That's right. But I have time to help you."

The look on Maria's face was priceless, and it warmed Diana's heart.

Maria shuffled over to the table beside the door and grabbed some individually wrapped slices of fruitcake, shoving them in Diana's hand. "One for my Cecilia and Addy, and two for you and your fiancé."

That warmed Diana's heart as well. Then Maria did something she hadn't done on the other two days. She leaned in and hugged Diana.

"I would never wish a stroke on myself, of course, but the best thing that has come out of this experience is having you come to visit. My life is a little less lonely with you in it." Maria stepped back and beamed at her.

Diana's eyes stung. They were probably just dry from the cold winter air outside. She was so good at keeping her emotions tucked away. At least she was until recently. "I'll see you tomorrow, Maria." She opened the door, stepped out, and walked to her car.

With a click of her key fob, she unlocked the doors, put the fruitcake slices on the passenger seat, and sat behind the steering wheel for a long moment. Her eyes still stung and her heart ached. All these weeks she'd been seeing Maria Harris and until this time loop happened she hadn't realized how lonely the woman was, or that Maria was related to the Pierce family. William probably would have noticed. He probably would have pried into Maria's life on the very first session and found out every detail. Diana used to think that was a bad thing, but Mr. Powell was right: The company was one big family, and that was good for someone like Maria.

Diana shifted her car into DRIVE and went to the Pierce house.

"It's nice to see you, Diana," Mrs. Pierce said.

Diana peeled off her winter coat and bit her tongue to keep from mentioning Maria. That was none of her business. "You as well. How's Addy doing today?"

"She's a moody teenage girl. That's normal, right?"

Diana laughed even though she'd heard that line four times now. "I think so, yes."

"What is it with a girl and her mother? They're either thick as thieves or two opposite poles on a magnet."

Diana thought of her own mother. Her relationship with Jackie, or lack thereof, was completely Jackie's fault. Even if Jackie were to start putting in more effort right now, it wouldn't be enough to close the gap. At this point, Diana didn't want to rekindle her relationship with her mother. Perhaps Mrs. Pierce—Cecilia—felt the same way about Maria.

"I'll just go check on Addy," Diana said. Then she turned back. "Um, here." She handed the fruit cake slices to Mrs. Pierce. "This is for you." She didn't reveal who had made the loaf. That was probably best left unsaid.

Mrs. Pierce smiled gratefully. "Oh, wow. We love fruitcake around here. Thank you for this." Gesturing down the hall, she said, "Work your magic. Good luck."

Diana was going to need it. Turning, she walked down the hall. She didn't want to say the wrong thing and upset Addy any more than she already was, but saying the right thing would be a nice change to this day. She stopped behind Addy's door and knocked.

"Come in," Addy called with a muffled voice.

Diana stepped inside and found Addy lying with her face pressed into a big, cushy pillow. "Hi, Addy. Everything okay?"

"No. My life is horrible, and it's not because I have can-cer." The girl rolled onto her back, freeing her face from the pillow. Creases lined her cheeks and forehead, telling Diana the girl had been smooshing her face into the pillow for quite some time.

"Want to talk about it?" Diana walked over and sat on the edge of the bed, knowing it wouldn't take much to get the teenager to unload all the things on her mind. "How about this? I'll tell you what's bothering me if you tell me what's bothering you."

Addy's eyes widened subtly. "Really? You never tell me anything."

"Well, today I'm offering up something juicy in exchange for you talking to me."

Addy looked skeptical. "Okay. You first. What's bother-ing you?"

Diana hesitated. She could go with some trivial detail, like saying her heater was on the fritz again, but that felt like a cop-out. "I'm currently stressing because I'm not sure I know how to be part of someone's family. My fiancé's family, to be exact."

Addy scrunched her brow. "What do you mean you don't know how to be part of a family?"

Diana shrugged. "I was raised by my grandmother. We didn't really act like family. We lived in the same house but that was about it. To be honest, the idea of holiday get-togethers kind of freaks me out. And the idea of a big wed-ding terrifies me."

Addy seemed to be soaking up the conversation. "Mean-while my family tries to suffocate me and I can't get a mo-ment's peace without my mom checking to make sure I'm still breathing."

"She loves you," Diana said, feeling vulnerable somehow. She hadn't even shared this exact truth with Rochelle, mainly because she knew her best friend would try to give her a ton of advice that wouldn't fix this situation.

"I know, and I guess I'm a little less annoyed at her now that I realize you didn't have that growing up. What are you going to do?"

"About what?" Diana asked.

"Well, are you still going to marry the guy? Because you'll be marrying his family too, you know?" Addy sounded so much like a mini adult.

It had never occurred to Diana to break up with Linus over his huge, overbearing family. She loved him. Of course she wasn't going to leave him just because he had an ideal, nurturing family environment when he was growing up, and she didn't.

"No. I'll just deal with it. I mean, I'll get used to having a family. How hard could it be?"

Addy coughed out a laugh. "Hard." She looked down at her hands and seemed to locate a spot of chipped polish on her nails. She began chipping more of the polish away as she talked. "That's why I don't see my grandma. She couldn't get along with my dad when he was still here."

"Oh?" Diana wondered why this aspect of Maria's and the Pierces' lives never came up before.

Addy nodded. "Yep."

"But that's not what's bothering you today," Diana said. "This is about a guy, right?"

Addy looked up and narrowed her eyes. "How'd you know that?"

"I was a teenager once."

To this Addy grinned. "It's weird thinking that you were ever a kid."

"Why is that?" Diana asked, feeling a little defensive.

"Because you're so serious all the time."

Diana let that sink in. Linus was one big adult kid and she was too serious to have ever been a kid. Opposites attract, but were they too opposite? From the moment she'd met Linus she'd known he was the one for her, but some part of her was also waiting for him to realize they weren't a good fit. There was this tiny fear inside her mind that he might leave her one day. "What's going on with the guy?"

A soft sigh tumbled off Addy's lips. "My boyfriend, Jay, is forgetting all about me. And now I hear he's talking to my best friend, Sierra."

"If that's true then he's not the right guy for you." Diana usually shied away from giving out personal advice, especially to her patients, but after having this discussion three times now, she couldn't hold her tongue longer. "And who knows? Maybe he's not into your friend the way you think he is. Maybe whoever is relaying this information to you is mistaken. Why don't you FaceTime with him?"

"FaceTime? Look at me." Addy pointed at her head. "My hair is falling out. My skin is dry." Tears welled in her eyes. "I look horrible. Whatever. Maybe he's better off with Sierra anyway."

"Hey." Diana placed a hand on Addy's back. "That's not true. You are beautiful. Don't think for a second that you're not."

Addy blinked back at her. "Bald and beautiful, right?"

"Yes, you're losing your hair. For the moment. But in time it will grow back. Life will move on, and maybe you'll be the one to decide this guy isn't worth your attention."

Addy sat up and visibly swallowed. "He's really nice, though."

"Then you should give him the benefit of the doubt and FaceTime him. Give him a chance to prove that to you."

Addy seemed to consider this. Then she looked at Diana and narrowed her eyes. "You usually shut down any conversation about my feelings. Why are you listening to me today?"

Was Diana really so awful before? "I usually try to keep you focused on the reason I'm here, which is to help you build endurance and strength. But emotional endurance and strength are important in your recovery too. I'm sorry if I haven't listened to you before now." *Great, now I sound like Rochelle.*

Addy chipped away more polish on her nails. "What if he sees me and doesn't want to talk to me anymore?"

"Then he's a jerk," Diana said flatly, making Addy's eyes round. "And you'll call me, and I'll come over with ice cream."

"You will?" Addy's pale lips parted slightly.

"Of course. As part of your therapy."

"Ice cream therapy. The best kind." Addy grinned. "Okay. Maybe I'll try to FaceTime him after school."

"Good."

"Diana? Thanks for talking to me like a real person. Like a friend." She leaned in and wrapped her arms around Diana, hugging her tightly, the way Maria had earlier. "It's kind of lonely in this room."

Diana resisted the tears that rose in her throat. She'd been coming to this girl's house for weeks. Addy never should have felt lonely, but apparently, she did.

Diana didn't want to be cold or heartless. She hadn't even realized that's how she came off to people. Grandma Denny was the same way. They weren't emotional people, or if they were, they just didn't show it. They were independent and didn't ask for help, out of necessity as much as anything else. Did Linus understand what he was getting into with her?

"I am your friend." Diana pulled back from the hug and looked at Addy. "And I'm also your physical therapist, so we better get to work."

When Diana arrived at Powell Rehabilitation Center later that afternoon, she walked up to Leann at the receptionist's desk. "I'm here for an interview with Mr. Powell at two."

Leann checked the clock. It was five minutes until the hour. "Have a seat. It'll just be a moment."

A couple minutes later, she led Diana into Mr. Powell's office.

Mr. Powell stood as she entered. "Good to see you, Diana."

"You too, Todd," she said with a ready smile.

"Can I get you some coffee?"

"No!" Diana practically shouted. Coffee had already ruined two of their interviews. Heat flushed her cheeks and she tempered her voice before speaking again. "No, thank you. I've already had my two cups today. Thanks."

"Ah, okay. Well, then, let's get straight to business, shall we?" He proceeded to ask the same questions as before, but Diana's answers came out differently.

"I'm not really sure why I would make a good leader. Maybe I wouldn't. I mean, I lead my patients, and I thought I was doing a great job, but a patient is more than just body parts, right? They have emotional needs too, you know?" She looked up at Mr. Powell. "And so do I?"

His expression was stiff. "Right."

"I think I've been neglecting those needs unintentionally. I thought I was being professional, but maybe not. Maybe sitting down to have a cup of tea with a patient isn't a waste of time. Or helping them pull down boxes of Christmas decorations from their attics. I mean, if it saves them from falling and further injuring themselves, that's therapeutic, right?"

"I guess so." Mr. Powell looked completely bewildered. Even so, his perfect smile was pinned in place.

"I'm not as personable as someone like William, but he spends just a little too much time socializing, in my opinion. My sessions are a happy medium between personable and professional. Not to criticize William. He's great." She was talking fast and this interview was dovetailing just like all the others. Of course it was.

Finally, Diana stood and shook Mr. Powell's hand, careful not to knock over his crystal picture frame.

"I'll be in touch," he said, although Diana wasn't optimistic. She headed past Leann at her desk and back out to her car in the parking lot. She didn't cry this time, even though she wanted to. She felt like she was losing her mind and this day on repeat seemed to keep getting worse.

Next on the agenda was drinks with Rochelle. Diana drove over and walked inside Sparky's Tavern.

"Happy birthday," she said, plopping down in her usual seat.

Rochelle slid a drink across the table toward Diana. "I ordered for you."

"Thanks." Diana took a sip and looked at her friend. "Any big news to tell me?" she asked, remembering how excited Rochelle had been about this new guy in her life yesterday.

Rochelle seemed to think for a moment and then she shook her head. "Nope. Same old, same old."

"A new guy maybe?" Diana prodded.

Rochelle snorted out a laugh. "I wish, but no. I'm still as single as the day is long."

And this was a very long day. "You didn't get flowers today?"

Rochelle sipped from her drink, looking confused. "No, why? Did you send me some?"

"No." But Diana had yesterday. And that had prompted Rochelle's dream guy to get her flowers too. And since Diana hadn't sent the flowers, dream guy apparently hadn't gotten the memo to do so either.

Sigh. There were too many balls in the air to juggle. Was this true for every day that ever existed? Were there a million choose-your-own-adventure options for every second of every hour?

"No, but it's your birthday and a girl deserves flowers on the anniversary of her birth."

"Aww. That's sweet. It's the thought that counts." Rochelle watched as Diana pulled her drink toward her and took a big gulp. "Diana," she said hesitantly, "I'm a little worried about you. You've been . . . distant lately."

That was the same thing Linus had said on December 3rd. "I'm not distant. I'm sitting right here. Three feet from you."

"Physically, yeah, but if I bring up your engagement or how you're feeling, you'd bolt in a heartbeat." Rochelle pursed her lips around her straw and sucked up the bright red liquid inside her glass.

"What exactly do you want me to say?" Diana huffed, her frustration building like a slow-moving hurricane, picking up random feelings that she'd been trying so hard to ignore. She was sick of repeating this stupid day. All it did was amplify what a mess her life was, and it was all her fault. "Do you want me to say I'm terrified of joining Linus's huge, hugs-obsessed family? That I'm worried I'll end up letting Linus down somehow and that he'll leave just like everyone else in my life?" Diana picked up her drink, took another gulp, and slammed the glass back down on the table with startling force, making the drink splash over the rim. Tears gathered behind her eyes. Blinking them away, she said, "Or that I hate it when you try to force me to look at things in my life that I don't want to see? I'd rather robotically go through my day and chase squirrels."

"Squirrels?" Rochelle repeated with a brow lift.

"Yes, squirrels." Diana pushed back from the table and stood. "Happy birthday, Ro. I've got to go."

"What? Why? Are you upset about something?"

Diana shook her head. "No, I just need some air. I'll call you later, okay? Tomorrow." Because tomorrow never seemed to exist anymore.

Rochelle looked like she wanted to ask if Diana was okay.

"I'm fine," Diana said.

"F-word alert." Rochelle offered a peacemaker smile.

Diana wasn't ready to make peace yet, though. She was doing her best, and she was making progress on this stupid day, but it wasn't enough. "Happy birthday, Rochelle." Turning, she walked out of the tavern. The cold stung her lungs as she inhaled deeply on her way to her car. She unlocked her door, plopped into the driver's seat, and rested her forehead on the steering wheel for several minutes. Then her phone buzzed with an incoming call. Diana glanced at the screen already knowing it would be Linus's mother.

Why does Joann keep calling?

Diana suspected Linus's mother was trying to form a familial relationship with Diana. At Thanksgiving, Joann had even told Diana to feel free to call her "Mom." *Sorry, Joann, but not everyone associates that word with positive attributes.*

On a sigh, Diana reluctantly answered. "Hi, Joann."

"Diana. I was just preparing to leave you a voice mail. I know how busy you are."

"You caught me at a good time, I guess," Diana said, even though it was crummy timing. There was never a good time on December 4th, though. "Is there something you needed?"

"Oh, no. I just wanted to check on you and see how the wedding planning was going. Do you need help with anything? Perhaps we can get together this weekend to start the planning."

"Thank you for the offer, Joann. I'll talk to Linus."

"Good. Please do. You'll be sure to let me know what I can do, won't you? I want to be involved in any way I can. You know, I've always wanted a daughter."

Yes, Diana knew that by now. And it touched her heart to know Joann would consider Diana enough to fill that void for her when Diana's own mother had acted like her child was a burden more than a blessing.

"Perhaps we can go dress shopping together one of these

days. Unless your own mother wants to do that with you," Joann said.

Diana inwardly flinched. Jackie Merriman wouldn't be caught dead dress shopping with her daughter. That would resemble too much of a mother-daughter relationship. "I'll let you know, Joann," she said as sweetly as possible. Diana really did like Joann. She didn't want to be so distant. Could people love you from afar? Could you really love them back? Tears blurred Diana's vision. "I really do have to go. I'm at work, so . . ." She trailed off.

"Of course. I just wanted you to know I was thinking about you. I'm so happy that you're joining our little family."

Little? Diana wanted to laugh as much as she also wanted to cry right now. "Thank you."

"We'll talk soon, okay?" Joann said.

"Mm-hmm. Bye." Diana's hand was shaking as she tapped the screen to disconnect the call. What was wrong with her that having such a simple conversation with her future mother-in-law was hard? Maybe she didn't deserve the Grant family.

Diana put her car into motion and drove to Linus's toy store next. He waved from the cash register where he was helping the same mom from yesterday. Diana walked around to the far aisle and spotted the little boy, Dustin, standing there and admiring the toys.

"Hey," Diana said in a hushed voice. "Do you remember me?"

The boy looked up and nodded. "Of course, I do. We talked yesterday."

Diana practically jumped up for joy. "So it's true? You're reliving the same day too?"

The boy gave her a curious look. "And tomorrow is supposed to be Christmas, but it never, ever is."

Diana knelt beside the boy and then just decided to sit on the floor where she was. "I think that's because we're doing this day all wrong."

Dustin gave her a knowing look. "Tell me about it. I'm trying to get off the naughty list—that's what my foster mom calls it—and it's just getting worse. No matter how good I try to be, I'm never good enough. I have no hope of getting any gifts on the big day."

"Hmm." Diana nodded. "I'm learning that trying is futile. I think, in your case, you have to actually want to be nice versus naughty. Not just until the big day, but afterward too."

Dustin fidgeted with his hands as he said: "Do you think being nice will get me out of this awful day?"

"Maybe. I'm still trying to get out of it myself," Diana admitted. Albeit, she wanted to get out of it with a few major changes. "What is it that's on your Christmas list anyway?" she asked.

Dustin looked down at his feet. "It's kind of stupid."

"I doubt that." She tapped a finger against the toe of his shoe, gaining his attention.

He looked back up at her.

"Is it in this store? You spend a lot of time on the doll aisle. Do you like dolls?"

Dustin looked offended by the question. "No. My foster sister does."

This made Diana smile. "That's sweet of you to think of her. So, what is it that you want? A remote-control car?"

Dustin shook his head again. "I'll whisper it to you," he finally said.

"Oh. Okay." Diana leaned toward him, lifting her ear to his mouth.

"A family," Dustin said in such a small voice that Diana wondered if she'd heard him correctly.

She pulled back and looked at him, knowing once she saw the vulnerability on his face that she'd heard him right. Her heart broke into a million little pieces.

"See? It's stupid. I told you so."

"No." Diana shook her head. "It's not stupid. It's great."

"There you are!" The child's foster mother turned onto the aisle and glared at Diana just like she had the day before.

"Hi," Diana said, feeling guilty even though she'd done nothing wrong. "We were just . . . um, chatting."

Dustin went to the woman. "She's reliving the same day over and over again too," he told her excitedly.

Diana felt her cheeks burn. "Um, or it just feels that way. Being patient for Christmas is tough." She let out a nervous laugh.

The woman didn't look amused. "Come on, Dustin. Let's go home. We never should have stopped here. With your behavior lately, you'll be lucky to get anything at all."

Dustin turned back to Diana as his foster mom tugged him down the aisle. Diana watched the duo leave the store. Then Linus turned onto the opposite end of the aisle and headed in her direction.

"Why are you here? And why are you sitting on the floor?"

Diana reached up a hand for him to help pull her up. "I bombed the interview with Mr. Powell and had an argument with Rochelle. My day has been miserable so far."

Linus rubbed his hands along the sides of her arms. "So you decided to try your luck with me? Should we argue about something?" he asked, teasing her.

Diana smiled. "I don't want to argue with you again. I just want to spend a little time together. Maybe I can help out at the store? Or . . . ?" she said, trailing off.

"Or?" he asked.

"Maybe you can close early and spend some private time with me."

He narrowed his eyes. "You know I can't do that."

"Why not? You own the store, right? It's cold and icy outside. People should be going home anyway." She went up on the tiptoes and kissed his mouth. "We could do things," she whispered.

"Things?" he asked.

"Things." She waggled her brows, hoping he got the message.

"Oh. I see. *Things.*" A grin lined his lips. "That's tempting. You haven't been all that interested in 'things' lately. I was starting to take it a bit personal."

She tilted her head, wondering if that was true. "Well, I'm interested now." At least in one of the things. "Say yes. Close the store for the evening. It's just fifteen minutes early."

"Then what's the rush? Can't you be a little patient?"

"No." She shook her head as Linus grinned wider.

"As soon as this woman and boy leave, I'll lock the door. How's that?"

"They already left. Just now. You're right. That woman really is awful," Diana said.

Linus gestured for her to follow him back to the cash register. "When did I say that?" he asked.

Diana cringed. He'd said it on a day that he no longer remembered. "Oh, maybe you were talking about someone else." She cleared her throat. "Do they come in a lot? The boy and his foster mom?"

"Dustin usually comes in on his own. He doesn't live too far from here. He likes to look even if he can't afford to buy."

"That's sad."

"I don't have a lot of sympathy for people who steal, except for him. I've caught him hiding items in his pockets a time or two."

Diana took a seat on the stool that Linus pulled up to the counter for her. She had a momentary flash of the first time she'd seen Dustin. He'd been hiding something under his coat. "Oh, no. Really?"

"I called his foster mom the first time. After I witnessed how she reamed him out, I never contacted her again. That woman has no business caring for children."

"If she's so awful, what was she doing here today? Is she shopping for Dustin?"

Linus scoffed. "As if. She has a daughter, who she showers with gifts. It's no wonder the boy acts out. With parents like that, who needs enemies?" Linus flinched. "I'm sorry. It's a figure of speech."

He was thinking about Diana's own parents. "It's okay. It didn't bother me."

"Good. Because word on the street is that there will be *things* in my future. I don't want to mess up my chances." He winked. "So, I'll meet you at home?"

Diana tipped her head to one side. "Or you could . . . meet me in the back room."

"With the toys? That's a bit creepy, don't you think?" he teased. "I don't think I can with the new Wetty Betty doll staring back at me."

Diana just didn't want to be on the roads. The roads are where everything spun out of control—literally. She couldn't lock the doors and hold him prisoner here, though. Could she? "Fine. But we're putting your bike on the rack and I'm driving just as soon as you close up the store." Because if she drove, she could control the speed limit. She could keep watch over everything. She could save Linus and this horrible day.

"Deal," Linus said.

"And we aren't talking on the drive home," she said, wringing her hands. "Not one word. I need to focus."

Linus furrowed his brow, but the corners of his mouth curled into a tiny grin. "Okay. No talking. That just gives me time to think about all the *non*-talking things we'll do when we get home."

Chapter 15

It wasn't dark yet. Diana could see clearly through the windshield. Ice hadn't formed on the roads. She clutched the steering wheel with two hands and kept her eyes pinned in front of her.

"Tell me about your meeting," Linus prompted.

"Shh. No talking, remember?"

"I thought you were kidding about that. Why wouldn't we talk?"

"Because I need to focus." Diana was hypervigilant, attending to the side roads and the left lane. Traffic was light tonight and they were only ten minutes from home. No taking the long way this time.

Linus reached over and touched her thigh, running his hand down its length toward the knee.

"What are you doing?" she asked.

"Teasing you. T-minus ten minutes to closed doors, right?"

Diana didn't look over. "Yes, but only if you keep your hands to yourself and stop talking." She lifted his hand off her thigh and pressed it back in his direction.

Linus shifted in the passenger seat. "You're acting very

strange today, Di. And what was that conversation you were having with Dustin in my store?"

Diana pulled up to a STOP sign and looked both ways. There were cars passing in front of her so she finally looked over to meet Linus's gaze. "He thinks Santa won't come because he hasn't been a good boy. And he told me what he wants for Christmas."

"Yeah? What is it?" Linus asked, looking interested.

Diana's throat felt tight just thinking about it. "A family." She swallowed thickly, checking the roads again. Cars were still coming. She heard the sirens of an ambulance nearby and sat up straighter. "Do you hear that?"

"Of course, I do. He told you he wanted a family?"

Diana nodded. "I hate that he lives with that awful woman. I wish I could take him home with me." It was out of her mouth before she even realized what she was saying.

Linus grinned and reached for her hand. "We've never discussed having kids before. It's interesting to hear you talk like that."

They actually had discussed children. He just didn't remember.

The sirens were growing louder, making Diana anxious.

"I would take Dustin home with me if I could too. Especially now that I know you wouldn't be opposed."

Diana met his gaze. "I'm not sure I'd be any better than that woman, though."

"Well, I'm sure enough for both of us." Linus lifted her hand to his mouth and kissed it.

Finally, the ambulance came into view and sped past them. It wasn't for Linus. He wasn't the one who needed help this time. Diana released a breath and finally lifted her foot off the brake. "Almost home," she whispered, focusing once again on the road.

"I can't decide if you're excited to get home because you're so turned on by me or because you think this world is out to get us. Judging by the way you're acting, I'm guessing it's the latter."

Diana looked over. "I'm fine."

A horn honked and Diana jerked her eyes forward.

"Next time, I'm driving," Linus said.

"No next time. We're going to make it this time." Diana's palms were slick against the steering wheel. Their apartment complex was in view now. She held her breath and drove. Then she pulled into the lot, parked, and exhaled loudly. "We made it! I can't believe we made it!" She turned to Linus and laughed out loud as tears filled her eyes. She didn't care. Relief and joy poured over her. "We're finally home!"

Linus's brows hung heavily as he pulled back and looked at her. "Did you ever doubt it?"

She swallowed. Then she launched herself across the middle console, wrapped her arms around his neck, and kissed him with everything she had. "Let's go inside," she said.

"*Now* you want me to touch you," he teased. "Will I be allowed to talk as well?"

She lifted a brow. "Depends on what you're saying."

"I'm not sure what's going on today, but I kind of like it." He grinned and pushed his passenger door open. "*Brr.* I can't get over how cold it is this year."

Diana stepped out as well, feeling the sting of winter on her cheeks. She also felt exhilarated. No way could Linus get into an accident now that he was home. They hurried past the sidewalk Santa, who was still ringing his bell. Diana reached into her purse, pulled out a five-dollar bill, and placed it in his pail.

"Merry Christmas to you!" he said.

"And to you!" Diana called back, feeling all the Christmas spirit running through her. Tomorrow would be Christmas Day. It had to be because the whole point of reliving December 4th was to save Linus, which she'd done. Whatever lesson she was meant to learn, if that was even true, she'd learned it.

She poked the key in the lock and opened the door, stepping over the threshold and pulling Linus inside with her. His lips bumped against hers again as they wrapped their arms around each other. Then he kicked the front door shut with his leg and followed her to the couch.

"Here?" he asked.

"Here. There. Anywhere with you," she whispered between kisses. She looked up into his stormy blue-gray eyes. "I've missed you so much."

"You've been kind of aloof for a while, and now, suddenly, you seem . . . well, hot and bothered by me." A lazy grin lined his lips as he pulled her onto the couch with him. He laid back and she pressed her body to his.

"I guess sometimes you don't know what you have until it's gone," she said, feeling that to her very core. She'd never take a single moment with this man for granted again.

"I was never gone. I've been right here waiting for you."

Diana swallowed. If only that were true. It didn't matter anymore, though. She was getting a new chance with Linus. No more avoiding him. No more running from things like happily ever after or huge bear-hugging families. She still wasn't sure she was ready for family life, but she could tell Linus. Maybe they could start simple and set a date for a year from now.

"Hey? Where'd you just go?" Linus asked, concern etched over his features.

Diana blinked him into focus. "Oh. Into my head, I guess."

He lifted his mouth to hers in a small kiss. "That's okay. We have all night. What if you take a hot bath and get out of your head? And your clothes." He waggled his brows. "I'll pour us some drinks and wait patiently for you."

She smiled. That was just like Linus to consider her needs over his own. He was so considerate and thoughtful. She could talk to him about what was going on in her head, and he would never judge her. She knew that. "Yeah. That actually sounds amazing." She pulled herself off his body and sat up on the couch. "I love you, Linus. I know I haven't been the most present fiancée lately, but my feelings for you have never changed. Ever."

Wrapping his arm around her, he hugged her close.

She breathed him in, so relieved they'd made it home.

"I love you too, Di. Here, there, anywhere," he said quietly, pressing his lips to her temple. "Now you take a bath. I'll pour the wine."

Diana pulled a deep breath into her lungs, feeling more grounded now that they were safely locked inside their apartment. She stood. "Okay. I'll be right back."

"Take your time. We have forever."

Yes, they did. Forever was not a myth. Not anymore.

Diana closed the bathroom door behind her and set the bathtub faucet to run steaming hot water. She did need to get out of her head. Her thoughts were too loud to enjoy making love to her fiancé. But she couldn't wait to feel his arms wrapped around her again. She wanted to soak him in without the background of her worries about whether tomorrow she would wake up on December 4th or Christmas Day.

She had to assume tomorrow would be the latter. She had saved Linus after all. She'd done what she was supposed to. And tomorrow, life would be back to normal. She couldn't wait.

Tonight, though . . . Tonight, she and Linus were going to reconnect in a way they hadn't in a very long time. They were going to be the *us* he had pined for the other night. The *us* that had filled a void when she'd first met Linus. Was that the lesson she was supposed to learn from all this? That people were more important than a promotion at some job.

She peeled off her clothes and stepped into the hot water,

sinking her body into the tub's depths while listening to the roar of water rushing from the faucet. She closed her eyes and leaned back against the bath pillow on the far wall. She wouldn't grow apart from Linus again. From this point on she would make time for him. She'd make an effort with his family too. And she would be a better friend to Rochelle.

Diana soaked for another fifteen minutes and then pulled the drain of the tub and stepped out. She grabbed a towel and dried off her body before putting on a fresh set of clothing. She felt a lot more relaxed and was ready for that glass of wine. Actually, forget the wine. All she wanted was Linus.

Diana stepped out of the bathroom and looked around for him. Their apartment wasn't big so there were only so many places he could be. And he wasn't in any of them. "Linus? Where are you?"

She wandered into the kitchen and stopped short when she saw a note on the counter. His chicken-scratch handwriting was large and hard to read at first. Her breath caught as the jumbled words came into focus.

> *We were out of wine so I slipped out for just a second to fetch a bottle. I'll be right back. I love you here, there, and everywhere.*
> *Linus*

Panic flared in all the places Diana had just worked to relax. "No, no, no, no, no." He couldn't leave. He was finally here, and he was safe. She hurried to the door, threw it open, and looked out. Maybe she could catch him before he left. His bike was gone, though. The closest store was just a little way down the road. Maybe a five-minute bike ride. But the sun had already set and it was dark out. Ice would be solidifying on the roads, making them more dangerous.

Diana's hand covered her mouth as she swallowed back tears.

"You look like you've seen a ghost, dear. Is everything okay?" Mrs. Guzman stepped up to Diana as she made her way to her own apartment after walking Leonardo.

Diana looked at her neighbor. "No. Nothing is okay anymore."

Mrs. Guzman reached out and touched Diana's arm. "Is there anything I can do?"

Diana shook her head, her eyes reaching past Mrs. Guzman to the roads, looking for Linus on his bike. Then, suddenly, the sound of sirens filled the air.

Mrs. Guzman dropped her arm back to her side and turned to acknowledge the sound too. "Oh, no. I hope that poor soul is okay."

Diana shook her head as tears swam in her eyes, overflowing onto her cheeks. She didn't have any hope. Not anymore. She knew that poor soul was Linus, and she also knew that he was not okay.

Chapter 16

Bah! Humbug!

The sound of the shower running stirred Diana in her bed. She moaned softly, resisting the light from the blinds in the window. When her mind caught up to her body, her eyes popped open.

Not again.

She couldn't go through this horrible day one more time. Not if she wasn't able to fix fate. Diana sat up in bed and waited for the bathroom door to open and for Linus to appear. When he finally did, he looked at her with a lopsided smile.

"Good morning, sleepy girl."

She wanted to sob. How many times could she watch this man get into an accident? This was torture—for the both of them. "What's good about it?" she muttered.

Linus's brows rose high on his forehead. "Someone woke up on the wrong side of the bed. I don't want to argue this morning, okay? I'm sorry about last night."

Diana threw off her covers. "Me too."

"That's one thing I love about our relationship: We don't

stay mad. That bodes well for our marriage." He crossed the room, heading toward his closet.

She already knew he was going to pick the lavender tie with the dogs on it. She already knew which lavender button-down shirt he was going to match with his trousers. She knew everything that was going to happen today, and she couldn't change it. She was going to see Maria and then Addy. Addy was going to be upset over a boy. After leaving the Pierce home, Diana was going to go to an interview that she would bomb completely and miserably. She would probably do even worse than she did yesterday and the day before that. Afterward, she'd meet up with Rochelle for drinks, and Rochelle would try to analyze Diana's every thought and action.

Then, finally, Diana was going to go see Linus at the store. And no matter what she did or said or tried, he would get into an awful accident this evening.

Diana's heart sunk into the pit of her stomach. She looked up as Linus walked out of his closet holding the lavender tie with dogs on it and the lavender button-down shirt.

"I have a meeting with a distributor this morning," he told her.

"Yeah, I know. But your truck isn't going to start because you forgot to put gas in it yesterday. So, you're going to have to take your bike because, even though I offer to drive you to work, you're going to argue that you need the exercise. In which case, you better go ahead and get dressed so that you're not late to meet the distributor. And I guess I need to get dressed as well because I need to see Maria and make sure she doesn't break her ankle."

Linus blinked back at her. "You're acting very—"

"Bizarre? Yes, I know. I'm getting stranger by the day." But he didn't know the half of it. Nobody did except for Dustin, who Diana would see this afternoon. The child who was naughty, but wanted to be on Santa's nice list so that he could get a family of his own.

Diana wondered if Dustin was having any luck changing fate. The thought of going through this day again just to find out was exhausting, though. She'd rather stay in bed with the covers pulled over her head and wait it out. Then again, she'd probably just wake up again tomorrow in the same miserable, horrible day.

"Are you all right?" Linus asked. That question would normally evoke a reassuring response from Diana. Normally she would reflexively answer, "*Of course I'm okay. I'm always okay. I'm fine.*" Today, however, she answered differently. "No, I am not all right. I am so sick of this day, and it's only just gotten started. All I want to do is spend the next twelve hours with you instead of running around and doing things that maybe I don't even care about."

Linus looked completely dumbfounded. "You love working with your patients. What are you even talking about?"

"Yes, I love working with my patients, but I have an interview for a promotion this afternoon. And I don't know if I even want to go, because maybe I don't want to be behind a desk all day. Maybe I want to spend more time with my patients. Maybe I want to be with you." She was talking quickly, and the more she said, the higher Linus's eyebrows rose.

"Di, you're just nervous about your meeting. You've been talking about this interview and preparing for it for a while now. Just relax. Maybe take a couple extra minutes to take a hot bath."

Memories of last night when he'd suggested the same came to mind. "No! I don't need a bath! I never want a bath again!"

Linus's brows drew together as he looked at her with concern. "Do you want me to call Rochelle for you?"

Diana shook her head quickly. "Just ride your bike to

work for your meeting, and I'll come see you later. I'm fine. I promise," she reassured him with a fragile smile. She was lying through her teeth, though, and she suspected he could tell. A person who was living the same awful day in a loop was as far from fine as one could get.

Linus offered a slight nod and then jingled his keys. "It's freezing outside. As much as I would love to get some exercise, I think I'll drive the truck this morning."

Diana didn't argue. He would learn soon enough that his truck wouldn't start.

He gave her a kiss before heading out the front door. She waited until she heard it close, and then she got ready for the day, moving much slower than she had the day before.

A text pinged on her cell phone. She stopped to take a look.

Linus: *How did you know?*
Diana: *Lucky hunch.*
Linus: *OR you funneled the gas out of my tank last night while I slept. Looks like I'm taking the bike after all. Love you.*

Diana stared at the text with tears in her eyes. She blinked them away, mainly because who had time for crying? She did apparently. She suddenly had loads of time, but she could only manipulate it in her favor a tiny bit. She texted back.

Diana: *Love you too.*

Then she continued with her day. Just like yesterday and the one before that, Diana called Maria and begged her to wait to pull out the Christmas decorations. Then she drove to Maria's house and pulled the Christmas boxes from the attic.

"All right, let's get down to business. I'm sure your arm is stiff today so let's stretch it out," Diana said.

"How did you know I was stiff?" Maria asked, looking perplexed.

"Probably because of the weather," Diana said, unable to hide the irritation in her voice. She loved Maria, she did. She just couldn't help herself today. Everything was rubbing her all wrong. She could make Maria feel less lonely today, but it would all be erased tomorrow. None of it mattered. Diana couldn't fix anything except apparently Maria's ankle.

"You seem troubled," Maria noted after a few minutes of stretching. "Do you want to talk about it?"

Diana shook her head. "What is talking going to do anyway? Nothing. Nothing changes anything. I just want to be done with this day," she practically shouted as Maria's eyes rounded.

Diana tried to take deep breaths, but the air didn't seem to reach her lungs. Was she having a panic attack? Seeing her fiancé get into an accident night after night would do that to a person.

Maria pulled her arm from Diana's and took an exaggerated moment to sit up.

"What are you doing?" Diana asked.

"You are having a rough day so instead of focusing on me, we're going to focus on you." The older woman stood and shuffled toward her kitchen. "I'm making you tea."

"That's not necessary. Maria, I'm here for you. For your therapy."

Maria glanced back, but continued walking. "Sometimes helping others is good therapy. Come. Sit. Would you like a slice of fruitcake?"

Diana followed Maria toward the kitchen. "No. Thanks." She'd been given enough fruitcake this week. And she probably shouldn't sit down for tea with Maria versus providing therapy because this wasn't her job. It wasn't professional. Her focus should be on Maria, not her own problems.

Maria flipped her hot water kettle on and pulled two mugs from her cabinet. "Want to talk about it?" she asked again.

"Not really," Diana said.

"That's fine. What *do* you want to talk about?" Maria asked.

Diana watched as Maria dropped a tea bag into each mug. "You. You said it's your fault that your daughter doesn't talk to you anymore, and that's one of the reasons you're lonely. I think you should try to reach out to her again."

Maria poured hot water over the mugs. Then she shuffled one mug over to Diana and slid it in front of her. She turned back and retrieved her own mug before facing Diana. "How did you know about my daughter?"

"You told me," Diana lied, knowing Maria would fall for it because she had the last time.

"Hmm," Maria finally said.

"Hmm?"

"My daughter told me she never wants to talk to me again. What more can I do?"

"You're her mother. You do what you need to show her you care." Diana thought of her own mom coming to see her every holiday. It wasn't enough. "Otherwise, you're as bad a mom as you think you are."

Maria's lips parted.

Diana cringed and shook her head. Okay, *that* was curt. "You know what? I'm sorry. It's not my place to say that." She took a sip of her tea and then pushed the mug away. "I'll come back tomorrow, Maria. I know it's not my day, but I owe you physical therapy. And I'll help you put up your tree as well." She got up and headed for the door, needing air. "I'll see myself out."

"Take care of yourself, Diana," Maria called after her.

It was rude to leave without responding, but Maria would soon forget just like everyone else.

Diana hurried out the front door and closed it behind her. Then she got inside her car, cranked the engine, and immediately shifted into DRIVE. She should probably cancel the rest of the day with the way things were already going, but instead she drove to the Pierce home. When Mrs. Pierce answered the door, Diana exchanged a short greeting, and walked down the hall and banged on Addy's door.

"Come in," Addy called.

Diana stepped inside and shut the door behind her. "Okay, here it is. My advice is to stop sulking and do something about what you want. If this guy of yours doesn't like you anymore, then he's not worth your time or attention."

Addy pulled her face away from the pillow she had it pressed into and rolled onto her back. "Tell me what you really think," she said sarcastically. "And how do you know I'm upset over a guy anyway?"

"Long story that you'd never believe anyway. That's why I'm not going to get into it with you. Not because I don't want to share things with you. Which I will—another time. Right now, I want to tell you that you're beautiful and smart, and you deserve to be treated as such."

Addy sat up in bed and heaved a forlorn sigh. "Well, the problem is, my friend Sierra apparently has a crush on the guy too. She's been eating lunch with him and passing notes, stuff like that." Addy looked down at her clasped hands. "Jay always said he wasn't into her that way, but, I don't know, maybe now that I'm MIA, he's changed his mind."

"This Sierra person doesn't sound like a true friend," Diana said, sparing nothing today.

Addy flinched. The truth sometimes hurt. "Well, you know how friends are."

"I know how mine are." Diana wished she could have a few words with this Sierra girl. *Actually, yeah, that's a good idea.* "Is she one of your contacts in your phone?"

"Of course."

Diana reached for Addy's phone on the bedside table and handed it to Addy. "Unlock this for me."

Addy's smooth skin wrinkled as she scrunched her face. "Why?"

Diana tipped her head toward the phone. "Just do it."

Addy complied and then Diana took the phone, pulled up the contacts, and found Sierra's name. "Sierra Reynolds?"

"That's her," Addy confirmed, reaching to swipe her phone back.

Diana tapped the contact and stepped away from Addy's reach.

"What are you doing?" Addy asked, eyes going wide with panic. "Are you calling her? Please don't say anything."

Diana listened to the ring tone until a girl's voice answered.

"Hello?"

"Hi, is this Sierra Reynolds?" Diana asked.

"Um, yeah. Who is this? And why are you calling from Addy's phone?" Sierra asked. "Is she okay?"

"She's fine. I'm calling to tell you that friends don't make plays on the other friend's guy when the other friend is down. Or ever for that matter. Friends are supposed to be there for one another." Rochelle had always been there for Diana, but maybe Diana hadn't always reciprocated.

"Diana . . ." Addy whined. She stood off the bed and reached for the cell phone again.

Diana whirled to keep her back to Addy and continued talking. "You should be glad to have such a great person in your life like Addy."

"What are you even talking about, lady?" Sierra said on the other line. "Are you spying on me or something?"

"If I was, would I see you hitting on Addy's boyfriend?"

There was a silence on the other end of the line. "We're just hanging out, okay? There's nothing else going on, I swear," Sierra said. "We're mostly talking about how much we miss Addy."

Diana turned back to Addy, who was close enough to hear what Sierra had said through the speaker.

Addy took the phone finally and held it to her ear. "Is that true?"

"Of course, it's true," Diana heard Sierra say as Diana stepped back. "You stopped talking to both of us, and I guess Jay and I have that in common. I mean, other than you being the only thing that we have in common because we both love you," Sierra told Addy. "Otherwise, he's kind of annoying, if you ask me."

Diana blinked the burn from her eyes. A misunderstanding? Days of enduring Addy's bad mood was over something that wasn't even true? "You two talk it out. I think my work here is done," Diana said quietly.

Addy looked at Diana and offered a tiny smile as she continued to talk to Sierra. "She's my physical therapist," she explained. "She's pretty cool. And maybe a bit weird."

Diana waved and headed out of Addy's bedroom. Then she walked down the hall and out the front door without talking to Mrs. Pierce like she normally would. It didn't matter. She was stuck in an endless loop of this day anyhow.

As soon as Diana got into her car, she pulled out her cell phone and called the florist. Rochelle's crush hadn't made a move yesterday because Diana had missed that step, and maybe she was a crappy friend, but she could at least send her best friend flowers on her birthday.

With the call behind her, she put her car into DRIVE. Next stop, Mr. Powell's office.

Diana blew out a breath and drove toward the edge of town. She wasn't even nervous this time, and she certainly wasn't about to race home to polish up. Not after the last several debacles. She wouldn't even have gone except she'd feel like she'd wasted the entire last couple of months if she didn't. She'd been pouring all her energy and time into getting into management, climbing the success ladder, and making something of herself.

Fifteen minutes later, Diana arrived at the rehabilitation center and sat in her car before getting out. Every other time she'd been here, she'd been beside herself with nerves. Not this time. Before going inside, she grabbed her phone and tapped out a text to Linus.

Diana: *Hey, just want you to know that . . .*

What did she want him to know? For the last three weeks, she'd been going to see him in the hospital, wanting so much for him to open his eyes and look at her. There was so much she wanted to say, but if she had to articulate it all . . . she really wasn't sure what she wanted to tell him. *"I love you"* seemed too simple. Too clichéd. But it was the most there was in the English language. Or any language.

She loved him so much that the thought of him never waking up from that coma was just too crushing to even consider. But even worse was the thought of Linus getting into a tragic accident time after time. How many times could she lose him? Was he feeling the pain with each accident? She had to assume he was because *she* was feeling it, more and more, deeper and deeper.

And she was realizing with each passing hour that one more day wasn't really a gift at all. Not if it was this one. It was more of a curse.

Chapter 17

Leann looked up and smiled as Diana entered the rehabilitation center. "I'm here to see Mr. Powell." Diana tapped her fingers impatiently as the receptionist looked at the schedule.

"Yes. Please have a seat and—"

"You'll let me know when Mr. Powell is ready." Diana nodded. "Got it. But he'll be ready in about thirty seconds so there's no point in me sitting down. I'll just stand right here and wait."

Leann's smile drooped. "Oh. Okay. Well, I'll let him know you've arrived." She picked up the receiver of the phone, her gaze flicking to Diana as she told Mr. Powell that Diana was here in a hushed voice. Then she placed the receiver back in its cradle and stood. "He's ready for you."

Diana felt a little frazzled and out of control, which probably wouldn't serve her best going into an important meeting with her boss. Not that it mattered. This day didn't matter one bit, just like yesterday and the day before. She followed Leann inside Mr. Powell's office, walked straight up to Mr. Powell and shook his hand. "No need to offer me any coffee, Todd. Let's just get to business, shall we?" she said as she sat down and crossed her legs.

Mr. Powell took a seat across from her, looking a bit bewildered. "Perfect." He ran through all the questions from yesterday and Diana answered them robotically until he got to this one: "What makes you think you would make a good manager?"

She shook her head. "I don't think that, actually. I have no idea if I'd make a good manager or not."

"Oh?" Mr. Powell's brows lifted with surprise.

"I mean, you want total honesty, right? That is my honest answer. Actually, if I'm honest, maybe I'm not cut out for this promotion at all. I have no idea why I'm even here." She ignored Mr. Powell's slowly sinking smile. "In fact, I'm wasting both of our time right now, aren't I? This interview isn't going to go well no matter what I do, so I'm going to get up and leave now, and spare us both an awkward attempt at proving to you that I'm better suited for the job instead of William." She stood abruptly and offered her hand to Mr. Powell.

Mr. Powell was speechless for a moment. "You're leaving?" he finally asked. "I didn't think this was off to such a bad start."

"Well, give it time and it would have been. There *is* no time, though," she said, feeling more frazzled and out of control by the moment. This whole day was a train speeding toward a tragic ending. "Or there is time, too much, but not for things I don't even know that I want."

Mr. Powell finally shook her hand. "Well then, thank you for coming in, Diana," he said politely.

When she pulled her hand away, she purposefully knocked the crystal frame off his desk and watched it shatter at her feet just like this train wreck of a day. It didn't matter. She'd be back here again tomorrow. "Thank *you*," she echoed. Then she turned and walked out of the office, past the receptionist's desk, and out into the cold afternoon. She hurried to her car, got inside, and didn't cry this time. In fact, she felt a little numb.

After a few minutes, her phone buzzed with an incoming text. That would be Rochelle. She checked the screen.

Rochelle: *You sent me flowers?!*

Diana tapped a message back.

Diana: *It's the least a crappy friend can do on your birthday.*
Rochelle: *You're not crappy. Thank you. You're not blowing off drinks, are you?*
Diana: *Nope. I need a few drinks, actually. See you in a bit.*

Diana was about to set her phone down, but it started to ring. That would be Joann. "Hello, Joann," she said without even checking the caller ID.

"Oh, Diana. I'm so glad I caught you. Are you busy?"

"Well, I am at work." Diana glanced around the lot where several cars were parked. The rehabilitation center had a home health branch, but it also saw patients inside the small gym area here. "I can spare a quick second for you to invite me and Linus over for dinner this weekend, though."

Joann stammered. "W-well, yes. That is exactly what I was going to suggest. We really enjoyed seeing you at Thanksgiving and we were hoping to spend some more time together. We could start planning that wedding of yours too," she said, her voice climbing a hopeful octave.

"That's a really nice offer, Joann. Our answer will depend on whether or not Linus and I can make it home in one piece tonight, I guess."

Joann laughed nervously. Diana guessed she thought Diana was joking. She wasn't.

"I'll discuss it with Linus," Diana added.

"Please do. Maybe we can go dress shopping sometime soon too. Me, you, and your mother."

Diana resisted the need to expel a loud, painful sigh. "My mom isn't really in the picture, Joann. She probably won't even attend the wedding."

"Oh." Joann was quiet for a moment. Diana guessed Linus had never filled his mother in on Diana's side of the family. "Well, that's okay. I've always wanted a daughter, you know. I know I won't be your real mother, Diana, but I will love you as if I were."

Diana swallowed hard. Her agitation about the repeating day seemed to dissolve for a moment. She couldn't hold on to that promise, though, even if Joann was sincere in making it. Because tomorrow, Joann would have forgotten this whole conversation and Diana would be the worse for remembering it. "I've got to go."

"Of course, you do. Talk to Linus and get back to me."

"I will. Goodbye." Diana disconnected the call and took a breath. Next train wreck was Sparky's Tavern.

When Diana arrived at Sparky's, she headed back to Rochelle's table and plopped into the chair with a heavy sigh.

Rochelle had a plate of fries and two drinks in front of her. She slid one drink toward Diana. "Here. I ordered for you."

"Because you are an awesome friend. And I am a crappy one."

Rochelle's smile slid down at the corners. "Something you want to talk about?"

Diana looked at her friend for a moment. "Yes. I don't like it when you try to be a counselor with me. You're not my counselor. You're my friend."

"Loosely the same things," Rochelle teased, wobbling her head back and forth. "I just happen to have a degree in counseling so I'm better than your average Joe."

Diana lifted her drink to her mouth and took long sips, wondering if Rochelle could fix her problems. Maria couldn't. Addy and Mr. Powell couldn't. "Okay, if you want to be a counselor to me so badly, here goes. I'm in a time loop and reliving this day, December fourth, over and over again, like a broken record. Today is December fourth. But it's really supposed to be Christmas Day and no one else knows that except this little boy at Linus's store."

Rochelle angled her face slightly, giving Diana a strange look. "What do you mean that today is supposed to be Christmas?"

"I mean, yesterday was December twenty-fourth and I met you here for our traditional Christmas Eve drinks." Diana sighed. "Linus was in a coma and I was sad and—"

Rochelle held out a palm. "Hold up. Linus was in a coma?"

"Right. On December fourth, the first one, he got into an accident while riding his bicycle home. He was in the intensive care unit of the hospital for one week. Then they deemed him hopeless, pretty much, and moved him to New Hope Long-Term Care."

Rochelle's eyes went wide. "Is this some kind of joke or some sort of mental health crisis that you're having?"

"It's none of those things. This is really happening. Anyway, my neighbor, Ms. Guzman, picked up a snow globe that Linus had given me. She told me to shake it and think of the one that I had loved and lost, and that I would get one more day with that person. So I did, and I thought of Linus, and now I'm trapped here in that day from three weeks ago. But it's the day that he got into his accident, so I hope that if I can stop the delivery truck from hitting him, I can keep him from going into a coma."

Rochelle swayed her pointer finger around in the air, talking with her hands. "Okay, if—*big if*—this is a repeat of some day from the past, then you think this day will record over the one that already happened? Effectively erasing it from history?"

"Exactly." Diana blew out a breath. "Finally someone speaks my language."

"Or . . ." Rochelle said, trailing off as she picked up another French fry and swirled it in her ketchup.

"Or?" Diana waited impatiently for Rochelle to continue.

"Or it's just a chance to see Linus again and say goodbye." Rochelle bit into her fry and chewed. "Not saying I believe this story at all, because I don't. If I'm reliving December fourth again, seeing that it's my birthday, then that kind of means I've jumped another year in age, and I am not okay with that."

Diana blinked, focusing on the first thing Rochelle had said. "I don't want to say goodbye to Linus. We're going to grow old together. We're going to have a family and pets. We don't even have a dog yet." Tears welled in her eyes. "We haven't even set our wedding date." Which was, of course, all her fault. "No, I'm going to think positive. I'll go back to the store before he closes."

Rochelle let out a disbelieving laugh. "I'm starting to think you really believe this crazy story, Diana."

"That's because I do." Diana reached across the table and grabbed one of Rochelle's fries. She popped it into her mouth and chewed. "Whatever. It doesn't matter anyway."

"That is so typical of you."

"What do you mean by that?" Diana asked, hackles rising. She finished off her drink and flagged down the waitress for another one, which probably wasn't the best idea because she had always been a lightweight. She didn't care anymore, though. If she was just going to wake up in the same day tomorrow, that meant she wouldn't have to endure the hangover.

"I mean that you won't allow yourself to ever let people in on what you're feeling. Because if you did, maybe we would realize that you don't have your shit together. Well, guess what, Diana? No one has their shit together. None of us. And that's okay. We don't have to. What you can't do is shut everyone out. I'm not trying to psychoanalyze. I'm trying to be a good friend, but you won't let me and you won't let Linus be a fiancé either. So, what's going to happen is that, one day, you're going to wake up and these walls you've built around yourself will have become your prison. I'm sorry. That might sound harsh, but it's true."

The waitress slid another drink in front of Diana. Without thinking, Diana picked it up and took several large gulps. "You're telling me that my life is spiraling down the drain because I don't whine, complain, cry, and throw a tantrum about all the injustices I've been served in life? That letting it all out and having one big breakdown would save the world?"

Rochelle rolled her eyes. "Yeah. Basically." She shrugged. "It would save *your* world at least."

Diana tipped her glass back and drank the rest of its contents. Her mouth tasted like alcohol. She felt nauseous and dizzy. "I'm not trying to save myself. I'm trying to save Linus, and I can't," she said, voice cracking.

Rochelle gave her a sympathetic look. "I don't know what you're talking about, Diana. I really don't. But I do know that all Linus wants is for you to let him in. He loves you. If you're going through something, tell him."

Hot tears filled Diana's eyes. She looked down at her empty glass, feeling suddenly sick to her stomach. Some little element of truth was waiting there in Rochelle's words for her to realize, but she felt too nauseous to grasp onto it. "What time is it?"

"Time for you to stop drinking. I'll drive you home."

"No. I can't go home. I need to go to the toy store."

"When I said to talk to Linus, I didn't mean after you've been drinking. Wait till you sober up, okay?"

Diana pushed back from the table and stood quickly. The blood rushed to her head and the room started to spin.

"Whoa. I'm not carrying you out, Diana. Slow down."

"I need to get to him. He's going to be in an accident,"

Diana slurred to Rochelle. Those two drinks must have had a lot of alcohol in them. Had she eaten today? Maybe drinking on an empty stomach wasn't such a good idea.

"Mm-hmm. Just like he's been in an accident for the last several days in a row. I'm taking you home. You owe me, by the way, because I was supposed to meet up with this guy for dinner. It's my birthday, and I'd much rather be having a steak than holding your hair while you puke."

Diana leaned heavily into Rochelle. "The guy works in the office next to yours. He drops off your mail sometimes. Today, he saw the flowers I sent you, realized it was your birthday"—Diana hesitated as acid reflux burned the back of her throat—"and he went down the street to get you an even bigger bouquet. Because he likes you."

Rochelle blinked. "I didn't tell you that."

"You did. You told me yesterday. No, not yesterday because I forgot to send you the flowers yesterday. It was the day before." Diana turned toward Rochelle. "I'm not losing my mind. This is real. And Linus is going to ride his bike home from the toy store tonight and be hit by a delivery truck. Or if he takes a vehicle, he'll still be hit because this universe is cruel and unforgiving."

Rochelle's lips parted just slightly. "I almost believe you."

"Almost?" Diana's head was pounding. She was such a bad drinker. Why did she do it?

Rochelle hesitated. "I can't take you into the toy store drunk."

"Then drive us there and you go in," Diana said. "You can talk to a little boy on the doll aisle. His name is Dustin. He's worried about being too naughty to be on Santa's list. And all he wants for Christmas is a family of his own." A tear slid down Diana's cheek. *Damn it.* Since when had she become a crier?

Rochelle sighed, linked her arm with Diana's, and helped her toward the exit. "Fine. I'll drive you to the toy store. On

my birthday. Instead of having dinner with a hot guy who
bought me flowers. And I'll talk to this kid. If he's even
there."

"He'll be there," Diana said, her world spinning as she
walked.

They stepped out into the cold and Diana took a deep
breath. Then her stomach gurgled, lurched, and all its contents projected up and onto Rochelle's boots.

Rochelle screeched in horror. "Well, happy birthday to
me," she finally muttered.

Diana groaned. "Sorry."

"Come on, let's go." Rochelle tugged her toward the car.
"Do not puke in my car or this friendship is called off."

Diana held onto the door handle as Rochelle annoyingly
drove one mile under the speed limit. "You have to drive
faster."

"So you can get sick in my car?" Rochelle asked. "I love
you and all, but I don't think so."

"He's going to be in an accident." Diana pressed her eyes
closed to bar the nausea.

Rochelle exhaled. "He doesn't close up the store until six,
right? It's five forty-five. We have plenty of time to get there."

Diana opened her eyes for a second and saw Rochelle
wave her hand off to the side.

"Not that I believe you," Rochelle said.

Fifteen minutes. That was enough. It only took ten to drive
to the store. That left five minutes to spare, and Linus never
left as soon as he closed. He needed to clean up and count the
register first.

Diana pulled out her cell phone.

"What are you doing?" Rochelle slid her gaze over. "Drunk
texting is never a good idea."

"It's fine when it's your own fiancé." Diana's stomach rolled
as Rochelle turned left.

"You only drink when you fight with someone. That's a sign that you're uncomfortable with your emotions. Instead of feeling them, you drink them away."

Diana glared at Rochelle. "Are you going to psychol-i-size this guy you like too? Because that won't go well."

"Just you," Rochelle said.

Diana couldn't see straight enough to text so she pressed CALL instead and held her phone to her ear, waiting for Linus to answer. After a moment, the call went to voice mail. She dialed again, nerves wrapping around her chest and squeezing, making it hard to pull in a deep breath.

"He's probably just checking out a customer. We're almost there. Relax," Rochelle said before sirens could be heard somewhere down the road.

"Do you hear that?" Diana sat up straighter.

"It could be anyone." Rochelle reached a hand across the seat. "Linus is at the toy store. It's not even six."

Diana pressed a hand to her chest, forcing herself to take a deep breath, but there didn't seem to be any air in her lungs. Rochelle stopped behind a line of traffic, waiting for whatever had happened up ahead.

"It's not anyone. It's Linus." Diana pushed open her car door, not stopping as Rochelle called her back. Then she started half walking, half running in the direction of the sirens. Her head was pounding and alcohol swished around in her stomach. She ignored it all. It was as if fate knew she was going to try to get here early and it had forced Linus to leave before closing. She couldn't stop this damned day.

Diana saw the delivery truck. It was surrounded by red and blue lights. She kept running, the cold stinging her cheeks. "Linus? Linus!"

"Ma'am. Stay back," a deep voice instructed.

She ignored the warning and kept going, only stopping when she saw Linus's bike on the road. Its front wheel was twisted along with the handlebar. "Linus!" she screamed. He wasn't there with his bike. Where was he?

"Ma'am?" The deep voice belonged to a man in a blue uniform. Officer Crane. He'd come to her front door on the first December 4th.

"The bike is Linus's. Where is he?" she asked, whirling to face Officer Crane.

He looked apologetic. "He's in the ambulance, Diana."

She turned toward the emergency vehicle and ran in that direction as the paramedic moved to shut the back door. "Wait! He's my fiancé! I need to go with him! Please! I don't want him to be alone. He can't go through this alone," she begged. She couldn't go through this alone either.

The paramedic opened the door and helped her step up. "We have to hurry," he said, pointing to a small bench near the stretcher. "Have a seat."

Diana slid down on the seat, her gaze pinned to Linus. She reached for his hand and held it. His skin was cold. She used her other hand to sandwich it, willing the warmth of her body into his. "I'm here, Linus. Hang on. I'm here."

Linus stirred and his eyelids fluttered open just a crack. "Di?"

She gasped and leaned in as tears washed her cheeks. "Hey. It's me. You've been in an accident. We're taking you to the hospital. Stay with me, okay? Keep your eyes open. Please." Maybe she could keep him from drifting off into some nowhere place in his subconscious that he couldn't come back from. "Stay with me. Don't leave."

"Di?" he asked again. His eyes weren't focused anymore. Instead he was looking past her.

Diana remembered what Rochelle had said about her being too closed off and not letting anyone in. She tried to handle everything on her own and that's not how relationships worked. "I can't do this life without you, Linus. I don't know if I ever told you this, but I need you. You have to stay because we're going to get married, remember? I've been too scared. Too stupid. Too in my own head. But—"

"Di?" Linus asked again.

She stopped talking and looked at him. "Yes? What is it?" His eyelids fluttered closed.

"No! Linus, open your eyes! Wake up! Don't leave me!" She squeezed his hand. "Please," she cried. "Please don't go. I'll marry you tomorrow. Any day you want if you just stay."

He didn't reopen his eyes, though. He was gone, again.

Chapter 18

"There you are," Rochelle said.

Diana looked up from the chair in the hospital waiting room where she was sitting with several of Linus's relatives. Diana had texted Joann from Linus's room before the doctors and nurses had ushered her out. "Hey."

Rochelle sat down in the chair next to hers. "How is he?"

"In surgery. They haven't told me yet, but he's going to pull through." Tears swam in her eyes. "He has a broken femur and some cracked ribs. His brain sustained the most injury."

Rochelle reached for her hand and squeezed tightly. The gesture was supposed to be supportive, but it made Diana want to cry. She didn't want to break down, though. Not here. Not in front of Linus's entire family, even if his Aunt Ruby was sobbing loudly on the other side of the room. Linus had told Diana that Ruby was a tad histrionic. He wasn't wrong. "Are you still going to tell me that you've lived this day before?" Rochelle asked quietly.

Diana nodded, her gaze moving to a row of chairs with Linus's cousins. They all had their phones out and seemed to be rapid-fire texting. Mr. Grant had a Pop Tart poking out of his pocket that he kept breaking a piece off from and sneaking it into his mouth, as if eating at a time like this was a crime. "It's true." Diana swallowed. "And I don't think I can keep going through this same day. It's the hardest day of my life, watching him in so much pain. I can't stop it from happening. I can't fix it, no matter how hard I try."

Rochelle squeezed her hand again. "I'm sorry, Diana. I don't know what to say."

Diana looked over. "What? You're not going to tell me that I'm acting irrationally? That I need to hang onto hope?"

Rochelle shook her head. "No. I'm just going to sit here with you, if you'll let me."

Diana looked down at Rochelle's hand in hers. She wasn't sure Rochelle had ever held her hand before. It felt like a lifeline that she could hold onto. "Please don't go. I want you to stay with me. I'm sorry to ruin your birthday though."

"That doesn't matter. It's just a day."

Diana blew out a breath. "And you'll have another one tomorrow."

"Mrs. Grant?" A surgeon stepped into the waiting room and looked around.

"Yes?" Diana said at the same time that Linus's mother said yes.

Diana shared a look with the older woman. Right. Diana wasn't a Grant yet.

The surgeon looked between them.

"I'm his mother," Joann said. "How is he?"

"Well, your son is a fighter, that's for sure. He pulled through the surgery. We'll have to wait and see if he wakes up."

Joann nodded. "Can we see him?"

"Of course," the surgeon said. "One at a time, though. Would you like to go in?"

Joann gestured at Diana. "You go. If there's anyone that can wake up Linus, it's you."

Diana stood shakily. "Thank you." She looked at Rochelle. "Will you be here when I get back?"

Rochelle's lips parted. She looked surprised that Diana would admit to needing her. "Of course, I will. If you want me to be."

Diana gave a small head nod. "Please."

Rochelle leaned back in her chair and crossed her legs to prove her point. "In that case, I'll stay all night."

At five minutes till midnight, Diana sat in a chair watching the man she loved lying helpless in a hospital bed. Rochelle was asleep in the visitor's chair by the window. Linus had been moved to a room on the second floor, which allowed more than one visitor. Diana was thankful for that because she didn't want to be alone right now—even if her support system was snoring softly in the corner.

Who could sleep at a time like this? Not Diana. She was wide awake as the clock ticked closer to midnight. The only positive thing she could think of right now was that, in five minutes, she'd wake up as if all of this were a dream—it wasn't—and then she'd see Linus. His eyes would open, his lips would offer a small smile, and the sound of his voice would fill the silence as he whispered, "Hello, sleepy girl."

Diana waited for that. "Linus, I'm sorry," she whispered. "I'm the reason you keep going through this horrible day. It's all my fault." She swallowed past the growing lump in her throat. "I just wanted to be with you one more time. That's all. But I don't even deserve that because when I had you with me, here, alive and well before the accident, I was too busy." She swiped at a tear on her cheek. "I was too scared. Too cut off. Too everything."

Diana jumped as Linus squeezed her hand. She blinked past her tears and looked at him, studying his face. "You squeezed my hand. Are you there? Are you listening? Linus?"

She watched his hand inside hers. He'd squeezed. She hadn't imagined that. Her gaze swiped to the clock. Three minutes to midnight. She shook Linus's hand and leaned over him. "Linus, wake up! . . . Come on, come on."

His fingers flexed against hers once more.

Diana laughed out loud.

"What's wrong?" Rochelle asked, opening her eyes and blinking sleepily.

"Linus is waking up. He's not going to be in a coma this time. Maybe we'll make it out of this okay." And wouldn't that be a Christmas miracle?

Rochelle stood and stepped over to look at him.

His eyes were still closed.

"He squeezed my hand. Twice," Diana said, excitedly. "He heard what I was telling him."

"What were you telling him?" Rochelle asked, looking confused.

Diana tried to remember. "That I was sorry. That I wished I had been there with him before the accident. I told him there was so much wasted time." She looked at Linus and squeezed his hand. "I won't waste another second if you wake up right now." They would set a wedding date just as soon as they could. Maybe they'd even get married tomorrow.

Diana checked the clock. T-minus thirty seconds. "Right now, Linus! Please! Open your eyes!" she demanded. "Wake up!"

Chapter 19

Dashing Through the Snow Globe

"Wake up, sleepy girl."

Diana's eyes fluttered open to see Linus hovering over her with a lazy smile. He was already dressed and wearing his lavender tie with the dogs on it. "What?"

"You overslept. I would have woken you, but I assumed you would eventually get up," he said. "If you don't hurry, you'll be late to see your first patient."

Diana blinked up groggily. "I overslept?" She groaned and grabbed her head with both hands. "My head aches."

Linus chuckled and straightened. "If I didn't know better, I'd think you were hungover."

Diana sat up in bed. She had drunk a lot last evening, but that should have been erased.

"I happen to know for a fact that you didn't drink last night, though," he said. "Instead, you went to bed without saying a word to me."

Diana lowered her hands. "It's still December fourth?"

Linus gave her a strange look. Then he bent to kiss her forehead sweetly. "Yes, and I've got an important meeting with a distributor. And you have your big interview with Mr. Powell this afternoon." He pulled back from the kiss. "I hope it goes well for you. You deserve this promotion. It's yours for the taking."

"Fat chance," Diana muttered.

"Hmm?" Linus turned back to look at her, his brow still deeply furrowed. "Did you say I look large in these pants?" he asked, one corner of his mouth quirking into a playful smile.

Diana burst into unexpected laughter. "That's the most absurd thing I've ever heard. You wear your belt on the second to last notch to even keep the pants on."

Linus grinned at her for a beat. "The fact that you're laughing maybe means you've forgiven me for what I said?"

"There's nothing to forgive. You were just expressing your feelings. Whereas my patient seems to think I don't have any of those. I'm an Elsa."

Linus shoved his hands in his pockets. "Well, the Queen of Arendelle is very popular on the shelves this year, and for the last many years, come to think of it. What is it with little girls and queens and princesses?" he asked, still grinning.

"They all want to be one."

"Did you?" he asked, pausing to look at her.

Diana shook her head, her gaze lowering to her hands in her lap. "My grandmother didn't believe in raising a child with such fantasies. She preferred that I play teacher or doctor."

"And look at you now. After today's interview, you'll be running that rehab clinic."

"Not exactly." Diana draped her legs off the edge of the bed. She was so tired of playing out this day. "You better go. You'll be late."

Linus looked at his watch. "I have plenty of time."

"Not if you're riding Byron to the store."

Linus chuckled. "I love to pedal, but it's a bit cold out this morning, don't you think?"

"Then you better take your coat," Diana offered. She was

so exhausted, and her body felt sore and achy all over. Was she sure that she wasn't the one being hit by the delivery truck every night?

Linus laughed, obviously thinking she was joking. Then he turned and headed out of the bedroom, calling behind him, "We'll celebrate your promotion tonight! I'll bring the wine!"

She heard the jingle of his keys as he picked them up from the counter. "I love you," she called after him.

"And I love you. Always and forever. Good luck today."

The front door slammed shut. Diana stood and dragged her feet on the way to the bathroom. Yeah, she did feel hungover, but not from the drinks she'd tipped back at Sparky's. This time loop was endless suffering for both of them. It had to stop, and yet, she was seemingly helpless to make it end.

Diana used the bathroom, dressed, and went about fixing her hair and brushing her teeth. Then she grabbed her keys and purse, and headed outside. The temperature seemed to have warmed a tiny touch from yesterday. The winter sun was bright, warming her cheeks despite the chilly air.

"Good morning, Diana," Mrs. Guzman said, walking toward her with Leonardo on a leash.

"Morning, Mrs. Guzman."

"I just saw Linus head off on his bicycle."

Diana nodded. "His truck is out of gas."

"Ah. Well, it's a touch warmer than yesterday, but the babbling forecaster on the TV is calling for snow later today, you know? Linus won't be able to ride his bike home in that weather."

It didn't matter. Diana didn't even want to go through this day one more time. She'd given up on saving Linus. All she wanted to do was keep him from getting hurt again. "Mrs. Guzman?"

The older woman turned back from her dog walking. "Yes?"

"I know you don't remember, but you put this spell—I'm sorry, enchantment—on a snow globe that I had. And I shook it and I got to relive this one day. This awful day. I thought that was what I wanted, but now I just want to take my wish back. I want to unshake that snow globe and unmake my wish."

The old woman didn't seem surprised in the least by what Diana told her. "Hmm. I guess that's why they say to be careful what you wish for."

"Well, I don't want this day anymore. Can I take back what I asked for?" Diana looked around to make sure no one would overhear.

Their neighbor, Mr. Zitnik, waved as he walked by.

"Of course, you can, dear," Mrs. Guzman said.

"I can?" Diana felt the tiniest prick of hope inside her heart. She was willing to do anything. "How?"

"Just like you said. Turn the snow globe upside down and shake it. Or unshake it." Mrs. Guzman said this as if it were the most obvious answer in the world.

"Shake the snow globe upside down?" Diana repeated. "That's it?"

Ms. Guzman smiled back at her. "Well, you could say something over it if it makes you feel better. It's more fun when the words rhyme, but it's not necessary," the older woman said, matter-of-factly.

Diana tilted her head. "So, when you said all those things over my snow globe, they weren't necessary?"

Mrs. Guzman chuckled. "It's not about the words, Diana. It's always about what's in the heart." She reached up and tapped her fingers against Diana's breastbone.

Diana shook her head, trying to make sense of this conversation. "What you're saying is, if I find the snow globe and shake it upside down, I can break the time loop and get back to real time?"

"Well, of course you can." Ms. Guzman shivered and used

one hand to hug her coat more tightly around her. "I have to go home and make some hot tea. Would you like some, dear?"

"Maybe another time." Diana had a tiny ember of hope warming her belly. "I have to go find a snow globe."

"Good luck to you. What day would real time be, anyway?" Mrs. Guzman called to Diana's back.

Diana glanced over her shoulder. "It should be Christmas."

Her neighbor's eyes widened. "Oh, my. I better do my holiday shopping, then. Do you like wine?"

Diana wasn't sure she'd ever accept another gift from Mrs. Guzman again. She certainly wouldn't accept another enchantment. "No need to get me anything. Just stop by on Christmas and join us for dinner." Not that there would be an *us*. Linus wasn't getting out of his coma. Diana had to accept that, and she needed to say goodbye.

Mrs. Guzman allowed Leonardo to tug her toward her own apartment. "Christmas dinner sounds lovely. Count me in."

Diana hurried back inside her apartment and ran to Linus's closet. All she needed to do to stop Linus's suffering was turn the snow globe upside down and unshake it. She reached past the curtain of ties, expecting her fingers to bump against the box that held the snow globe. But it wasn't there. *What?* In a panic, she threw the ties down to see with her own eyes that the gift-wrapped box was gone. Where was it?

A thought occurred to her. Maybe Linus hadn't purchased it yet. He could have gotten it anytime between now and his accident, and then returned home to hide it. Of course, that would mean leaving the store and Jean had been out with vertigo. There's no way he could have left.

Diana frantically searched the area surrounding the ties. What was she going to do if it wasn't here? She needed that globe in order to get out of this dreadful day. Otherwise, she and Linus would be stuck here on December 4th, and Linus would continue to get hurt, day after awful repeating day.

Swallowing back her tears, she tried to think of where Linus would go to purchase such a charming novelty item. If she could figure that out, she could purchase the snow globe herself. Yes! *Think, Diana, think.* Snow Haven was a small town. Eloise's Trinkets and Gifts was the only local place that would have something like that. That had to be where he had gotten it from.

In a mad rush, she hurried out of her apartment and past the sidewalk Santa on the way to the parking lot. She stuffed some cash in his bucket and heard him call "Merry Christmas" behind her. Then she got into her car, cranked it, and waited impatiently for the motor to warm as she dialed Maria's number. As soon as her patient answered, Diana said, "I'm calling out today, Maria. I'm not feeling quite myself. Whatever you do, please, do not pull your Christmas decorations down from the attic. I'll be back tomorrow, and I'll get those boxes for you. I promise." Because tomorrow would return to real time.

"How did you know I was planning to go into my attic today?" Maria asked.

At this point, Diana could practically say every word out of Maria's mouth before she said it. "Hunch. No boxes, okay?"

Maria chuckled. "You are a good therapist, Diana. Looking out for me in ways that aren't even necessary."

"That's because your well-being is important. *You* are important. Maybe you should, I don't know, give your daughter a call today."

"How'd you—"

"You told me. I think she'd love to hear from you, Maria. It's worth a try, isn't it?" Diana couldn't seem to help herself. She wanted this time loop to end better for someone, at least.

Maria hesitated. "Maybe so."

"Great. I'll see you tomorrow, and we'll put up your tree together, okay?"

"Wow. Yes. That's worth waiting for, indeed," the older woman said on a small chuckle.

Diana disconnected the call and then pulled up Mrs. Pierce's contact, called, and canceled Addy's session.

"Please tell Addy I'm sorry to miss her session today," Diana said.

"She does look forward to seeing you. She doesn't talk to anyone from school anymore. You're her closest friend these days," Mrs. Pierce joked quietly. "I know you're not friends exactly."

"Yes, we are. I can be her physical therapist and her friend. In fact, I'd like that." Diana's voice cracked a little.

"Are you okay?" Mrs. Pierce asked.

"Yes. Or actually, no. Not really. My friend Rochelle says I need to stop hiding my feelings and ask for help instead of trying to do everything myself. And I've finally decided that maybe she's right."

"That's good advice. Is there anything I can help you with? You've helped me and Addy so much."

Diana was about to say no, but she reconsidered. "Yes, actually. You're going to get a call from someone today. You're probably not going to want to answer, or if you do, you're not going to want to listen. Just try, though. Life is too short for grudges and unforgiveness."

"I'm not following," Mrs. Pierce said.

"That's okay. You'll understand later. I've got to go." Diana disconnected the call and drove to the corner of Main and Burgess Streets where Eloise's Trinkets and Gifts was located. Then she got out and headed inside the tiny store. It was dimly lit by fairy lights inside that draped from one end of the wall to the next. Every spare nook and cranny held something unique and interesting. Diana could stay in this place for hours and not grow bored. She didn't have hours, though. What had Mrs. Guzman said before? When a person realized that time wasn't unlimited, their priorities shifted?

"Welcome to Eloise's!" a woman called from the back counter.

Diana headed in that direction. "Hi, there. I was wondering if you could help me. I'm looking for a snow globe. It has a model of Snow Haven inside. Do you have one like that?" Diana asked, hopefully.

Eloise was a short woman with jet-black hair and a thick layer of red lipstick. She was younger than Diana expected a woman with such an old-fashioned name to be. "I had one, yes. But I sold it yesterday."

"Yesterday, as in December third?"

The skin pinched between Eloise's eyes. "I guess so."

"Who did you sell it to? Do you remember?"

"Um, yes. It was a man. He was tall. I don't know his name. He owns a toy store around here, I think. He gave me a gift card to buy presents for my daughter in order to get the snow globe down to twenty dollars. I was hesitant, but his gift card is worth more than the amount I took off the globe."

Diana blinked. "That's Linus. He's my fiancé." How many men owned a toy store in this small town? "You sold the snow globe to my fiancé?"

"I guess I did." Eloise laughed quietly. "I think it was a gift for you, though. So you might need to pretend you don't know about it. Would you like to get him something while you're here?"

"No. Thank you. I'm in a bit of a hurry, but I'll come back to shop," she promised. "You have a beautiful store." She backed away and turned to leave.

"Oh, I remember something else," Eloise called after Diana.

Diana stopped walking and turned. "What is it?"

"The man told me he was starting a collection for you. He said you've never collected anything and that he wanted to fix that travesty. That's what he called it. He said everyone should be a collector of something."

Diana felt frozen for a moment. She'd told Linus once that Grandma Denny didn't believe in collections. They were frivolous, costly, and took up too much space. She'd said that people developed silly affections for things that didn't really matter in the long run. Of course, everything was frivolous in Denny's eyes. "He's starting a snow globe collection for me?"

Eloise smiled. "He said he'd order another one next Christmas. I'm ruining his gift, aren't I? Act surprised, okay?"

Diana nodded. "I will. Thank you." She started to walk out of Eloise's Trinkets and Gifts when something caught her eye. She turned to look at a display of brightly colored tie-dyed scarves. A purple-and-gold one stood out to her and practically screamed Addy's name.

"Find something you fancy?" Eloise asked with a hopeful rise to her voice.

"Yeah. I think one of these scarves would be just the thing to give one of my patients." Diana reached for the scarf and carried it back to the register where Eloise was waiting.

"These are handmade by one of the locals in town. I try to purchase all of my items from locals."

Diana inserted her debit card into the reader. "The snow globe too?"

"Mm-hmm. My husband makes them. The one I sold your fiancé is one of a kind."

"Wow." Diana watched as Eloise placed the scarf in a pink-hued paper bag.

"There you go." The storeowner handed the bag over the counter. "Thanks for shopping and please tell all your friends."

"I will." With a wave, Diana turned and headed out of the store. She got into her car and checked the time. 1:45. Her meeting with Mr. Powell was in fifteen minutes. Everything would work out as long as she got to the snow globe before Linus left work tonight. She needed a chance to say goodbye. That's what tonight was about—one last goodbye.

Diana checked her reflection in the rearview mirror and cringed. She grabbed a ponytail tie from the dash and pulled her hair back to hide what the weather had curled and frizzed. Then she put her car in drive and headed over to Powell Rehabilitation. She walked inside and headed directly to Leann at the receptionist's desk. "Hi, I have an appointment with Mr. Powell at two o'clock."

Diana flicked her gaze to the clock hanging on the wall. It was 1:55. Early. She flashed the receptionist a confident smile. She didn't feel so nervous this time, probably because she'd already been through this interview too many times.

"Yes. Please have a seat. I'll call you when he's ready."

Diana turned toward the waiting area and took several deep breaths. When Leann called her forward, Diana was ready. She followed her down the hall and turned into Mr. Powell's office, heading straight toward him with an outstretched hand. "Hi, Todd. Nice to see you again."

He shook her hand and smiled perfectly. "You too. Can I get you some coffee?"

"No, thanks. I've had my two cups today." And she didn't fancy spilling it on herself or her boss this afternoon. Not this time.

Mr. Powell sat down behind his desk. "Well, then, we'll get to business. I must say I was surprised when you put in for the promotion."

"I surprised myself," Diana said. "But I think I have a lot to offer in management. I've been at this company for nearly ten years. I know the ins and outs, and sharing my knowledge with others would be very rewarding. Not to say that seeing my patients isn't rewarding, but I'm ready for a new adventure."

Wow. Diana was impressed by how confident she sounded. She was answering Mr. Powell's questions before he even asked them. But, unlike yesterday, she didn't feel frazzled and out of control. She'd let off some steam during yesterday's rampage, and her emotions felt settled. "Take William Davis, for example. I've given him a lot of support since he's started working here. He's still learning the ropes after two years, and I'm seasoned enough to show him." *Well said without throwing William under the bus.*

The skin between Mr. Powell's eyes pinched. "Oh? I didn't realize William was still learning."

"Well, we all are, aren't we? Even after ten years, I'm learning." *Humility for the win.*

"True enough." Mr. Powell folded his hands in front of him on the desk. "Tell me, why do you want to be in management, Diana?"

Diana swallowed. Her answer had changed over the last few repeats of this day. At first she'd wanted the promotion because she thought she deserved it. She'd worked hard for it, and it was the next right step in her career. At least that's what she was telling herself.

The truth was that the main reason she'd ever taken interest in this promotion at all was because it was an excuse not to focus on wedding planning. She knew she wanted to spend her life with Linus, but once he'd slid the ring on her finger, a million fears had surfaced. She'd never been a part of a family, and Linus was all about family. She didn't want to let him down or lose him, so instead she'd started pushing him away, which made no kind of sense at all.

"Diana?" Mr. Powell asked, reminding her that her boss was still sitting across from her and waiting for an answer.

"I want the management position because . . . Well, the reason is . . ." She trailed off. "It's . . ." The interview had been going so well until this moment. Now, suddenly, she was at a loss for words. "I'm sorry." She stood from the chair, careful not to knock over Mr. Powell's crystal frame. Then she walked over to the open space near the coffee machine and began to pace.

"Are you okay?" Mr. Powell asked.

"Yes," Diana answered honestly. "I'm fine. I mean, I'm not fine. I'll never be fine again, but that's okay." She stopped pacing and looked at Mr. Powell. "I guess I just realized that I don't want a desk job. I love being out in the world with my patients. I love getting to know them, and I even enjoy getting into the middle of their teenage drama."

Mr. Powell smiled. "Your patients love you too, Diana." He gestured at his laptop. "Can I share something with you?"

"Um, okay." She took a hesitant step closer.

"Maria Harris sent me an email earlier today. She wanted you to be recognized by the company for all of your efforts."

Diana approached his desk. "She did? What does the email say?"

Mr. Powell put on a pair of reading glasses and angled his laptop screen toward him. He lifted his gaze to Diana before lowering it again and reading.

> *To whom it may concern:*
>
> *After my stroke, I hit a low point in my life. I couldn't do a lot of the things I enjoyed and I became depressed. Then Diana Merriman started coming to my house and she started stretching my arm and giving me exercises to get better. She made me feel hope, which is something you can't buy at stores. More than that, she listened to me. Really listened. I'm an old woman and most of my friends have grown tired of listening to my stories. They've already heard them a hundred times. Diana didn't*

know them, though, and she genuinely seemed to enjoy them. I guess she made me feel seen for the first time in a while, and I'd say that that's worth getting sick over. Sometimes things happen for a reason, and your physical therapist, Diana Merriman, coming into my life was the reason for this.

So, I don't know if there's an award or something you do to honor your employees, but if there is, she deserves it.

Sincerely,
Maria Harris

Mr. Powell took his reading glasses off and looked at her. "Maria Harris thinks very highly of you."

Tears clouded Diana's eyes and one slipped free, sliding down her cheek. She quickly wiped it away, feeling foolish. She wasn't one to become emotional in front of others, least of all her boss. "Sorry."

"Don't apologize. I got choked up when I first read it too. You're a good therapist, Diana. Perhaps you'd make a great supervisor as well."

Diana blinked away her tears. *Wait, what?*

"You could still carry a small caseload if you want. It wouldn't be a complete desk job. Think about it."

"I will. Thank you for considering me, Todd."

"You're welcome. I'll be in touch later in the week," he said.

Diana shook his hand, careful not to break his crystal frame, and left his office. She walked past the receptionist's desk and out into the wintry air. It was feeling more and more like snow. The clouds hung heavily, threatening to sprinkle white flakes at any moment.

When she got into her car, she sat there behind her steering wheel for a long moment. That had actually gone well. Fifth time was a charm? Maybe she'd get that promotion after all. *If* she wanted it. No matter what, Linus wouldn't be there to celebrate with her.

She swallowed thickly and checked the time. There were still a few hours before Linus closed the shop. If she hurried, she could find the snow globe and head off to see him before shaking it upside down like Mrs. Guzman had instructed.

Diana's eye caught on the scarf that she'd bought Addy. If today was going to be the one that stuck, like the first snowflake of a white Christmas, she wanted to make things right for Addy too.

Chapter 20

Diana pulled into the Pierces' driveway, grabbed the scarf, and got out. She practically ran to the front door and pressed the bell, jogging in place to stay warm. She hadn't taken the time to put on her coat because she was in too much of a hurry. The rest of the afternoon needed to go like a well-oiled machine.

"Diana? I thought you weren't coming by today?" Mrs. Pierce said when she finally answered the door. She was wearing a food-splattered apron and her hair was pinned in a messy bun. She welcomed Diana inside out of the cold and looked at the scarf in Diana's hand. "What's that?"

"I have a gift for Addy. I didn't have time to wrap it." Diana grimaced. "Do you mind if I go back and give it to her?"

"Sure. She's having a rough day. I think it's a boy problem, but she won't talk to me." Mrs. Pierce's expression looked strained. "I'm making her favorite meal to cheer her up. She barely eats these days, but I'm hoping maybe she'll eat a little more if it's her favorite."

"That's a good thought," Diana agreed, already heading down the hallway toward Addy's room. "I'll just be a minute. I'm in a hurry." Diana was halfway down the hall, but she turned back. "Did you by chance get a phone call from anyone yet?"

Mrs. Pierce shook her head. "No. Who is it that I'm expecting a call from?"

Diana shook her head. Maybe Maria wasn't going to take Diana's advice after all. "It doesn't matter." She continued forward and knocked on Addy's door, but didn't wait for Addy to answer before turning the knob and stepping in.

Addy stirred from an apparent nap, blinking sleepily at Diana. "Diana? What are you doing here?"

Diana held out the scarf. "Merry Christmas."

Addy slowly sat up and looked at the scarf, a slight smile lining her thin, pale lips. "But it's December fourth."

"Believe me, I know." Diana sat on the edge of Addy's bed. "I wanted to give this to you early, though. I saw it at a boutique, and I thought it'd look really pretty on you."

Addy took the scarf and ran her fingers along the silky fabric. "It's beautiful. These are my favorite colors."

"I took a wild guess." She gestured at Addy's walls and décor. "You can knot it around your head. I think the colors will bring out your eyes."

Addy gave her a full smile now. "I can't believe you bought this for me. Thank you."

"You're welcome. I can't stay long," Diana said. "I have something I need to take care of."

"What is it?" Addy asked.

Diana remembered how much it had meant to Addy when she'd shared a little bit about herself the other day. "There's an important conversation I need to have with my fiancé. I've been putting it off, but if I put it off any longer, we'll never get to have it."

"That sounds serious," Addy said. "Probably adult stuff that a kid like me would never understand."

"You get maturity points for being so kick-ass these last couple of months," Diana told her.

Addy's eyes rounded and Diana laughed.

Diana held out her palm. "Here, let me help you put the scarf on."

Addy handed her back the scarf. Then she climbed out of bed and slowly headed to the bathroom. She stood in front of the mirror, bracing her hands on the sink in front of her.

"I'll get you a chair." Diana pulled one up for Addy to sit on like she did every day. "Energy conservation, remember? Save your energy for the important stuff."

"Like?" Addy asked, draping the scarf over the top of her head.

"Like talking to Jay."

Addy's gaze connected with Diana's through the mirror. "How do you know about Jay?"

"Long story. You'll just have to trust that I know what I'm talking about," Diana said.

Addy looked down for a moment. "The doctors and nurses told me to trust them too. I guess I'm getting better so listening to their advice worked out."

"Great, so you'll FaceTime Jay in a minute?"

Addy's jaw dropped as she connected gazes with Diana again. "I can't do that."

"Give me one reason why not?" Diana asked.

Addy's lips molded around words that didn't come out. Finally, she said, "What if he's not into me anymore?"

"Then it's his loss. But I think you should give him the benefit of the doubt. Your mom says that Jay and your best friend have tried to call you." It was just a tiny lie, but enough to give Diana an edge on the conversation.

Addy looked down at her hands. "I don't have anything to say to them anymore. We have nothing in common."

"Yes, you do." Diana squeezed Addy's shoulder, making her look back up. Then she helped Addy tie the scarf around the back of her head and smiled back at her through the mirror. "You look amazing."

Addy smiled too. "It's pretty."

"You're the pretty one. Now go FaceTime Jay and get the real story of how he's feeling firsthand."

Addy reluctantly got up from the chair and moved to her bed. "You're staying, right?"

Diana slid her gaze to Addy's bedside clock. It was four o'clock. She still had a little time left before Linus closed his store. "Of course. If you want me to."

"I do." Addy reached for her cell phone and held it with shaking hands. "I'm so nervous. He hasn't seen me since I started chemotherapy and radiation."

"But he's tried?" Diana asked.

Addy looked down for a moment. "Yeah. At first. I answered one night and told him to leave me alone. I told him I didn't want to see him anymore."

Diana's lips parted. This was new information. "You broke up with him?"

"I didn't mean it. And I didn't mean that he should start hanging out with Sierra." Addy blew out a breath. "Aren't guys supposed to fight for you?"

Diana shook her head. "If you ask them to leave you alone, they're supposed to respect your request. They're not mind readers, you know?"

Addy rolled her lips together. Then she tapped her finger along her screen.

Diana assumed she was pulling up Jay's contact. "You're sure you want me to stay?"

"Just for a couple minutes. In case he tells me he doesn't like me anymore and doesn't want to talk to me."

"That's not going to happen. Press Dial."

Addy sucked in a breath and tapped her screen. Then she held her phone to her ear.

Diana heard the beep of a connection and held her breath, hoping this guy didn't break Addy's heart any more than he already had.

"Addy?" a male voice said. "Hey."

"Hi, Jay. Um, how are you?" Addy's cheeks were now flushed against her pale skin.

"I've been missing you," he said. "A lot."

"Really? I've missed you too." Addy gave Diana a sheepish look. "But . . . I hear you're hanging out with Sierra now. She's keeping you company."

"Yeah," he said. "We've hung out a few times. To talk about you. We both miss you, Addy."

"You've been talking about me?" Addy brought her folded legs to her chest and propped her phone on her knees as she looked into the screen. Diana was so proud of this girl.

"Not about you in a bad way. We were scheming on a Christmas present for you. Or, more like a Christmas get-well card. It's not done yet."

Diana felt a wave of relief crash over her. This boy wasn't going to break Addy's heart. It sounded like he genuinely liked her.

"Wow. That's cool," Addy said.

"I like your scarf," he said. "It looks nice on you."

Addy flicked her gaze at Diana again, a grateful smile tugging at the corners of her lips.

Diana gestured toward the girl's door and waved as she backstepped out of the room. Addy didn't need her listening in on her call with her boyfriend, and Diana needed to get to the next item on her list: locating the snow globe in Linus's closet and *un*shaking it.

Chapter 21

"You sent me flowers?" Instead of texting, Rochelle had called this time.

"Yes, I did. Happy birthday," Diana told her.

"This isn't your way of trying to get out of meeting me for our birthday drinks, is it?"

Diana went quiet. She hadn't tried to get out of meeting her best friend at Sparky's the first several times, but this time, she really couldn't spare a moment out of this day. "I'm really sorry. Please don't be mad. I'll make it up to you."

"You're ditching me?" Rochelle groaned into the receiver. "You better have a good excuse."

"I do."

"Okay, let's have it," Rochelle said.

"I'm ransacking my apartment to find the gift that Linus got me for Christmas."

There was silence on the other end of the line. "I said *good* excuse. You're supposed to wait until he actually gives you the gift, Diana. On Christmas."

"I know. This is a special situation, though. And before you ask, I'll just say that you wouldn't believe me if I told you." Although Rochelle had kind of believed her yesterday. "Hey, I know this makes me a crappy friend, but I want you to know you are the best friend I could ever want," Diana said, remembering how Rochelle had held her hand yesterday and stayed with her at the hospital all night. "I don't know what I would do without you."

"Okay, what's going on? You never get mushy on me. Are you dying or something?" Rochelle asked, genuinely sounding concerned.

"No. I don't think I am, at least. I've just come to realize that time is short, and it's all just wasted if you spend it shutting people out and not telling them how much they mean to you. Or chasing dreams that aren't really yours." Diana paused in front of Linus's closet. She'd already checked it once, but what if he hid it somewhere other than behind his rack of ties in this timeline? Maybe she hadn't looked hard enough.

"Something is definitely going on with you. If I was standing in front of you in person, I might just give you a hug."

"And I might just let you. Oh, make sure you prominently display those flowers I sent. I want to make sure your office neighbor sees them when he comes by."

"Why is that?" Rochelle asked.

"I just think flowers were meant to be shown off."

"And how do you know about my office neighbor?" Rochelle sounded increasingly suspicious.

"You've mentioned him before," Diana said.

"I don't think so. In fact, I'm pretty certain I haven't."

"Hmm. Well, happy birthday, Ro," Diana said, changing the subject. "I'll call you later." She disconnected the call before Rochelle could ask any more questions. Then she stepped back into Linus's closet. Her gaze caught on his silly ties that hung there on his tie rack. He hadn't used that hiding place this time. Why not? She knew he'd bought the snow globe already. Eloise had said as much. So it had to be here somewhere.

Browsing through his shirts of various shades of blue, pink, and purple, she noticed a box on his wire shelf above his vast collection of sport coats. She reached up and balanced on her toes to grab it. With a grunt, she pulled it to her and placed it on the floor at her feet. She lifted the lid and peered inside where Linus kept a few old things from his childhood. There, among photographs and letters, old awards from grade school and a movie ticket stub from their first date, she also saw the wrapped gift for her.

Her hands shook as she grabbed the gift-wrapped box with a big sealed envelope and her name on the front.

Bingo.

She carried the box to the bed and leaned over it, hesitating because Rochelle was right, this was wrong. Opening a gift before the giver had even given it was a sure way to end up on the naughty list like Dustin. At this rate, though, Linus would never get a chance to give it to her. She had to open it. But first, the card. There hadn't been a card when she'd found this gift before now. At least something had shifted in the universe.

Diana tore open the envelope and pulled out the folded card. "Forgive me, Linus," she said as she opened it and read.

> *My love.*
> *This is the first of what I hope will be many in your snow globe collection. It's okay to get attached and to want more. To start off small and grow. That sounded good in my head, but on paper, I just sound mushy, don't I? Regardless, I propose we start a second collection, the two of us. Let's collect all the tiny moments—the good, bad, and boring—and let them gather, like the snowflakes in this globe, to equal our forever. I promise I will be there for you when it counts. I promise I*

will never leave. You can count on me to love you,
no matter what comes our way. Always.
   Yours,
   Linus
   P.S. Someone smart once said the world was his
oyster. I say it's really a snow globe.

Diana blinked away her tears and pulled the gift toward
her. Then she slowly peeled the paper back, carefully, not
wanting to rip it in case she needed to cover her crime. But if
what Mrs. Guzman said was true, tomorrow would be
Christmas—a lonely one without Linus.

Diana flicked her gaze at the card. He'd just promised to
be there for her no matter what, but he wouldn't be. A
promise, by nature, was meant to be broken. That was her
experience.

She slid her finger under the lid of the box and wriggled it
open. Then she peered down at the snow globe inside. The
little town of Snow Haven was quiet below. As ridiculous as
it sounded, all she needed to do was turn this globe upside
down, shake it, or *un*-shake it, and get back to real time.

She reread the card. Linus wanted to start a snow globe
collection for her. He'd wanted her to get attached. To commit. To buy-in to forever. Those things didn't come naturally
to Diana. Grandma Denny had made sure of that.

"Don't ever depend on someone else if you can help it.
And don't let people depend on you either. That way life
hurts as little as possible."

Why was she still taking advice from Grandma Denny?
Grandma Denny had done her best by Diana, but Diana
could make different choices now. She wanted to depend on
Linus, lean on her friends, and share her life with those
around her. She wanted to get attached to her patients and to
a silly collection of snow globes. And she wanted the happily
ever after that Linus had offered her.

Diana left the gift in the box, picked it up, and stood. She had to see Linus before she shook this snow globe. If this day was all she got, it was time to say goodbye.

She grabbed her keys and hurried out the door, running into Mrs. Guzman on the way. The gift box shifted and nearly dropped from her hands, but Diana snatched it back to her midsection.

"You're in a hurry," Mrs. Guzman said. "Where are you off to?"

"The toy store, to see Linus."

"Is that the snow globe you were asking me about?" her neighbor asked.

Diana hugged it more tightly to her side. "It is."

"Oh, dear. Well, then, I guess tomorrow is Christmas. I hope future me did all her shopping."

"I'm sure it'll be okay."

"It always is. Better hurry. It's going to snow." As Mrs. Guzman said it, something wet hit Diana's arm.

She looked down at the crystalized drop. "I think that was a flake." She looked up and laughed softly. "It's snowing!"

Mrs. Guzman smiled back at her. She didn't seem surprised at all. "I hope it sticks. Maybe it'll be a white Christmas after all."

"Maybe. I'm sorry, Mrs. Guzman, but I've got to go."

"Yes, of course. See you tomorrow, dear. On Christmas!"

Diana hurried past the jingling sidewalk Santa and got into her car. She carefully placed the snow globe in the seat beside her and checked the time on her phone. It was one hour until Linus got off work. There would be plenty of time to get to him, but it would never be enough to say all she needed to.

Her phone rang from inside her purse. Right. Joann.

"Hello, Joann," Diana said as she held the phone to her ear. It was getting easier to answer the phone with Linus's mom. At least that was progress. Perhaps they could still be friends when December 4th was over, even if Diana never married into the Grant family.

"Oh, Diana. You answered," she said.

"You sound surprised."

"Well, I know you're busy. I just wanted to invite you and Linus to dinner this weekend. Do you think you can spare an hour or two to come visit your future in-laws?"

Diana pressed a hand to her chest, wishing the Grants would in fact be her in-laws. She didn't have active parents, but they might fill that void for her. "That sounds nice, Joann. We'll be there," she said, knowing the weekend she was referring to probably wouldn't happen. Linus would be in a coma by then and all their hearts would be broken irreparably. "My mom was never really in the picture for me, Joann."

"Oh? I'm sorry to hear that, Diana. I didn't know."

Diana glanced out her windshield, taking in the scenery around her. "I always wanted a mother like you, though," she said, flipping the script.

Joann was quiet for a moment. "Well, I never believed blood was what bound a family anyway. And we don't have to wait for the wedding either, dear."

Diana's eyes swam with tears. "That means a lot. Thank you, Joann."

"Of course." She sniffled on the other line. "Talk to Linus. We'll see you this weekend, okay?"

"Okay," Diana said. "Goodbye."

She disconnected the call. Then she put the car in DRIVE and pulled onto Main Street. Linus was going to look at her like she had two heads, but she didn't care. She didn't care if all his customers thought she was out of her mind. She wanted to spend every last second she had left of this day together, whether it be fighting, kissing, or just staring into each other's eyes. It didn't matter. All she wanted was to soak up his smile, his face, his voice. She wanted to memorize all the things about him that she'd missed so completely over the last three weeks.

Diana pressed the gas pedal a little harder, edging over the speed limit as she raced toward Linus's toy store, suddenly desperate to get to him. Tears gathered behind her eyes as she mentally prepared for this goodbye. The last goodbye. What kind of gift had Mrs. Guzman given her? This repeating day hadn't done her or Linus any favors. Yes, Mrs. Guzman had told her that this day wouldn't change anything, but how could Mrs. Guzman know that for sure? Especially since it had spun things around for Maria and Addy?

A few minutes later, Diana pulled into the parking spot closest to the store's entrance. She turned off the ignition, but didn't get out just yet. This was it. The next hour was all she had with the love of her life.

The little boy—Dustin—exited the store, carrying a bag.

Diana got out now and hurried over to catch him. "Hey."

Dustin stopped walking. "Hey."

"How's your mission to be good going?" she asked, her breath making white puffs of air as she spoke. The air seemed to be colder and full of moisture.

"Not very well. I'm just a bad kid, so what's the point?"

Diana stepped closer to him. "You are not a bad kid . . . What's in the bag?"

Dustin hugged it closer to his body. "A doll. But I didn't steal it."

"If you had stolen it, it wouldn't be in a bag, now would it?" It would be stuffed under his coat like it had been the first time she'd run into him.

"The man inside gave it to me. Mr. Linus."

"Oh?"

Dustin offered up a small smile. "I'm going to give it to my foster sister. She wants one of these. I could never afford it on my own, but Mr. Linus told me that sometimes he likes to play Santa."

Diana laughed, blowing white frosty air from her mouth. "Sounds like him. I'm sure your foster sister will love it. You wouldn't rather pick something for yourself?"

Dustin shrugged.

"I think you're a better kid than you know, Dustin. From where I'm standing, you're a pretty awesome kid, actually."

Dustin's jawline clenched. "Well, my foster mom doesn't think so. She can't wait to get rid of me. I heard her telling somebody on the phone. She's just waiting until after Christmas so she doesn't ruin the holiday for Jacy—my foster sister. Then I'm going back into the system."

Diana's mouth fell open. "Oh, Dustin. I'm so sorry."

"I'd run away if I didn't know I'd be back where I started tomorrow morning. There's no escape from this stupid day."

Diana forced a smile. "Well, there's good news on that front. The time loop ends today. I'm ending it."

Dustin swiped a snowflake from his eyelashes. "You can do that?"

"I think so. I hope so, at least. Then tomorrow when you wake up, it'll be Christmas Day."

Dustin looked sadder than any child deserved to be. She knew she'd been that sad as a child growing up in Grandma Denny's home, though. She recognized herself in him. "It's never Christmas Day for a kid like me."

Diana wanted to hug him. She was thinking about it when Dustin blinked and a tear slid down his cheek. Then he crossed the distance and wrapped his arms around her waist for a brief second. Pulling away, he looked up at her.

"At least if you end this day, I get a chance to try to be good with a new family. If someone ever takes me again. Do you think I can be good?" he asked.

Diana's heart broke for him. She remembered wondering

if her mom would stay if she was interesting enough. If she got all As on her report cards to show her mom on her yearly visits. "It doesn't matter how good you are," Diana said.

Dustin looked down at his feet. "I thought so."

Diana tapped his shoulder, making him look up at her again. "It doesn't matter because you don't have to be good or bad. You just have to be you. You're enough."

Dustin swallowed hard. Then he clung to the toy store's bag at his midsection. "If today is ending, I need to get this to Jacy. I want her to have it. It's special."

Diana nodded. "Be careful on your way home." She inwardly flinched, knowing Dustin didn't consider where he was going to be home.

He started walking, glancing back once to look at her and then running off into the distance. Once he was out of sight, Diana faced the front of the store and headed in that direction, wondering how she was going to say goodbye to the man she was supposed to spend forever with.

Chapter 22

"Diana? What are you doing here?" Linus asked as Diana stepped up to his counter.

"I'm here to see you, of course." She looked around the store, noting that the aisles were empty. "Am I the only customer?"

"For now. And with the way the weather is acting, it might stay that way."

"Snow in Snow Haven. Can you believe it?"

Linus grinned. Then he leaned forward and pressed a kiss to her mouth. She resisted pulling him to her and holding him there. "Maybe we'll get snowed in tonight and have to stay home in bed together all day tomorrow."

"Mm. That sounds like heaven. Can we? Please." Because that sounded like a day worth repeating.

"Come sit back here with me. I'll pull up an extra stool."

She rounded the counter and sat on the stool that was already there while Linus retrieved another one for himself. Then they sat together, staring out the storefront at the falling snow. "Maybe we'll be snowed in here and never leave," she fantasized. That would just leave them back in the time loop, though, which wasn't good for her, Linus, or Dustin.

"How'd the interview go?" Linus finally asked.

"Actually, I think I might get the promotion." She released a heavy sigh.

"Don't get too excited," Linus said with a hint of sarcasm. "Isn't that what you wanted?"

"I thought so. Maybe I can do more good as a full-time therapist working with my patients, though. Maybe I don't even want to work in home health anymore. Maybe I want to work with children."

Linus's eyes rounded. "That's a leap, isn't it? Have you ever worked with kids?"

"Not really. Just Addy. I think I'd be good with kids, though. Maybe. Like you said, it's an acquired talent."

"You'll be great no matter what you do," Linus said. "I believe in you." He nudged his elbow against the side of her arm.

Diana turned to him. "Maybe I would rather focus on planning a wedding and marrying you. And being your wife."

Linus's grin grew wider. "You don't have to choose between your work and me, you know? You can have us both."

"I know. Work was my excuse, and it was a weak one. I'm sorry."

"What do you mean?"

Diana took a breath. "Your family intimidates me. Or they did. There are a lot of Grants that come with you."

He reached for her hand and squeezed. "I can't really change that."

"And I wouldn't want you to. I'm warming up to the idea of having an adoptive family. I wish I could be a part of the Grant clan. More than anything."

"You can. Marry me."

Diana squeezed his hand back, staring up into his blue-gray eyes. "You've already proposed and I said yes, in case you've forgotten. And I have no regrets on that front, in case you're wondering."

"Let's do it this weekend, then. We'll find a justice of the peace or someone who can officiate. It doesn't have to be big. I don't even have to include any of my family."

Diana shook her head, knowing that wasn't what he truly wanted. Linus was sentimental. He lived for special moments with loved ones. "Let's marry on Christmas evening, after the huge meals and presents. Everyone will already be gathered. We can do it then and there."

Linus's eyes lit with excitement. "We'll already have the tree and the lights. There'll be no need for more decorations."

"And we'll have the food and your family."

"Your family too," he said, giving her a meaningful look.

Diana swallowed. All she had was Jackie Merriman, who still only came around once a year. But what if what Joann had said were true? That blood didn't make a family. Rochelle was Diana's family. Maybe even Maria and Addy. "It'll be perfect," she said quietly.

"What about the honeymoon? If you take on this promotion, you might not get time off for a while."

"You come first. *Us* comes first."

"I love *Us*," he said, his voice dipping low.

"Me too."

Linus leaned in and kissed her before pulling back and looking at her for a long moment. It was like he was memorizing her face while she was doing the same. "I'll lock up the store and then we can go home. How's that sound? There are no customers anyway, and if we get snowed in, I'd rather it be where the food is." He winked as he stood.

Diana felt a flutter of panic inside her belly. Last time she'd shaken the snow globe, her wish hadn't come true until the next morning. What if the same was true for unshaking the snow globe? Another night of Linus getting into a tragic accident was too much. She couldn't allow it to happen again. She wouldn't.

Linus jingled his keys in front of her. "Ready? I'll lock up and we'll go. I'm glad you're here. There'll be no riding my bike home in the snow tonight."

Diana stood on wobbly legs. She followed him to the front door and stepped out into the snowy evening, waiting for him to lock up.

When he was done, he turned to face her. "Shall we?"

"Linus?" she said quietly.

"Yeah?"

She didn't know what to say. What *could* she say? Snowflakes covered her lashes. She blinked them away, trying to keep her gaze on him. "I'm s-sorry."

"For what?" He stepped closer to her, his eyebrows knitting with concern.

She shrugged and shook her head simultaneously, on the verge of tears. "For everything."

"Don't be silly. Let's go before you freeze to death." He grabbed her hand and gently tugged, hurrying to her car.

"Put your bike in the back," she instructed. "I'll drive. No. Actually, you should drive." Because every time she drove, they got into an accident.

"You got it."

Diana dipped into the passenger seat, watching Linus in the rearview mirror. Her heart was hammering through her chest. Her hands were shaking. On a deep inhale, she picked up the snow globe, turned it upside down, and shook it. When nothing happened, she shook it again. And again.

"What are you doing?" Linus slid into the driver's seat beside her.

"Making a wish." She continued to shake the globe in an upside-down position, just like Mrs. Guzman had told her to.

"You opened your gift early?" he asked, realizing what she was holding. "And without me?"

"Sorry, but it had to be done." She shook the globe even harder.

"Diana, stop! You'll break it!" Linus reached for her forearm and squeezed gently. "Diana?"

When he pulled his hand away, she accidentally let the snow globe slip from her grasp. It dropped in slow motion, shattering in the middle console between them.

Diana gasped softly and looked at the liquid glitter and broken glass. Then she looked up at Linus, feeling like she might combust just like the snow globe had. "Everyone in my life has left me, Linus. I'm putting my trust in you to be different. Don't leave me too. Whatever you have to do to come back to me, please, just do it." Her voice was shaking as she pleaded with him. "You promised me forever, and I believe in you. Forever isn't a myth. I want all the tiny moments you wrote about in your card—the good, the bad, the boring. They all equal up to a future that I want more than anything."

He reached for her hand. "I'm not sure what you're fretting about, but don't worry. You're stuck with me. I'm not going anywhere for a while yet." He looked down at the mess she'd made. "Even if you open your Christmas gift early, and without me, and break the gift inside your car."

She sniffled softly. Her heart was beating fast—too fast. Her breaths were coming out shallow—too shallow. How could she let go of the one person who'd ever come into her life with a promise to stay unconditionally? Even Grandma Denny had always made sure Diana knew she wouldn't always be around. There was an expiration date on their relationship.

"Diana?" Linus asked, gently touching her forearm.

She closed her eyes and counted to ten, taking deep breaths that didn't feel like breaths at all. The harder she tried to pull in a breath, the less air she seemed to pull into her lungs. She was hyperventilating and suddenly her world was spinning off its axis.

"Di? Are you okay?"

She loved the way he looked at her with a deeply furrowed brow when she wasn't making any sense. She loved the way he kissed her, gently at first and then like a man in love.

"Di?" he asked.

"I'm f-f . . ." She wasn't fine, though. She opened her eyes and looked at him. "Here's the thing. We're going to have an accident on the way home, and you'll be injured."

Linus's forehead wrinkled. "What do you mean?"

"You'll go into a coma and the longer you're there, the less probability there is that you'll wake up. I've tried to fix this, to change this. But I think some things are just fated, and they can't be altered." Tears swam in her eyes. She blinked them away and focused on Linus's face. "I know you don't understand, but I want you to know that I'm sorry I couldn't save you." Her tears finally streamed down her cheeks. She couldn't keep them at bay any longer. "Linus, I'm so, *so* sorry I let you down."

"Di, I haven't got a clue what you're talking about right now." He reached up and swiped a lock of hair from her cheek. "But you did save me. I had no idea what I was on this earth for until I met you. I just took up my dad's toy store because he couldn't run it after his heart attack. I felt unsettled and unanchored. Then you walked into the store and I knew, from the moment you said hello, that you were my reason for breathing."

Diana searched his blue-gray eyes. She'd felt the very same way when she'd met him. Even though he'd been recommending the most horrible toys for her to buy for her coworker's daughter. "Why me?"

"Because there's something about you that makes me feel like I can do anything."

She was doing her best not to start sobbing right here in this snowy parking lot. "If that's the case, promise me that whatever happens between here and home, you'll come back to me. Swear it, Linus."

He held her gaze. "As long as I'm alive on this earth, I will always come back to you, Di. That's a promise that I will never break."

Chapter 23

One Enchanted Christmas

Diana opened her eyes and blinked up at the ceiling. She looked at the empty space beside her. Then she turned to look toward the bathroom. The door was open and the lights were off.

"Linus?" She sat up and looked around as if he might be hiding in the closet, looking for just the right tie. He wasn't. "Linus?"

Reaching for her cell phone on the bedside table, she pressed the bottom button to bring up the home screen, where today's date popped up.

December 25th.

It was Christmas. A mix of emotions swirled around inside her chest. Linus wasn't here. December 4th was finally over, and she hadn't saved him. She swallowed thickly and got up, shuffling to the bathroom. After she was done in there, she went to make herself a cup of coffee and looked at a few messages on her phone while it brewed.

She didn't really know how all the versions of December 4th had altered, or not altered, the day she was in now. Did she get the promotion at work? Had Maria broken her ankle?

Had Maria reconnected with Mrs. Pierce? What about Addy? Was the teen girl talking to Jay and Sierra again? There were so many unanswered questions. The only thing Diana knew for sure was that Linus was in a coma, and he might never wake up.

The coffeepot grumbled noisily to its finish. She grabbed a mug from the cabinet and poured herself a full cup. As she drank the nutty brew, the first Christmas text of the day came through.

Rochelle: *Ho, ho, ho! Merry Christmas!*

Diana smiled.

Diana: *Same to you!*
Rochelle: *You okay?*
Diana: *Unfortunately, Santa didn't come.*

That was an understatement.

Diana: *How are things with you and the new guy?*
Rochelle: *Actually . . . Brian is here.*
Diana: *Really? You're spending Christmas Day together?*
Rochelle: *I am. I'm taking him home to meet my parents.*

Diana blinked at her screen. The hot guy in the neighboring office had stuck! Diana wasn't sure what had happened in the days since December 4th, but something had changed for Rochelle. At least *her* life had improved with the time loop.

Diana: *That's amazing, Ro! I'm so happy for you.*
Rochelle: *Your invitation to my parents' house is still open. If your current plans fall through.*

Diana nibbled at her lower lip. She had no idea what was lined up for her today.

Diana: *What exactly are my current plans?*

Her phone rang and Rochelle's name flashed on the screen. "Hey," Diana answered.

"That was a weird text, so I'm making sure you aren't drunk or being held hostage and sending me a cryptic message."

Diana let out a small laugh. Even at her lowest point, her best friend could cheer her up. "Neither of those things. It's a long story, but if you could tell me where I'm supposed to be today that would be helpful."

"Linus's parents' house. They invited you and you actually said yes."

"I did?"

"I know, right? I'm surprised too," Rochelle said. "I'm so proud of you these days."

"What time am I supposed to be there? Do you know?" Diana asked.

Rochelle hummed quietly in the receiver. "You're acting very weird this morning."

"I know," Diana said. "I haven't had my first cup of coffee yet."

"Whatever you say. I believe you said you were going to the Grants' house at noon. But first you're going to visit Linus."

Diana's heart sank a notch in her chest. "At New Hope?"

"Where else would he be? I'm being serious, Diana. Do you need help?"

"No, I'm fine," she said reflexively.

"F-word alert," Rochelle shot back. "I'll be there in ten."

"No. Stay where you are. I'm okay. Really. Enjoy your morning with the guy. Is he your boyfriend now?"

Rochelle cleared her throat. "I'm calling you later to make sure you're okay because you seem to have hit your head or something."

"Maybe that's true. So is he? Your boyfriend?" Diana repeated.

Rochelle chuckled. "Yes. For two weeks now. Where have you been, Diana?"

Diana sipped from her coffee. "I'm not really sure," she said honestly. "I'll talk to you later, okay? Merry Christmas."

Diana disconnected the call and stood. Then she headed to her bedroom, quickly dressed, and prepared to go see Linus at New Hope. It felt weird, knowing he was back to lying in that dreadful bed. She'd just seen him last night. He'd been awake and happy. They'd planned their wedding to take place at Christmas with all his family present. They'd finally set a date! And Diana hadn't felt the least bit intimidated by that thought. The idea of it actually felt perfect to her.

She swallowed, wishing those plans could come true. But Linus was back in his coma. She couldn't humanely keep him in that horrible day, destined to be in one accident after another. How could she say she loved him and allow that to be the case? She couldn't. He'd promised that he'd fight for her, though, and even if everyone in Diana's life had left her, she believed in him. If there was a way, Linus would find it. He wouldn't give up.

Grabbing her keys, she headed out the front door. The jingling sidewalk Santa was gone. Diana guessed he was celebrating with his own family today, if he had one. Or sleeping in after flying all over the world to leave presents under kids' trees during the night.

Linus was the real Santa. Diana knew it, and the fact that he'd given Dustin that doll yesterday proved it. Diana wondered what Dustin was doing this Christmas morning. Were there presents under his tree for him to open? Did he even have a tree? Diana would like to think his foster parents were good people. But, if what Dustin had told her was true, they weren't a match for him. He was a sweet boy. The woman Diana had seen him with at Linus's store seemed bitter and cruel.

Diana pressed the gas pedal a bit harder. Her chest began to constrict the closer she got to New Hope Long-Term Care Facility. It had only been a few days since her last visit, but it felt like forever ago. As she approached the facility, she slowed her vehicle and turned into the parking lot. The SUV with the Rudolph hood ornament wasn't parked in its usual spot. Most people were likely home with their loved ones this morning.

She cut the engine, grabbed her purse, and stepped out into the cold. *Brrr.* Her steps quickened until she pushed through the front entrance and was enveloped in heat and the smell of cinnamon and bleach. The giant Christmas tree was still in the corner of the front room, even larger than she remembered. Her gaze fell to the popsicle-stick ornament with Linus's name on it. It looked like something a child might have made.

"Diana! Merry Christmas!" Ernest said as he pushed his mop forward.

"Merry Christmas to you as well. You don't even get a day off on December twenty-fifth?"

He chuckled. "This place is my home. I wouldn't want to be anywhere else. Tell Linus hello for me."

Diana nodded. "I will." She headed past him, walking by a nurses' station where a couple of employees were chatting about their plans for later in the day.

Meeka Jamison, the charge nurse, looked up as Diana passed. "Hey, Diana! Happy Holidays!"

"You too," Diana said, slowing long enough to ask a question. "How is Linus?"

"Handsome as ever," she said cheerily.

She wasn't wrong. Even in his coma, Linus was still the

handsomest man Diana had ever known. He wasn't Linus without his lavender dog tie, though. Or his lopsided smile, quick wit, and self-deprecating humor.

Diana continued toward his room and rounded the corner. She couldn't help it. Some part of her fantasized that he'd be sitting up. He had promised her last night, after all. Did he remember that? Was he really there? Maybe these last few days had only been a dream. If that were the case, though, Rochelle wouldn't have woken up with her new boyfriend this morning.

Diana stood behind Linus's door a moment, closed her eyes, and envisioned him sitting in bed eating Jell-O. Then she opened her eyes, took a breath, and turned the door-knob. Her heart plummeted into her empty belly. He wasn't sitting up or eating anything. She shut the door behind her and approached his bedside. "Hey," she said as she sat on the chair beside his bed and took his hand. "Remember me?"

Not a single muscle on his face moved. Not one.

"Merry Christmas." She squeezed his hand and waited for him to squeeze back. When he didn't, she continued to talk. "We've had an interesting few days, haven't we? At least I have. All I know is December fourth will never be the same for me. Although I haven't decided if it's a good day or a bad one. It was definitely a strange one."

She breathed past the ache growing in her chest like an un-ruly weed that needed to be plucked. "A few things have changed. Rochelle has a boyfriend now. And I think, maybe, I might have gotten the promotion at Powell Rehab. I guess I should be happy about that, but without you . . ." She trailed off as she held his hand and studied his face. "I didn't know what I had before all of this happened. I was sleepwalking through life and letting all these fears and worries keep me from just living in the moment. A million tiny little moments in a day, all seemingly so unimportant, but they mean everything once they're gone. Snow globes are great, but it's those tiny, wonderful moments that I want to collect," she whispered.

The door to the room opened and Diana quickly blinked her tears away. Then she turned, expecting to see Meeka. Instead, Joann stood there wearing a heavy wool coat with a red-and-white-striped scarf around her neck.

"Diana. You're here early."

Diana stood and went to greet Linus's mother. She was just planning on a small hug, but Joann wrapped her arms around Diana in a huge hug and didn't let go for a full minute. Diana couldn't remember what had transpired from December 5th to the 24th, but based on this hug, maybe she and Joann had grown closer.

Joann pulled back and turned to look at Linus for a long moment. "I just want to shake him, you know? The boy I raised would never be sleeping in on Christmas morning." She looked at Diana sheepishly. "Nothing would have kept him in bed on this date. He had the flu one Christmas, and he was still the first one up. Granted, he was throwing up as he opened his presents." She chuckled softly, her gaze falling to her feet for a few seconds. Then she looked back up at Diana. "How long have you been here? Do you want me to leave so you two can have some private time?" Joann's cheeks flushed as soon as the words left her mouth. "I mean, I know you don't need private time. Not the kind *that* sounded like, at least."

Diana had never really realized the way Joann talked herself in nervous circles. It was endearing in a way that reminded Diana of Linus. "I don't need you to leave. I wasn't planning on visiting for long."

"Well, neither of us can afford to, can we? Not if we want to eat this afternoon, right? You're still planning to come, aren't you? You're my helper. I need you."

"Oh. Yes. Um, remind me what you need me to do," Diana said, feeling like she was the one who'd hit her head.

"Cook, of course. The family will be arriving promptly at two thirty and I always have the food done by arrival. I used to insist that I didn't need help, but this year, with all that's happened, I'm grateful you offered. I'm not too proud to accept help. Not anymore." She reached for Diana's hand and squeezed.

It seemed the last December 4th had bridged Diana's relationship with Joann in a big way. Diana had opened up to Joann on that day and she'd told Joann about her own mother. Then she'd confessed that she always wanted a doting mother like Joann. And now they seemed closer than Diana could have imagined. What else had happened in the last three weeks? Diana wished she could remember. "I'll be there to help you in the kitchen. Of course." She shook her head. "I just . . . I didn't get my first cup of coffee yet this morning," she lied. It was just a small fib. She'd had only one cup and she could definitely use a second.

"You left the house without having coffee?" Joann practically gasped. "I'm not sure how you're upright right now."

Diana smiled. She really did like Joann. They could be friends, if not family.

Joann turned her attention to Linus. She stepped up to his bed, dipped, and kissed his cheek, leaving a plum-colored lipstick stain. "I love you, son. I miss you. Merry Christmas." She watched him quietly for a beat and then turned to Diana. "What else is there to say at this point? I say the same thing every day when I come. He probably feels like he's reliving the same day over and over again."

Diana could relate. She looked at Linus as well. "I wish I knew what he was thinking."

Joann gestured to the chair beside his bed. "Do you mind if I sit here?"

"No. Actually, I'm going to head out. I have a few things to do before I go to your place."

"At noon," Joann said, raising a finger.

"I won't be late." Diana left Linus's room and passed the nurse's counter. Meeka waved as Diana hurried toward the front lobby. When she stepped outside, she gulped the cold air into her lungs. She leaned over her knees, feeling like she might throw up or pass out—one or the other. Then she heard her phone buzz inside her purse. She took a few more breaths before reaching into her bag and pulling it out. The text was from an unknown number.

Unknown: *He's ready when you get here. The address is: 105 Sandy Run Road.*

Diana stared at the screen, rereading the text a second time. Who was ready? She straightened and continued walking toward her car. She guessed she'd find out when she arrived at the given address.

Chapter 24

Diana turned onto Sandy Run Road and drove slowly until she reached the mailbox that read 105. She pulled into the driveway, wondering what to expect. For all she knew, the text was from a wrong number. Then again, she didn't remember what had happened over the last twenty days, so it was a good bet the message was meant for her.

There was a child's bike tossed on the ground in front of the small one-story house. One of the screens on the windows was torn and hanging down. Diana got out of her car and walked toward the porch. There was no Christmas wreath. No welcome mat at her feet. Instead, she saw a sign that read BEWARE OF DOG.

She didn't hear a dog inside the home, though. Instead she heard a woman yelling. Diana froze momentarily. The woman didn't sound like she was in danger. It wasn't a call for help like Diana had heard from Maria on the original December 4th. This was more of an angry yell. Whoever was inside wasn't having a merry Christmas so far.

Diana swallowed past a growing lump in her throat, climbed the porch steps, and pressed the doorbell. The yelling inside the house immediately stopped. Heavy footsteps approached the front door and then the door swung open and a woman who seemed to be in her forties, maybe late thirties, appeared. Her cheeks were still flushed with anger, but she tried to hide it with a smile.

Diana recognized the woman from the toy store. She was Dustin's foster mom.

"Your timing is perfect." She bent to grab a bag off the floor. Then she opened the screen door and heaved the bag in Diana's direction. "Here you go. Everything he owns is inside."

Diana blinked. She looked down at the black duffel bag with superhero iron-ons. *What is going on?* When she looked up, Dustin was standing behind the woman, his eyes round with an unmistakable look of fear. "I'm sorry. Remind me what's happening right now," Diana said, not for the first time this morning.

"Oh, I see." The woman's smile dropped quickly and she folded her arms over her chest. "Now you're going to try to back out? You're all talk until it's time to act, huh?"

"No. I just . . . I need a reminder, that's all." Diana looked down at the bag in her hand. It was heavy. What was inside?

"Here's your reminder," the woman said. "Dustin is yours now. The expedited paperwork was approved yesterday after he was already in bed. You said you'd come first thing this morning to get him."

"Paperwork?" Diana repeated, trying to make sense of this conversation.

"Congrats. You're a new foster mom. Everything the boy owns is in the bag," the woman reiterated.

Diana felt her mouth hang open. She met Dustin's eyes. He still looked frightened and she had the sudden need to scoop him up and carry him far away from this house. Did he remember the last twenty days? Was he as lost as Diana was? "It's Christmas," Diana said. "Where are his toys?"

The woman laughed dryly as if that were an absurd thing

to wonder. "Christmas doesn't come to kids who behave the way he does." She turned back to glare at Dustin. Who could hate a child? This woman could, evidently. "When you behave the way you do, you get kicked out of the warm home that invited you in and from the warm food you've been given. Eventually, you'll run out of people willing to take a chance on you, you know?" she said, speaking in a harsh tone.

"Dustin?" Diana said.

He looked past the woman to Diana. "Yes?" he asked so quietly that Diana almost didn't hear him.

"Come on. It's time to leave."

Relief washed over his expression. He timidly stepped onto the porch where Diana was standing.

"Is the bike on the lawn his?" Diana asked. There was no need for smiles or friendly pretenses. She didn't like this woman any more than the woman seemed to like her or Dustin.

"No. It's going to the thrift store first thing tomorrow. Trust me, you'll thank me for not giving it to him. He used that thing to ride all over town causing mischief in his wake."

Diana placed a hand on Dustin's shoulder. "Come on, buddy. We have a busy day ahead of us." She walked the boy around to the passenger side of her car and opened the door for him. Then she tossed his bag into the back seat. Once she was in the driver's seat, she looked over. "Apparently, you're with me now."

He nodded silently, keeping his head low.

"Is that okay with you?" she asked, suddenly concerned this wasn't what he wanted. She wasn't exactly the family he'd asked for on his Christmas wish list.

He nodded again. "It's okay with me," he said quietly.

"Do you remember the last couple of weeks?" she asked, hopefully.

This time he met her eyes. "You told me you'd do every-thing you could to bring me home with you. I didn't really think you meant it. Until now." His eyes shimmered with tears that he seemed to be working hard to hold in. "I got ex-actly what I wanted for Christmas," he said. "Thank you, Diana."

She was working hard to hold in her tears too. Diana wasn't sure what exactly had transpired to lead her here, but she wasn't sorry.

She slid the gear into DRIVE and reversed the car. "You de-serve more than me for Christmas." She glanced over with a sudden idea and a growing smile. "And you're going to get more." She directed her vehicle toward her next destination and talked to Dustin as she drove. "So, you do remember the last few weeks?"

"Kind of. You followed me home one day and Mrs. Keller was yelling at me. You told her you had a friend who would help you become my foster mom."

Rochelle?

"We were repeating the same day over and over. Do you remember that?" Diana asked.

Dustin nodded in her peripheral vision. "But Mrs. Keller never believed me."

"I can blame her for a lot, but I can't blame her for that. It's a tall tale. How about we just keep that a secret between us?"

Dustin nodded again. "I really tried to change how I acted. I thought that's what I was supposed to do. Mr. Linus gave me a doll and I brought it home to Jacy. Then Mrs. Keller ac-cused me of stealing it. She threw it away to hide the evidence and told me I was rotten."

Diana's heart broke. "I'm sorry, Dustin." She parked in front of Linus's toy store. The lights were off. It was closed today because Linus was at New Hope in a coma. As far as Diana knew, his part-time employee, Jean, had been operat-ing the store for the last three weeks. "Let's go inside. It's

Christmas Day after all. And I can't say for sure if you've been behaved or not, but I can say that you deserve good things."

Dustin's eyes lit up. "You're going to let me pick out a toy?"

Diana laughed as she pushed open her car door. She stepped out and dipped to speak to Dustin, who was still in the passenger seat. "You can pick out ten toys and a new bike. How's that sound?"

The boy whooped and threw open his door.

Why not? Diana was certain Linus would have done the same. "I don't have any kid stuff at my place so we're going to need to stock up, aren't we?" she asked, walking alongside him toward the front entrance.

Dustin jumped up and down just like a kid at Christmas should. Diana's heart warmed watching him.

She used her spare key for the store to let them inside and flipped on the lights. "Merry Christmas, Dustin."

He let out another cheer and took off running down the aisles to pick out whatever he wanted while Diana watched with tears clouding her vision. She wished Linus could be here right now. He loved to see children searching for the perfect toy. She understood the reason now. It was simple and innocent, and she loved the feeling too. She loved having a child to bring to the store.

She was a foster mom now. Her? The one who'd dragged her feet and made excuses to delay marrying Linus because she wasn't sure she could be part of a family. Now she'd taken on a child and she was spending the day at the Grants' home. A lot had happened since that first December 4th, and maybe Linus was still in his coma, but life had changed, some of it for the better.

At noon, Diana rang the doorbell for the Grant home. Dustin hadn't stopped smiling since they'd left the toy store.

He'd picked out the ten toys and a bike, and he'd given her at least a dozen hugs in between.

Joann opened the door. "There you are! Just in time. This must be Dustin," she said, looking down at the boy.

Diana guessed she'd already filled Joann in on her plans. "Yes, it is. I am officially a foster mom now."

Joann opened her arms wide, wiggling her fingers. "Give me a hug, son."

Dustin hesitantly stepped into Joann's arms, disappearing under her layers of clothing.

"Welcome to the family, Dustin." Joann pulled back. "Are you going to help us cook too?"

Dustin hedged, his gaze skittering to Diana. "I'm not supposed to touch stoves because one time I set something on fire. But I promise it wasn't on purpose."

Joann laughed hard and loud. "My son Linus did that one time too." She wrapped an arm around Dustin's shoulders and led him into her home. "I'll be with you today so it's okay to touch the stove."

Diana stood back and watched before stepping inside and closing the front door behind her. When they reached the kitchen, Joann handed her an apron. She also handed one to Dustin.

"And this one belonged to my son when he was your age, Dustin. You can wear it. I'm sure he'd be happy to share."

For the next couple of hours, they prepared sweet potato casserole, rolls, winter squash, deviled eggs, ham, pies, and cookies. Then Linus's aunts, uncles, and cousins began to arrive. By midafternoon, the house was full of people who belonged to Linus, not Diana. At least that's the way she had felt back at Thanksgiving. Now she felt differently, though. With each hug, she felt a little more integrated. She could tell Dustin wasn't quite there yet. He was quiet and stuck close to her side through the prayer and meal.

"Is Mr. Linus going to wake up one day?" Dustin asked after they'd cleaned up.

Diana looked over. "I hope so."

"Will he be upset that I moved into your house?" Dustin asked, looking small and worried. She could relate to him, never feeling like she had a place in this world. Even Grandma Denny had made sure she understood what a sacrifice she'd made taking Diana in. Diana and Dustin had a lot in common.

"No. Mr. Linus would be happy you're staying with us." In fact, Linus was the one who'd mentioned fostering a child one day. Diana stood and reached her hand out to Dustin. "I didn't get much time with Linus this morning. Do you want to go visit? You can thank him for the toys we took from his store."

Dustin looked suddenly worried as he reached for her hand and stood. "Did we steal them?"

Diana shook her head. "No. No, of course not. I gave them to you, and it's okay. I paid for all of it. They're gifts."

Dustin visibly exhaled. "Okay. Let's go see him. Maybe he'll wake up while we're there," he said hopefully.

Diana admired that hope. She envied it. "Maybe so."

Chapter 25

Dustin pushed open the door and ran ahead of Diana, rushing to Linus's bedside. Once again, Diana's fantasy that Linus would be sitting up and eating Jell-O didn't happen.

Dustin touched Linus's arm. "Hey, Mr. Linus?"

Diana watched from the doorway. She needed a moment to collect herself. Having one more day, or five, hadn't helped. In fact, it made seeing Linus like this even harder.

"Mr. Linus, it's Dustin. Do you remember me?" the boy asked.

Finally, Diana stepped over and laid a hand on Dustin's shoulders. "He can't speak back," she told him, "but he can hear you. Go ahead and talk to him." She pulled up a chair and sat as Dustin told Linus all about Christmas at the Grants' home.

"Your mom is so nice," Dustin told Linus. "You're so lucky she was your mom when you were growing up. She made cookies with me and let me eat one as soon as it came out of the oven. And your sister lady was so cool. She had kids my age and we got to play with all our new stuff. Thank you for that, by the way. Ms. Diana let me into your store. I hope that's okay. I picked out a Lego set and some superhero figures. And a bike. It was so cool! This was the best Christmas ever. I just wish you could have been there too. I'm sorry you're in a coma." Dustin looked over at Diana as if he'd said too much.

She smiled reassuringly at him. How had she become responsible for an eight-year-old child? What universe was she living in?

"But Ms. Diana says that one day you'll wake up. That'll be cool," Dustin told Linus. "Maybe next Christmas you'll be at that house too. I mean, I might not be there. No one keeps me for long because I'm a bad kid."

"Dustin," Diana said softly, "no more talk like that, okay? You are not bad."

He turned back to look at her. "You only just took me in. This is called the honeymoon stage. Next week, you'll be regretting taking me."

Diana gave his arm a gentle tap. "You and I might be good for each other, you know? I don't have anyone right now, and neither do you."

Dustin seemed to think on that. "You could have fooled me. There were a lot of people at Christmas dinner. You have all of them."

"Yeah. I guess I do. I kind of think you do too. The Grants are the kind of people who stick."

This made Dustin smile. "Okay," he said simply. Diana wasn't sure if that meant he believed her or he was just humoring her. Then he broke into a yawn.

"You tired?" Diana really didn't know the first thing about taking care of a kid. It had been a long day for her too, though. "We should probably head out."

Dustin looked at Linus one more time. "Don't worry. We'll be back tomorrow. Maybe you'll be up then."

Diana stepped up to Linus's bed. "You're probably a little confused, if you're listening," she whispered, leaning in for only Linus's ears—if he could hear her. "He needed me and I needed him. We'll be here waiting for you when you wake up." She kissed his forehead and then straightened and turned toward Dustin. "Come on. Let's go home."

After Dustin had fallen asleep on Diana's bed—she was taking the couch—Diana retreated to the living room and sat with her cell phone. She tapped off a quick text to Rochelle.

Diana: *Thank you for helping me with Dustin.*
Rochelle: *Of course. How'd today go?*
Diana: *Best Christmas ever. Or it would have been if Linus was here. Yours?*
Rochelle: *Best Christmas ever.*
Diana: *What do I do with Dustin when I go to work tomorrow? I can't just leave him in the apartment alone.*
Rochelle: *What are you talking about?*

Diana stared at the question. It felt off and she was suddenly aware that she was missing another piece to the puzzle.

Diana: *I can't take Dustin to work with me.*
Rochelle: *Why not?*
Diana: *Because I treat patients. I can't bring a child to their homes.*
Rochelle: *Are you okay?*
Diana: *Yes. Why?*
Rochelle: *Because you quit your job two weeks ago.*

"I did?" Diana said out loud. Why would she do that?

Diana: *I know this will sound weird, but where do I work now?*
Rochelle: *. . .*

Rochelle: . . .

Rochelle: *You're right. That does sound weird. Are you sure you're okay?*

Diana: *I'm better than okay. It's just been a long day. A long month, actually.*

Rochelle: *You quit Powell Rehabilitation. You got the promotion, but a week later, you decided you never really wanted to be someone's supervisor.*

Diana: *No? What do I want?*

Rochelle: *You want to sell toys. At least for now. You're running Linus's store. And I think Dustin will be a great helper.*

So, she had gotten her promotion and was supervising fifteen home health therapists, and then she'd decided to run a toy store instead?

Rochelle: *You keep saying you're just holding down the fort for Linus. But I see how happy you've been. You like it. If it makes you feel closer to Linus, it's a good thing.*

It *was* a good thing for Diana. She loved her home health patients, but when she really stopped to consider her life, she wanted a change. And becoming a supervisor at Powell Rehabilitation wasn't it. She'd spent most of her life keeping her feelings tucked inside, but now she wanted to feel them—all of them, even the messy ones. What better source of raw emotion than being around children?

Diana: *This is also going to sound weird, but . . . is there anything else that's happened over the last couple of weeks that I should know about?*

Rochelle: *Other than becoming a foster parent and quitting your job to run a toy store?*

Diana: *That's right.*

Rochelle: *I think that's enough change for one month. Are you experiencing amnesia or something?*

Diana: *Something like that.*

Rochelle: *Well, just don't forget about New Year's Eve drinks with me. It's tradition. And in case your memory is failing, Linus's mom is watching Dustin that night.*

Diana: *Thanks. I'll be there.*

Rochelle: *You better!*

Chapter 26

Let It Snow, Let It Snow

New Year's Eve

The bell over the front entrance to the toy store jingled.

Diana looked up from the counter and hurried over to greet her incoming customer. "Addy! Mrs. Pierce! What are you two doing here?"

"Oh, we were out doing a little after season shopping, and Addy wanted to stop by and say hello," Cecilia Pierce said.

"How's the new therapist working out?" Diana asked.

"He's so annoying." Addy rolled her eyes. She was wearing her purple-and-gold scarf today—the one Diana had purchased for her at Eloise's Trinkets and Gifts. "I miss having you come over. For one, William is a guy and he has no fashion sense whatsoever. He also tries to be my best friend, and I'm sorry, but he's just not. Sierra is my best friend."

Diana had to admit, she got a little thrill over the fact that Addy didn't like William as her physical therapist as much as she'd liked Diana. Diana also had to admit that William made a decent supervisor. His over-the-top need to accommodate others made for a decent work environment for the staff.

Diana had discovered that she was looking for a change of

pace, though. She'd heard that there was a position for a school PT opening at Dustin's elementary school in the new year. Maybe she'd apply for it. If Dustin and Addy had taught her anything, it was that she liked kids. Plus, this job would line her up with Dustin's same schedule. She could take him to and from school and keep an eye on him during the day.

"Well, you won't need therapy much longer," Diana told Addy. "When are you going back to school?"

"As soon as Christmas break is over." Addy's skin was glowing. She looked genuinely happy. And healthy.

"I'm sure your friends will be thrilled," Diana said, watching the girl's reaction closely.

"For sure. We're actually getting together tonight at my house for a little New Year's Eve party. Jay and Sierra are coming, along with a few others."

"That's great," Diana said.

"You can stop by too," Mrs. Pierce offered. "You've still never taken me up on dinner. Or what about tomorrow for New Year's Day? I always make black-eyed peas and collards. It's supposed to bring good fortune in the year ahead."

Diana used to quickly turn invitations like this one down, out of habit and her need to keep relationships in a nice little box where people couldn't hurt her. She was feeling differently these days, though. "Can I bring my foster son?"

"Of course, you can. We'd love to meet him," Mrs. Pierce said. "What's his name again?"

"Dustin. Warning, he's an active little boy. But he's a good kid. A great one, actually."

"Well, aren't they all?" Mrs. Pierce looked more relaxed these days as well. Diana had heard through the grapevine that Addy's mom and Maria were now getting together on a near-daily basis, repairing their mother-daughter relationship. What a difference a couple weeks could make. "Let's say noon tomorrow, then?"

"Sounds perfect. Thanks for stopping in."

Addy looked around the store before leaving. "It's so cool that you run a toy store now."

"Just temporarily, but it is a lot of fun. And it makes me feel close to my fiancé," Diana confided.

Addy offered a sympathetic look. That was the look Diana used to avoid. Then the girl stepped over and gave Diana a tight hug. Diana had avoided these as well, but hugs helped. Accepting support from others didn't make her weak or vulnerable. It only made her stronger.

Mrs. Pierce hugged her next. Then the two Pierces waved goodbye.

"See you tomorrow," Addy called behind her.

"Have fun with your friends later." Diana watched them leave before turning back to the aisles of toys. Linus had put together many of these things with his own hands. He'd told her once that he used to love coming to the store after school as a kid to hang out with his dad, and that he'd always known he'd wanted to work here when he got older.

Linus was steadfast. He didn't waver on what he wanted. Diana guessed that kind of confidence came from a stable home environment and a supportive family. Grandma Denny had offered Diana the best she could. Diana knew that, and she was grateful. Diana was doing the same for Dustin. That's why she'd finally taken Rochelle's advice on getting counseling. Her best could be even better if she worked on a few areas in her life.

"Diana?" Dustin came barreling from the back room. "When is Grandma Joann coming to get me?"

"Grandma Joann?" Diana raised a brow.

"That's what she told me to call her." Dustin shrugged. "Don't worry. I'm not getting too attached."

Diana stepped over to the boy and wrapped her arm around his shoulders. "It's okay to get attached. None of us are going anywhere. She's not your real grandmother, but you can adopt her as one if that's what you two decide."

"Adopt?" Dustin's eyes widened. "What about you? Can I adopt you too?"

Diana squeezed him to her in a side hug. "It goes the other way around, kid. And as a single person, I'm not as attractive a candidate as a couple who might want to take you in."

Dustin hung his head. "A couple isn't taking me in, though."

"Right now, you're with me and that's how it's staying."

"Maybe when Linus wakes up, you two can adopt me. As a couple." Dustin looked back up at her, a hopeful gleam in his eyes.

The more time that passed, the less likely it was Linus would wake. That was Diana's brain speaking. Her heart was leading these days, though, and her heart told her he would come back. He'd made a promise and Linus Grant didn't break promises if he could help it. "Yes, that's a good idea."

"Do you think Linus will agree?" Dustin asked.

"I don't think it, I know it," Diana said.

Dustin broke into a wide childlike grin as he bounced excitedly on his heels.

Then the bell upfront jingled again as Joann stepped into the store.

"Grandma Joann!" Dustin took off running toward Linus's mother.

She opened her arms and hugged him close. "I'm taking him to the movies and then home with me," she called to Diana. "You're free to go off with your friend tonight."

"Thank you, Joann!"

"Are you stopping by to see Linus after you leave here?"

"Of course," Diana said.

"Will you give him a kiss from me?" Joann asked, her arm still draped around Dustin's shoulders. "It's been a couple of days and I feel criminal for not visiting."

"I'm sure Linus understands. I'll kiss him for you." Diana grabbed Dustin's overnight bag and handed it to him. "Behave," she told the boy with mock sternness.

"I promise," Dustin said. "Or I promise to try."

Diana grinned. "Thank you. Have fun with your adopted grandmother." She shared a look with Joann.

Joann shrugged her shoulders again and looked down at the boy. "We are going to have so much fun together. I can hardly wait."

Dustin grinned, looking happier by the moment. "Bye, Diana."

"Bye. I love you. Call me if you need something," she told Joann. "And thank you."

Joann let go of the boy to hug Diana tightly. "And even though you and Linus aren't married yet, I'm claiming to be your mother-in-law." She pulled back and pressed her lips together. "The in-law part always feels like a negative thing to me. Can we just say that I'm your second mom?"

Diana swallowed past her sudden uprising of emotion. "Sounds good to me." She waved as Dustin grabbed Joann's hand and dragged her toward the exit. Then she followed behind them because it was closing time. She turned the sign in the window to CLOSED and locked the door. After closing out the cash register and sweeping the floors, she pulled on her heavy winter coat and grabbed her purse and keys.

The cold air nipped at her cheeks as she stepped outside. She stopped for a moment to study the tiny snowflakes that filled the air around her, holding out her gloved hand and letting the fragile flakes land in her palm. Delicate and lovely. The snow hadn't stuck on Christmas, but maybe a white New Year's would bring good luck.

Diana hurried to her car and slid inside the driver's seat. She let the engine warm for a few minutes before turning out onto the main road that led between the toy store and New Hope Long-Term Care. She drove slowly on the slippery streets until she pulled into the parking lot, taking her spot right next to the SUV with the Rudolph nose still covering its hood ornament. Hugging her coat over her chest, she hurried inside. The tree in the front lobby was taken down now. The corner looked barren without it. Now a chair sat in its place with a small table next to it and some business cards from various shops and companies around town.

"Hi, Diana!" Ernest had on snowflake-printed scrub pants today with a plain navy blue scrub top. "Is it still snowing out there?"

"It is. It's going to be a white New Year's," she told him.

Ernest chuckled as he pushed his mop forward. "It's a small miracle to get snow around here. On Christmas and now New Year's."

"I hope it sticks at least for a day." She walked by him and continued past the nurses' station.

Meeka looked up from her computer and waved.

"Hi," Diana said. Meeka looked busy so she didn't stop for any more conversation. She just wanted to get to Linus anyway. She opened the door to room fourteen and turned inside, stopping for a moment to let her fantasy of him sitting up and eating Jell-O crash and burn in her mind. He wasn't sitting up, eating, or doing anything other than lying in his usual position.

"Hi. It's me." Diana closed the door behind her. "Happy New Year's Eve." She stepped over to him and kissed his forehead. "That's from your mom," she whispered. Then she kissed his mouth, lingering for a beat and entertaining a *Sleeping Beauty*–type fantasy where her kiss would wake him. It didn't. "That's from me. More where that came from if you open your eyes," she teased.

She pulled up the chair and sat down, picking up his hand to rest inside hers. It was soft and warm. As she sat there, she told him all about business at the toy store and Dustin's latest shenanigans, which weren't all that troublesome. "He's calling your mom 'Grandma' per her request. That woman is desperate for grandkids, in case you didn't know."

Diana went on about Addy and her phone call with Maria this morning. "Maria is doing well. She's back to driving, which is huge for her. She and Addy's mom are growing close again. I hope that relationship works out. Maria is a nice woman, and everyone needs family." Diana squeezed Linus's hand, willing him to squeeze back just this once. She wished he would stir and wake, even if it was just for a moment. She missed those blue-gray eyes staring back at her. "I never thought I needed family, but I was wrong. Anyway . . ."

Diana trailed off and waited for more things to say. It wasn't easy carrying on a conversation by yourself. "Well, I have to meet up with Rochelle tonight for our traditional New Year's Eve drinks. You know us. Any excuse to have a fancy drink, right?" Diana stood and leaned over to kiss Linus's lips again. She lingered a moment, breathing him in. He'd smelled of pine needles once upon a time. Now he smelled like antiseptic and rubbing alcohol. She straightened and let go of his hand. "See you tomorrow, sleepy man."

Turning, she headed toward the door, so lost in her thoughts that she almost didn't hear the quick intake of breath and slight groan behind her. Everything in Diana's body stilled, even her heart, but she didn't turn. She was tired of entertaining fantasies of Linus waking up, even though she wouldn't, couldn't, give up on him. She never would.

The noise came again, louder this time.

Diana slowly looked behind her and gasped at Linus's open eyes. He seemed to startle at her presence too. Diana rushed over, reaching for his hand and leaning over him. "Linus? Linus, are you awake?"

"Diiii." He made noises from his chest, but his lips weren't yet moving. His gaze focused on hers and she saw the flicker of recognition there in the stormy blue-gray oceans of his eyes. He was still there. Her Linus was still there.

"Linus?" She turned to call over her shoulder. "Meeka? *Meeka!* Somebody?" She looked at Linus again. "Stay here. Don't move."

The corners of his mouth flicked into a maybe smile.

Meeka burst into the room a moment later. "You okay?"

"He's awake! Linus is awake!" Diana shouted as hot tears streamed down her face. She could barely see from the cloud of them filling her vision.

Meeka stepped over to look at Linus and gasped as well, confirming that Diana wasn't imagining this. "You *are* awake. Linus, can you hear me?"

His brow furrowed in that Linus way as if to say, *"You're acting bizarre."* "Yessssss," he croaked.

"His first word!" Diana jumped up and down on the balls of her feet. It was like he was a child who'd never uttered a single syllable.

"I'm getting Dr. Romani. I'll be right back." Meeka rushed out of the room.

Diana stepped back over to Linus. He was still watching her. He tried to sit up. "No, don't. You need to rest."

His brow furrowed again. "How long?" he asked in a scratchy voice.

"Hmm?"

"How long . . . have I been . . . here?"

She hesitated to tell him. He'd missed an entire month. One that felt like one long run-on day. "Since early December. Well, you were at the hospital for two weeks before coming here."

Linus frowned, his gaze sliding over to the tiny twinkling tree with tinsel and ornaments on his bedside table. Diana had been meaning to take that down. "What day is it?"

"December thirty-first," she told him. "It's New Year's Eve."

She saw the awareness pass through his eyes. He'd missed what was going to be their first Christmas together.

"Wow," he finally said.

"The only thing that matters is that you're back. You're awake." She laughed out of sheer joy. She almost couldn't believe this was real.

He narrowed his eyes. "I told you I would come back, didn't I?"

Diana's lips parted. "You remember that?"

"Hmm," he groaned weakly. "I remember . . . everything."

Diana was just about to clarify what he meant when Dr. Romani walked in. He looked surprised when he saw Linus as if he hadn't believed Meeka.

"Mr. Grant, how are you doing?" the doctor asked.

"Stiff," Linus said, making them all chuckle.

"Well, trust me, your fiancée here stretched your arms and legs every day," Meeka told him. "She deserves an award for how well she took care of you."

Linus slid his gaze to meet Diana's. Was this real? What had he meant by saying he remembered everything?

"The stiffness will go away," Dr. Romani said. "You'll need some PT to get up and moving again."

Diana raised her hand. "I think I know someone for that job."

Linus cast her a full smile now. That's when Diana knew, even before the doctors and nurses had run any tests to confirm. He was there, all there, and he was going to be just fine. Scratch that. He would be better than fine. And so would she.

Chapter 27

Winter Wonderful

Diana: *I'm sorry.*

Rochelle: *Uh-oh. You're ditching me for New Year's Eve drinks?*

Diana: *I have a good excuse.*

Rochelle: *Doubtful. What is it?*

Diana: *Linus is awake!*

Rochelle: *WHAT?!? Are you serious?*

Diana: *Completely!*

Rochelle: *You're forgiven. Tell him hello.*

Diana: *I will. Rain check?*

Rochelle: *Snow check. And yes. For sure.*

An hour later, Joann came into the room with Dustin trailing behind her. "Linus! Oh, my son! I've missed you so much!"

"Hi, Mom. How are you?" Linus's voice had gotten even stronger in the last half hour.

"That's for me to ask you." Joann took his hand and held it like she never planned to let go. That was a mother's prerogative, Diana guessed.

"I've been better." His gaze reached past her and landed on Dustin. "Hey, there, buddy. I hear you've moved in with us while I was sleeping."

Diana straightened in the chair. She hadn't told Linus that just yet. How did he know?

"Is that okay?" Dustin asked sheepishly as he stepped closer. "I mean, now that you're awake, do I have to leave?"

Linus offered his hand to the boy.

Dustin hesitated before taking it. "No way. I'm excited about having a new roommate. I hear you got to go shopping at the store for Christmas too."

Diana hadn't told him that either. Not while he was awake, at least. "Where did you hear that?"

Linus glanced over. "You told me."

"But . . . but you were in a coma. You heard what I said?" she asked.

Linus's dark brows dipped. "I guess I did. Being in a coma is strange. I had this bizarre dream."

"Dream?" Joann took a seat on the edge of his bed. "What kind of dream?"

Linus seemed to look off in space as if he was trying to put the sequence of it in order. "I was reliving the same day on repeat. It was kind of bizarre. And I kept getting hit by a delivery truck at the end of it."

Diana covered her mouth with one hand and reminded herself to breathe.

Joann looked at her. "What's wrong?"

Diana couldn't tell them the truth. Not the full truth. She shared a look with Dustin. He wasn't planning to pipe up about that day just yet either. It was their little secret to keep. "It's just . . . I had the same dream," Diana told them, her eyes burning.

"How odd is that?" Joann asked on a laugh.

Diana swallowed past a tight throat. "It was terrible."

Linus looked at her. "I don't know. It had its good moments," he said, his gaze holding hers. "Didn't it?"

Was he there? Was that even possible? Then again, was any of this experience possible? "Yes, I guess there were some good moments." She nodded as tears filled her eyes. She'd never cried so much in front of others. The moments that had made up the days she'd repeated had changed the course of her life. Of *their* lives together.

"You know, Diana has been running your toy store for you while you've been in here," Joann said.

"Yeah?" Linus shifted and tried to sit up higher. He was weak right now, but Diana knew that he'd grow stronger. She'd help him rebuild his muscles and his endurance. He had an aisle to walk down after all. "Thank you, Di."

"You're welcome. I actually kind of enjoyed it, much more than I would have thought." She tilted her head. "Not enough to wear silly ties or such."

"Ah, how I miss my tie collection," he teased, sounding more and more like his old self. "Please tell me you didn't ditch any of my favorites."

Diana laughed. "I didn't touch a thing. Except maybe that holey Snow Haven High T-shirt you always leave on the floor."

Linus's eyes went wide. "You didn't?"

She bent and kissed his lips. "I might have worn it a time or two, that's all."

"Ah, well, that's perfectly okay. Seeing you in my old T-shirt might actually be good for my health."

Joann cleared her throat. "Okay, I think I'll just give you two some private time." She looked around nervously. "Not that you need *that* kind of private time." She reached for Dustin's hand. "We'll just go back to my place for tonight. I'm sure you two want some time to catch up."

Diana reached for Dustin and pulled him in for a hug. "Be good for Grandma Joann, okay?"

"I will. I promise." Dustin walked over to Linus's bedside and gave him a hug as well. "I'm glad you're awake, Mr. Linus. Diana said you might adopt me once you're a married couple."

Heat scorched Diana's cheeks. That was a big decision. Maybe too big for a guy who'd just woken from a month-long coma. "Oh, um . . ." She looked between Dustin and Linus. "We can talk about that some more later, okay? Have fun with Grandma Joann."

Dustin nodded and headed out the door with a wave.

Once Diana and Linus were alone, he reached for Diana's hand. "I'm not sure what's real and what's not right now, but I know it's good to be here, with you. It'll be even better when I'm home."

"It's really okay that Dustin is staying with us?" she asked, hoping she hadn't guessed wrong. She loved having Dustin live with her. They'd bonded in a way that Diana guessed a mother would with a child.

"It's more than okay."

"If it's any consolation, I missed out on most of the month too," she told him. "I just remember December fourth, the day of your accident, and then landing myself here on Christmas Day, waiting for you to wake up."

"Why is that?" Linus asked.

"I guess . . . I guess I was just lost without you." She shrugged. "That's the only way to explain it, at least."

Linus squeezed her hand. "Well, now you're found. We both are. We'll have to celebrate Christmas privately when I get home." He closed his eyes. "I'm tired right now, though." He cracked his eyes back open. "I'm afraid if I close my eyes for too long, I'll slip back into my comaverse. Will you stay with me tonight?"

She squeezed his hand back. "I'll stay with you forever. How's that?"

"That sounds like a proposal if I've ever heard one," Linus said, blinking sleepily again.

Diana leaned in and lowered her voice to a whisper. "Linus Grant, will you marry me?"

"Name the time and the place. I'll be there," he said softly before closing his eyes for good.

"As soon as possible," she said, leaning back in her chair and wondering at all the things she couldn't possibly understand. Then she closed her own eyes and stopped trying. From now on, life was their oyster. Scratch that. It was their snow globe.

Epilogue

December 4th. The following year.

"Rise and shine, sleepy girl."

Diana rolled over onto her side, vaguely aware of Linus's voice above her. She groaned softly, resisting waking up.

His hand slipped beneath her arm and tickled her softly. "Wake up," he whispered, teasing her.

"That's just cruel," she moaned. "Tickling someone awake is the worst wake-up call."

"Oh, I'm sorry." His voice was anything but apologetic. Then he climbed over her and plopped into the bed beside her, making the mattress bounce softly.

Diana finally opened her eyes, deciphering what was going on. Linus wasn't in a hurry to get to work. Usually he was dressed by now and prodding her to do the same for the school job she'd taken on. "What's going on?"

Linus's fingers slid under her arm again, tickling the line that led down her ribs. She let out a tiny laugh and batted his hand away. "Stop it," she pleaded. "What are you doing?"

"Playing with you."

"You are one big kid, Linus Grant. *Stopppppp* . . . Don't you have to get to work for some distributor meeting or something?"

"I really should," he agreed, but didn't move to leave the bed. "But, you see, there's one slight problem."

Diana narrowed her eyes. "What's that?"

He attempted to tickle her some more but she rolled out of his reach.

"What's the problem?" she asked again.

"It's snowing outside," he whispered, leaning in close to her ear as if to confide a secret.

"A little snow shouldn't stop you."

"Not just a little snow. It snowed a lot while we were sleeping. We're snowed in."

Diana felt her eyes go wide. "What? What do you mean?" She launched herself out of bed and ran to the window, peeking through the blinds to look down on the town. Jingling Santa wasn't even there this morning. Instead, the entire ground was covered in a brilliant white snow. "I can't believe this. How deep is it?" She turned to look at Linus, lying with his head propped up on his arm.

"At least three feet. Maybe four and it's still falling. The roads haven't been cleared. Neither of us are going anywhere today."

"This wasn't in the forecast."

Linus reached out for her, luring her back to the bed with him. "Sometimes the best things in life aren't planned."

She stepped toward him and allowed him to pull her back onto the bed. Satisfaction made a wide smile curl on her lips. A day to be snowed in with her new husband sounded perfect. She and Linus had gotten married as soon as he'd left the hospital. Linus's grandfather was right. Forever *was* a myth. All they were guaranteed was the moment they were in. The next was a gift, and she wanted to collect all the moments she could.

"Let's just lie here all day," he said.

"Mm. Sounds perfect."

"Or," he said, "you lie there and I'll have my way with you. And I'm not talking about tickles."

Diana burst into more laughter. "I think I need coffee first. You?"

Linus sighed. "You will never turn me on to coffee. It will always be hot tea. In fact, I'm going to make us a cup right now along with breakfast."

Diana moved to get up. "Want me to help?"

"No. You stay here." Linus patted her thigh and then lifted himself up off the bed. "I'll make it and serve it to you in bed." He bent and kissed her temple. "Now get back under the covers where it's warm," he mock demanded.

She didn't argue. Instead, she crawled back under the covers and grabbed her phone. First text of the day was to Rochelle.

Diana: *Happy birthday! Did you wish for snow?*

Diana watched as the dots starting blinking on her screen while Rochelle responded.

Rochelle: *It's like I woke up in a winter wonderland. The only bummer is that we won't be able to have our traditional birthday drinks tonight.*

Diana: *Rain check. Correction—snow check.*

Rochelle: *What will you do with your free day?*

Diana: *Spend it with Linus.*

Rochelle: *Where's Dustin?*

Diana: *Grandma Joann's. She kept him overnight.*

Rochelle: *Very nice of her.*

Diana: *The woman spoils him rotten. Now I know why Linus is the way he is.*

Diana and Linus had officially adopted the boy this summer. All he needed was someone willing to love him unconditionally.

Rochelle: *Snowed in with your hubby sounds heavenly.*

Rochelle sent a GIF of a woman waggling her eyebrows and Diana laughed. Then she set her phone down and closed her eyes, savoring the stillness of the morning and looking forward to spending the day with the man she loved. She laid there long enough, with her eyes shut, that she started to doze off again.

"Wake up, sleepy girl," Linus said, walking back into the room with two plates of food. He handed her one.

"Mmm. How did I get so lucky?" She breathed in the delicious aroma wafting beneath her nose.

Linus sat down on the bed beside her and grinned as he bit off a piece of his bacon. "I could say the same about you."

"Have you ever made me breakfast in bed before?" she asked. Because maybe he had in some version of time that she'd completely forgotten. Time was a slippery thing after all.

Linus furrowed his brow as he thought on his answer. "I don't believe so. How about this for a new tradition? Every time we're snowed in, I'll make you breakfast in bed."

"I like that tradition." She somehow suspected Snow Haven would have a lot more snow in its future. Something had shifted, not just for her and Linus, but for Dustin and Maria. For Addy. For everyone. A lot could change in one day.

They ate their breakfast together, talking and laughing and being the "us" that Linus had longed for during their time loop.

"Can we just live like this?" Linus mused as he ran his hand down the side of her arm.

Goose bumps rose to the surface of her skin. "Every day from now on."

"We'd run out of food," he said.

"We could survive on love alone."

Linus grinned, looking equal parts adorable nerd and sexy toy salesman. "I like this mushy side of you, Mrs. Grant."

She finished off her second slice of bacon. "In that case, I also want to say I'm glad we found each other. I know I'm not winning any wife of the year award, but I love you."

"You *are* winning wife of the year award. At least in my book. And I love you back," he said. Then he got up from the bed and stashed his breakfast plate on the nightstand. "Okay, I can't wait until tonight. Let's open our gifts to each other now."

Diana laughed. "Are you serious?"

"Rarely. But right now, yes. Dead serious."

Diana shook her head. "You are one big kid, you know that?"

"Guilty as charged."

She placed her empty plate off to the side too and got up to retrieve his gift from inside her underwear drawer while Linus slipped into his closet. She guessed his hiding place was once again behind a curtain of silly ties.

Diana's brain stuttered to a stop when he stepped toward her holding out a cube-shaped box. She and Linus had discussed the snow globe. He knew about Mrs. Guzman's enchantment and he'd lived the time loop right along with her while he was in his coma. "Is that what I think it is?"

He handed the box to her. "Don't shake it."

Diana swallowed thickly. Then, slowly, she tore away at the paper, peeling it off until she was only holding a plain white box. Her hands shook as she lifted its lid and peered down at the contents. "A snow globe." Her heart kicked softly. She looked up at Linus and back down at the gift. Then she carefully pulled it from the box and inspected the intricate little town of Snow Haven. "It's just as beautiful as I remember."

"Mm. There's something magical about a snow globe, you know?" he said, sounding just like Mrs. Guzman.

Diana felt excited and panicked at the same time. "Aren't

you worried we might find ourselves stuck in another time loop?"

"Just keep Mrs. Guzman far, far away from this one."

Diana smiled, holding the snow globe tightly. "Deal. I love it. I love you." She tipped her head toward his gift now. "Open yours."

He picked the tiny package she'd gotten him up off the bed where she'd set it down and immediately shook it.

Diana gasped. "You're not supposed to do that. What if it's breakable?"

"It's not. I know exactly what this is." He tore at the paper, revealing a turquoise tie with tiny kittens chasing balls of yarn printed all over it.

"You can wear it on the off days when you're not wearing the dog-print tie," Diana offered, suddenly worried he wouldn't like her gift. The one he'd gotten her was special. It was one of a kind. Hers was just ordered from a catalog.

"This is perfect," Linus said, looking sincere. The man didn't know how to be anything less. "Thank you."

"You're welcome. What now? Should we put up the Christmas tree or go back to bed?"

Linus hummed on that thought. "There's more than enough time to do both. And if there's not, we can shake that snow globe of yours and make a wish to do this day all over again."

"No!" Diana said without hesitation, hugging the snow globe to her side. "Definitely not."

"In that case," Linus leaned in, brushing his lips to hers, "I choose going back to bed. The tree and the trimmings can wait. All I need in this moment is you."

"Ditto that." She smiled into their kiss, collecting one of many more beautiful moments to come. "All I'll *ever* need is you."

Acknowledgments

I am so deeply grateful for everyone who helped make this book possible. There are so many to thank and a simple thank-you doesn't feel nearly sufficient for helping to make my dream of writing my first women's fiction novel come true.

Firstly, a huge thanks goes out to Kensington Publishing for taking this book on and bringing it to readers. I am so honored to be working with such an amazing publisher. Thank you to Shannon Plackis, my editor for *Through the Snow Globe*. It was such a pleasure working with you on this first project.

Even though I have several published books under my belt, this novel felt like a debut because it was my first in the women's fiction genre. In some ways, I felt like I was starting over with my writing career because there was so much to learn. That was as exciting as it was intimidating, and I am eternally grateful to those who lent me their expertise. Thank you, Tif Marcelo! Time is a precious gift and you spent yours reading the early pages of *Through the Snow Globe*. Feedback from someone I admire and respect was invaluable. Thank you, thank you! I also want to thank Laura Apgar, who also read an advance copy. Your comments and suggestions were exactly what I needed to feel confident in this new genre. I have always enjoyed working with you in the past and I'm so glad we can continue here and there.

I can't forget my wonderful critique partner, Rachel Lacey, who was also one of the first readers for this book (and all of my published books). I am so glad we met at our little RWA chapter so many moons ago and became critique partners.

Thank you, as always, to my wonderful literary agent, Sarah Younger, who believed in this idea and helped me find a home for my women's fiction books. Your support over the years has been a godsend. I am so blessed to have you on my team and as my friend.

Thank you to my #GirlsWriteNite ladies: Tif Marcelo, Rachel Lacey, April Hunt, and Jeanette Escudero. You are my writers' family and I don't know how I could ever do this without you. I do know, however, that I wouldn't want to. You inspire and encourage me, and also crack the virtual whip when I'm not meeting my word count goals.

As I said earlier, time is a precious gift. I am so fortunate to have a supportive family who allows me to have the time needed to write the stories of my heart. Not only that, you support and encourage me. I love you all so much and I appreciate all that you do to help me in all the areas of my life. I am sure I'm not even fully aware of all that you give and sacrifice on my behalf. If my life were a book, you all would be the story's heroes. You are my heroes. So, from the bottom of my heart, all the way to the top and flowing over, thank you.

THROUGH THE SNOW GLOBE

Annie Rains

About This Guide

The suggested questions are included to
enhance your group's reading of
Annie Rains's *Through the Snow Globe*!

DISCUSSION QUESTIONS

1. In *Through the Snow Globe*, Diana finds herself repeating the same awful day. If you were given a day to repeat, would you choose one of the happiest or one of your worst, in an attempt to make it better?

2. Diana comes to understand that there is something she has to do in order to stop the endless time loop of December 4th. After reading the story, in your own words, what do you think it was that Diana needed to do or learn for the time loop to be broken?

3. If *Through the Snow Globe* had been set in the springtime instead of the holiday season, would the story have worked? Do you buy into the notion that there is something innately magical about Christmastime?

4. From beginning to end, how did Diana's character transform? If she had met Dustin before Linus had gone into a coma, would she have considered fostering him? Why or why not? What needed to change for Diana to open her heart to the idea of adopting a child?

5. If you could repeat a day and change it, would you? Do you think changing the past would alter the future?

6. People like to say that things happen for a reason. Do you believe that's true? If so, what would be the reason for Linus's accident in this story?

7. In *Through the Snow Globe*, Diana initially keeps her emotions shut-off and her friends and family at arm's length. As the story progresses, however, she opens herself up to the world around her. Do you relate more to the Diana at the opening of the story—turning inward when you're in dark times? Or do you relate to the Diana we see at the end of the story—seeking out comfort and solace from others? Do you think that one way is healthier than the other?

8. Rochelle is Diana's supportive best friend. She offers her support by giving Diana tough love and no-nonsense advice. If you were in Rochelle's role, what do you think the best way to help a friend dealing with grief would be?

9. In the story, Addy is Diana's teenage patient recovering from cancer. What role, if any, do you think Addy had in Diana's character transformation?

10. In *Through the Snow Globe*, Cecilia Pierce and her mother are estranged. How does this sub plot support the story's theme of second chances?

11. If you were handed a snow globe and told that you could have one more day with the one you loved and lost, would you do it? Who would you wish to spend that extra day with?

12. Diana receives another snow globe in the epilogue. What are the chances that the new snow globe is enchanted as well? If it is, do you think Diana and Linus would risk shaking that snow globe again?